BATTING STYLE

FRANKLIN U 2

LOUISA MASTERS

Batting Style

Copyright © 2024 by Louisa Masters

Cover: Tal Lewin @caravaggia13

Editor: Hot Tree Editing

All rights reserved.

No part of this book may be reproduced in any form or by any means without the prior written consent of the author, excepting brief quotes used in reviews.

This is a work of fiction. Names, characters, places, events and incidents either are the product of the author's imagination or are used fictitiously, and any resemblance to persons, living or dead, business establishments, events or locales is entirely coincidental.

To the extent that the image or images on the cover of this book depict a person or persons, such person or persons are merely models and are not intended to portray any character or characters featured in the book.

BATTING STYLE

Blaise

There are a few things I know for sure: I'm gay, I want to do costume design for film and television, and a supportive family is what other people have. Oh... and fate's not my biggest fan. That's fine, though—who needs fate? I've got friends I love, a welcoming community, and a plan. Graduate college? Check. Build up my portfolio? Whenever I can. Impress industry pros? Done. Save the money for my dream internship? Working on it. All I've gotta do is stick with the plan, and that internship is mine next year.

And then Jordan Marks walks into my life, and my plan turns into a loose guideline. Suddenly I'm learning about baseball and giving away shifts at work so I can watch him play. My goals are the same, but maybe there's room in them for the world's sweetest athlete.

Jordan

I'm pretty sure the gods of baseball don't care if I wear a suit on game day, but Franklin U and Coach do, so when mine rips, replacing it is an urgent mission. That's how I meet Blaise

Warner and my "I guess I could be bi" musings become full-blown "I wanna learn to handle a bat" demands. Blaise is smart, talented, and has goals... and he's more than happy to teach me a new batting style.

But as we go from casual to more, the things I never mentioned—like my dads' connections in the entertainment industry—become heavy secrets. Plus, while our friends know we're dating, nobody else does. That's not fair to Blaise, but do I really want to be the latest queer college ball player?

I don't get a chance to figure it all out before things fall apart, and now we both have to decide what our real priorities are.

AUTHOR'S NOTE

All FUKing titles stand alone and can be read without reading the others—though why would you want to? All these authors are awesome! If you're following the recommended reading order, this book is third and there's some timeline overlap with later books in the series. Happy Reading!

ONE

JORDAN

At first, I think the ripping sound is Boyle letting one rip—no pun intended. It's kind of his thing, which is how he got the nickname Farty Boyle. Though it probably helped that his actual name is Marty.

But there's no stink invading my nostrils or outcry from the guys closest to him. In fact, when I look up, everyone's staring at me.

"It wasn't me," I protest immediately, even though I know that's the dumbest thing I could say. Nobody ever believes that. I mean... he who denied it, supplied it, right?

"Dude," Polly—also known as Brad Polling, our pitcher—grabs my head and turns it toward my arm, "if you're going to deny shit, at least destroy the evidence first."

My confusion lasts for about three seconds before my eyes land on the mega-fucking-huge rip in the sleeve of my suit jacket. "Shit. How'd that happen?" And is Coach going to make me wait here until the area around the stadium is abandoned so nobody can see me leave? The season hasn't even started yet—today's preseason friendly barely got any turnout—so maybe he'll relax the stupid suits-must-be-worn-on-game-day rule. The athletics department must have been eating shrooms when they came up with that piece of bullshit.

"Did you snag it on something?" Laringo asks, and I shrug, then wince when I feel the gap widen.

"Don't think so, but I'm gonna take this off before I make it worse." They all watch while I wrestle my way out of the jacket, unfortunately making the hole bigger even though I'm trying to be careful.

"Why is it so tight?" Boyle shakes his head. "You trying to prove something?"

I roll my eyes. "I've got nothing to prove. Just ask your mom."

The guys jeer and laugh—including Boyle—and I turn my jacket to look at the rip in the sleeve. Polly bends his head closer, blocking the light. "Pol, you mind?"

"Sorry." He straightens. "Good news, that's just the seam ripping. It can be repaired." His dad's a tailor, so he's become our resident expert on things like this. Every year, he does a thirty-minute how-to-sew-on-buttons session for incoming freshmen players. Coach hates for us to look sloppy.

"Great." I don't sound enthusiastic. "Thanks, man. I'll get that done."

He claps me on the shoulder and grabs his duffle, following some of the other guys out. "Don't forget, Shenanigans tonight," he calls over his shoulder. That's the local bar, not an invitation to get up to no good. Though there's a chance we'll do that too.

I flip him a wave of acknowledgment, then go back to getting my stuff together and wondering if I could just sneak past Coach's office without him—

"Marks? Did I hear someone say you ripped your suit?" Coach's bellow precedes him, and I mentally curse my gossiping teammates. There goes that idea.

"Just the sleeve." I turn to face him as he stomps over. He's not that big of a guy, so fuck knows why he's got such a heavy walk. "I'm going to get it repaired."

He studies it with narrowed eyes. "Make sure it's done before next week," he orders. "And go out the side door."

I resist the urge to pump my fist in victory. "Yes, Coach. Thanks!"

He leaves without giving me another glance, and I yank on a hoodie and grab my shit before he can change his mind. Coach Penney is decent enough, but he doesn't like to show it. I kind of get why—we're middle of the road in the league. We win a few more than we lose, but it's been a long, long time since FU Baseball won any pennants. His career is kind of stagnant.

That's not to say we're not a good team. It's Division 1 baseball, after all. But we're not setting the world on fire, and with the exception of maybe Polly, who gets scouted sometimes, none of us are going to the majors, though I know a few of the guys have plans for the minors and hopes to work their way up from the farm teams. Not me.

I make my way as quietly as possible past Coach's office, in case he changes his mind, then out the side door. Nobody ever waits here, because the dumpsters smell like they haven't been washed since the beginning of time. Also, the middle-rank team thing. Girlfriends, family, and friends are usually the only ones who wait for players after our games. Sometimes the occasional little kid whose parents brought them to the game for a day out. I like that it's low-key. As much as I love playing ball, I don't want it to take over my whole life. During the season, my weekends aren't my own, and I know the big leagues would only be worse. I'm going to enjoy it while I'm at school, and then when I graduate I'll find a rec league or something. Baseball is going to be my hobby and something I love for my whole life—not the thing my whole life revolves around.

But that's a few years off yet, and in the meantime, I have to follow the school's rules—and Coach's—or I'm off the team, and that's something I *don't* want.

Back at the dorm, I dump my bag and collapse onto my bed, then dig out my phone. I need to find a tailor to repair my jacket, and I need them fast. It's after four on a Saturday, which means I'm probably shit outta luck, but I can at least find one to call tomorrow. Or... will they even be open tomorrow? Do I have to wait until Monday? How am I supposed to know all this stuff?

Faced with unanswerable questions, I do what any self-respecting nineteen-year-old does: I call my dads.

Uncle Luke—my adoptive dad—picks up on the first ring. "Are you in jail or on fire?"

Rolling my eyes, I reply, "I know you think that's funny, but I *do* call you. A lot. More than most of my friends call their parents."

He snorts. "Jordan, I've met most of your friends, and that's not the flex you think it is. Hold on, I'm putting you on speaker so Grant can hear us."

I wait, smiling a little. Ever since I can remember, Uncle Luke has been a constant in my life. I was eleven when he met—or re-met—Grant, but since then, there've been two men in my life I can rely on no matter what.

"Hey, Jordan," Grant calls a second later. "Do you need money?"

I open my mouth to indignantly deny it, then pause. Do I? No, my bank account is still good. "Why are you both like this?" I whine.

"You love us. So what's up?"

"What do you mean, what's up? Can't a guy just call his dads to check in, see how things are?" I'd feel guilty that I'm not actually doing that, but... nah.

"Sure he can. You're not, though," Uncle Luke says. His voice sounds like he's laughing, and I try to picture them. At this time on a Saturday, they're probably not doing much, or getting ready to go out for dinner. They're both workaholics, but they agreed years ago that if they were going to work weekends, it would be mornings only. Afternoons and nights are family time. They might be on the couch with the TV on, Grant's head in Uncle Luke's lap.

They still live in the house we rented when we first moved to Joyville, but I don't think they'll be there much longer. I get the feeling they're waiting for me to finish college and get settled, and then they'll leave Joyville. The new CEO at Joy Inc. has been grumbling a lot lately about Uncle Luke not being based out of head office in LA, and Grant's hit the ceiling in his career unless he moves someplace bigger. Neither of them wanted to uproot me—or Mila, before she left for college—so they've made it work, but now that we're both adults, they need to put themselves first.

I don't say any of that, though. "This isn't encouraging me to call you more often," I warn. "If I'm gonna be treated like this every time, maybe I'll start calling you less."

They both laugh, damn them, but I can't hold back my grin.

"It's a parent's job to make their kid feel bad about not calling enough," Uncle Luke reminds me. "Just like it's your job to call as infrequently as possible."

"Why aren't you busy, anyway?" Grant adds. "It's still afternoon there—don't you have a preseason game today?" Grant played ball in college, and when I showed skill and love for the game, he helped foster that. Even though he and Uncle Luke were barely dating at the time, he used to show up to all my Little League games and spent hours practicing with me in the backyard.

"That's done. We won." There's an edge of pride in my voice. We were playing Long Beach today, and they've got a pretty good team.

"Congratulations!" Uncle Luke sounds thrilled, even though the game doesn't really count. My childhood was messy at times, but he kept me and Mila grounded.

"Are your stats up online yet?" Grant asks, and even though he can't see me, I shrug.

"Maybe. But anyway, the thing is, I ripped my suit and now I need a tailor." I pause. Do I need a tailor? I know tailors make clothes, but do they repair them? "Or a repair place."

"How did you rip your suit?" Uncle Luke asks.

"Dunno. I put the jacket on, and it just ripped. Polly says it's on the seam and can be fixed," I parrot.

Uncle Luke makes a little hmm noise, and Grant says, "Told you he'd bulked up."

"What?"

"When you came home for Christmas, Grant thought you'd put on some muscle," Uncle Luke explains. "Is the jacket tight? What about your shirts?"

I think about it. "Uh, I guess? It's a lot harder to get on and off now, anyway. I just thought it'd shrunk or something." This makes more sense, though. I have been working out more since Nina, my girlfriend, broke up with me last November. A guy's gotta work off that excess energy somehow, and casual hookups only go so far.

"You thought it'd shrunk," Grant repeats. "Have you been washing your suit?"

"No," I scoff. Shit, was I supposed to? My dads get their suits dry cleaned, so I just assumed I wasn't supposed to wash it.

"Then how would it have shrunk?"

Uh. "Good question," I mutter, and they laugh again. "So anyway, do I need a tailor for this, and how do I find one? Because if it's not fixed before the next game, Coach is going to give birth to unicorns."

"Why unicorns?" Uncle Luke asks curiously.

"Eh, he can't be giving birth to kittens when he gets all ragey. They're too little and cute. Unicorns have those big pointy horns, though, and that would make a guy scream like Coach does."

"Oh my god, you had to ask," Grant mutters.

"If your jacket and shirts are tight, you're better off just getting a new suit," Uncle Luke advises, ignoring the pointy-horned birth. "There's no point repairing it if you're not planning to lose muscle. Which you won't, with the season starting soon."

That's true. Even if I stop the extra workouts, I tend to bulk up a little during the season. The extra muscle helps build stamina. "So I don't need a tailor, then?"

"Nope. How long have you had that suit, anyway? I can't remember when you bought it."

"Sure you do. You took me to buy it."

There's a stunned little pause, then Uncle Luke demands, "Are you telling me that's the same suit I got you for Homecoming your junior year?"

"Yep." When would I have bought another? And *why*?

"I just assumed you bought a new one when you went to college and needed one for dress code. How does it still fit you?" he exclaims.

"It doesn't," Grant deadpans.

"Hey, it was fine until now," I defend my poor suit. It's been through some tough times and deserves some respect. Though... this last year or so, it's been a little short at the wrists and ankles. But it was *fine*.

"I doubt that very much," Uncle Luke says dryly. "You need a new one. And some shirts, if you're still wearing the ones we bought with the suit." He sighs. "A couple of ties, too. Don't wear the same one every time, Jordan."

This is starting to sound complicated. "Okay, so... do you think you can get them to me before Saturday?"

Another little silence.

"Excuse me?"

"Like, I know you've gotta work, but if you call the store and tell them what you need, can they ship it express?"

Grant snickers. "I'm going to let you handle this and go crack open the whiskey."

"Make mine a double," Uncle Luke tells him. "Yes, Jordan, I'm sure they can, but that's not what's going to happen."

I don't get it. Why not?

"What if we pay them extra?"

"Oh boy," he mutters. "Kid, listen carefully. This is what we're going to do."

I smile in relief. Uncle Luke has a plan. I knew he would.

"I'm going to tell you how much I love and miss you, then go enjoy a drink with my husband while we wait for Jason and Dimi to come over for dinner. You are going to find somewhere near you that sells suits, and then you're going to go there and ask a salesperson for help buying a suit, shirts, ties—are you still wearing the same dress shoes?"

"Uh..."

"Okay, so get new shoes too. Put the whole lot on the emergency credit card. Got it?"

Panic wells up in me. "What places sell suits? Like, am I looking for a suit shop? A designer? Those fancy places where you need an appointment intimidate me, Uncle Luke."

"Then don't go there," he says patiently. "In fact, I'd prefer you didn't. That credit card has a limit. You'll be able to find suits at a good menswear store."

"And where do I find one of those?"

He sighs. "Did someone hit you in the head with a bat today? Should you be following concussion protocol?"

What? "No, of course—"

"The mall, Jordan. Go to the mall. Find a menswear store. Ask the salesperson for help. If you get lost at the mall, find an information desk and get directions. Understood?"

Ohhhhh. "There's no need to make it sound like I'm an idiot."

"Uh-huh. I love you and miss you, kid. Call more often, okay?"

Warm feelings rush through me. "Love you, too, Uncle Luke. Hugs to you and Grant, and say hi to Jason and Dimi for me."

I end the call and toss my phone aside. Okay, new plan. Tonight, Shenanigans with the team. Tomorrow, sleep off my hangover and go to the mall.

I've so got this.

TWO
BLAISE

I wouldn't mind working Sundays so much if I weren't in a dead-end job. Sorry, not a dead-end job—as my manager has informed me so many times, he'd love for me to go into the management training program. In a year, I could be assigned to my very own store! One day, I might even be an *area manager*.

Which is fine, and I guess I'm glad he thinks so highly of me, but working retail is not what I want to do for the rest of my life. Four years of college focused on garment design and marketing with a minor in theater and performing arts was supposed to get me closer to a career in costume design and styling. I'm not naïve—I know wardrobe supervisor on a movie or TV show isn't a job the newly graduated just stroll into. I'm prepared to put in the effort. I just wish all that effort was resulting in some kind of progress.

Stop being a whiny loser, I chide myself. Things could be worse, after all. I live in a nice two-bedroom apartment with a roommate who's hardly ever home, thanks to his job as a steward for a charter plane company. His dad bought him the apartment for graduation, and my rent is super low, since he doesn't want it sitting empty most of the time. Plus he's always got the *best* gossip, even if he can't name names. This job isn't my dream, but between it and the side work I do tailoring, plus part-time gigs as wardrobe assistant for a local theater company, my bills are covered. I'm slowly adding to the experience section on my résumé and saving up to apply for a wardrobe internship at Joy Inc.

So my life isn't that bad. I'm twenty-three, I have a job, a home, friends. I've cut the toxic parts of my family out of my life, and I've got goals. I've got a plan. The internship has a top-level reputation: do the year with Joy Inc., and even if they don't offer you a job, you're almost guaranteed to find work with other studios.

I've got an in, too—the guy who runs the program saw my work on Franklin U's film production my senior year, and he actually reached out to invite me to apply. When I said I couldn't cover my living expenses for a year, he gave me his number and told me to call him when I was ready to apply. It's not a definite acceptance, but it's a positive sign. I can deal with working retail for a while if it's going to get me where I want to be.

Even if it is mind-numbingly boring.

Focus on the end goal. Focus on the— Well, hello.

I eye the scrumptious snack that just walked into the store and is gazing around, slightly bewildered and, if I had to guess, very hungover. He turns slowly in a circle, taking in the racks of suits and separates and tables of knitwear, and his expression turns skittish, like he's about to bolt.

Hell, no. A customer is exactly what I need right now, and a good-looking one is even better. Pasting on my customer-service smile, I approach, sizing up his outfit. College uniform of jeans and a sweatshirt, but they're in good condition and not cheap ones. Beat-up Converse on his feet, but one of last year's styles.

"Hi! Can I help you find anyth— Okay, I'm going to take that as a yes," I say as both his hands latch tightly onto my forearm.

"Please," he begs. "Help me."

For a second I wonder if this is more than a shopping emergency—is he in actual danger?—but then he adds, "Why are there so many? I only need one," and I relax. Being in a college town, we get this type of customer a lot. Living away from home for the first time, needing to shop without their parents or older siblings to guide them, they have no idea what they actually need. I get to don my superhero cape and be all, Blaise to the rescue!

"If it's the right one, sure," I agree. "Don't worry, I got you. I'm Blaise, by the way."

"Jordan," he introduces, still looking a little terrified. "How do you know which one is the right one?"

"Well, first tell me what you need. We can go from there."

"A suit. And my dad said I should get shirts and ties and shoes too."

Aw, his dad said. "Job interview?"

He shakes his head. "Sports. School says I have to wear a suit on game day."

"Easy." He needs something that will survive having a jock shove it into his locker and weekly wear, not too ostentatious, and—since he doesn't strike me as the type who wants to buy a new suit every year—nothing too trendy. "Thirty-four waist pants?"

Jordan blinks, getting that same surprised look most men do when I accurately estimate their clothing size. It's kind of my job, and I'm damn good at it. "Ah... yeah."

"No problem. Come and tell me what you think of this." I lead him across the store to a rack of mid-range dark blue suits. They're suitable for any event a college student might need them for, durable, and not that expensive. Plus, the blue will look great with his eyes. "So, you're a freshman?"

He shakes his head, fingering a jacket sleeve. He doesn't reach for the price tag, which confirms my guess that money's not something he worries about. "Sophomore. I ripped my suit this week, and my dad said to get a new one since I'd had it so long."

I frown. If he's a sophomore, how long could he have had it? Most teen guys outgrow their clothes regularly. "Makes sense. So, do you like the blue?"

"Yeah, it's nice. Not too blue, y'know? I don't want anything that stands out too much—I'd rather let my game stats be what people talk about."

Of course he would. Typical jock. Myself, I want my outfit to be on everyone's lips.

"Okay, then these pants should fit, and..." I eye his torso. It's hard to get a good estimate with the sweatshirt. "Are you wearing a T-shirt under that?"

He blinks. "Yeah?"

"Mind taking the top layer off so I can get the right jacket for you? And some shirts, you said." I love a customer who needs a whole outfit. "Commission" is my favorite word.

He obediently strips off the sweatshirt, mussing his brown hair, and boosts the scrumptious factor up by a hundred percent. He's lean, but those arms... yum. "This one." I grab a jacket from the rack. "Let's get you set up in a fitting room, and I'll find you some shirts and ties... and shoes." I lead the way across the store, and he strides beside me all loose-limbed and confident.

"Thanks for this, Blaise," he says. "I'm sure you can tell I'm a novice at suit shopping."

"We all have to start somewhere." I hang the suit in an empty cubicle—which is easy, since they're all empty at the moment—and wave him in. "Start with the pants, and I'll be back in a second."

He flashes me a smile, all white teeth against tanned skin, and I resist the urge to fan myself as the curtain whisks shut.

Shirts, Blaise. The man needs shirts. What a pity.

I find him three—white, cerulean blue, and pale blue—in different styles and fits, then get a pair of black dress shoes. The ties can wait—they don't need to be sized. When I get back to the fitting room, the curtain is open again, and Jordan is standing in front of the huge mirror, turning to the side to get a better view.

"Nope," I declare, and his head comes around.

"No? I think it looks pretty good."

"Oh, it does, but that jacket's too small."

"It is?" He turns back to the mirror with a doubting look.

"Trust me. Here, do this." I put the shirts and shoebox on the big ottoman where friends and partners usually sit, then lace my fingers together in front of me and lift my arms, elbows out. My jacket, which is the right size and perfectly tailored to fit by me, tightens but still gives me decent range of motion.

Jordan mimics my movement, but freezes before his arms get too high. "Uh... I think if I keep going, I'll need to pay for this jacket."

"Too tight?" I try not to sound smug. The sleeves are definitely restricting him too much.

"Yeah."

"Take it off, and I'll get you a bigger size. We might need to tailor it in some places, though." Because this one is perfect around the waist.

He looks alarmed. "Can that be done before next Saturday?"

"No problem. Your pants need to be tailored a little, too, but it can all be done by Wednesday."

Visibly relieved, he takes off the jacket and hands it to me. "Should I try on the shirts now?"

"And the shoes. We might need to adjust the length of the pants. I can get everything pinned today for the tailor." Who is me. I mean, the store does have another tailor we use when things get busy, but since I graduated and started working here full-time, I'm the one who does most of the tailoring. Being able to sew is kind of a requirement for garment and costume designers.

He sits on the ottoman and opens the shoebox, and I take the jacket back out to the front of the store. The next size up isn't where it's supposed to be on the rack, and before I start a storewide search, I check inventory on the computer. We supposedly have three, which probably means Rob sold one and didn't restock the rack. He's notorious for that. A quick foray into the stockroom later, I head back to the fitting room.

And stop.

Jordan's gone back into the cubicle, but the curtain is half open, and I can see him as he unbuttons the white shirt and strips it off. His pants are open, probably because he wanted to tuck the shirttail in, and my eyes trace his six-pack alllllllll the way down to the beginning shadow of his pubic hair just above the band of his underwear. I swallow hard. His torso is just as tanned as his face, making me think he must have gone somewhere warm over the holiday break, and all that smooth skin is begging for my tongue.

"Is that for me?" he asks, breaking my trance, and I muster a smile, pretending I wasn't just ogling him unprofessionally.

"Sure is. How are you going with the shirts?"

"The white one was too tight, but the blue ones were good. Especially the light blue."

The white was a slim fit, and I didn't really think it would work. He's not broad, but he's got some muscle. "If you prefer white, I can get that color in the same style as the pale blue."

He shrugs, and sweet baby Jesus, all those muscles flex. "Yeah, my dad said to get a few shirts. And I like the dark blue color too."

"We'll sort you out," I assure him. "Uh, if you put one back on, you can try the jacket too, get the whole picture." Though it's a real shame to cover all this up. My eyes drift back down to his torso.

He chuckles, and for a second I'm worried I might have said that last bit out loud, but when I jerk my gaze up, I realize I didn't have to. I'm being kind of obvious.

I pull a rueful face. "I'm so sorry. I hope I haven't offended you."

"Nah." He shrugs again. "My dads are gay. I'm not offended that a man finds me attractive."

That's reassuring. "So I'm guessing there wasn't much need for secret experimentation in your early teens," I joke. "Equal opportunity dating endorsed." I regret the words immediately. What a stupid thing to say.

To my surprise, he pulls a face. "I mean, sure, nobody would have batted an eye if I'd started dating guys," he says, "but how do I know if I want to?"

Uhhh... is that a serious question? I study his face, but it doesn't look like he's kidding. "Usually the first sign is that you're attracted to a guy. Um... are you into women, or..." Is this an ace or aro situation? Because I might not be the best person to guide him on that.

"Oh yeah," he assures me confidently. "I like dating and sex with women. And, like, some men are hot, right?" His face goes red and he looks away, then sneaks a peek back at me.

It might just be embarrassment about the conversation, but maybe...

"I'm gay myself, so I don't have any experience in being attracted to women," I begin, moving closer to the cubicle and stopping right outside. "But I've been told the feelings are the same regardless of gender. When you're into someone, being around them makes you a little warm. They get close, and you get tingles. Your stomach fills with butterflies; your mouth gets dry." I lean in closer. "Your heartbeat picks up and you breathe a little faster."

Fuck, my dick is so hard right now. If he looks down, he'll see exactly how into him I am.

He swallows and lets out a shaky breath. "I think," he croaks, then stops to clear his throat. "I think it's safe to say I'm attracted to men, then."

I smile. Safe to say he'll be open to me slipping him my number later. "Welcome to the club." Stepping back, I half turn away to grab the new jacket from the ottoman but freeze at his next question.

"But how do I know if it's just surface attraction? Maybe I like the idea of liking guys, but don't actually want to have sex with one."

Again, I'm not sure if that's a genuine question. Sure, romantic attraction and sexual attraction are different things, and it's absolutely possible to be romantically interested in a particular gender but not sexually. But somehow, I get the feeling that he's not as confused about this as the question makes it seem.

Sure enough, when I look at him, he meets my gaze boldly, a smirk on his lips and challenge in his eyes.

Never let it be said I walked away from a challenge. Especially not when it has full, kissable lips, messy dark hair, and washboard abs.

Grabbing the jacket, I walk back to the cubicle, and this time, I step inside. Hopefully nobody comes into the store for a while. We should be safe—Sunday mornings are quiet, hence me being the only staff member here. "That's something else I can help you with, if you like." I hang the jacket on a peg and quirk a brow at him. We're close enough that I can see the pale freckles on his high cheekbones.

"Oh yeah? How?" He's full-on grinning now.

"Well…" I reach out and put my hand, palm flat, between his pecs. The grin falters, and his chest rises as he takes a deep breath. "How does that feel? Still attracted?"

He nods, and I slowly slide my hand downward, pausing on his abs when he shivers. "What about now? Any ick feelings?"

"Uh, no. No, this is… good."

I mock frown. "Only good, huh? Okay… so what if I…" My fingers dance over the sensitive skin below his navel and tease along his waistband, the heel of my hand pressing lightly against the bulge below. "Hmm… I'd say this answers your question."

He coughs lightly. "Yeah. So. Definitely. Sex with men."

Looking him in the eye, I toy with the fastening of the suit pants and say, "It's such a shame to waste a hard-on like this…"

"I… yeah. Maybe… uh… could…"

The store is empty—and likely to stay that way until after lunch—so I take pity on him and sink to my knees, keeping my gaze locked with his. "I could take care of it for you."

He nods so fast, I'm surprised his teeth don't rattle. "Yeah. That would be great. Thank you."

Smiling, I open the waistband and unzip, then free him from his underwear. "Don't thank me just yet." His cock is gorgeous, not too big but more than a mouthful, flushed red, fully hard, and throbbing after just a little teasing, and it makes me feel like the sexiest man alive. I blow lightly on the head, loving the way he twitches, but I don't really have the time to tease him. The store is open, someone could come in at any time, and I didn't even close the curtain to the cubicle. I definitely can't afford to lose this job.

So I mentally farewell the thought of anything fancy and take him in my mouth as deep as I can. He sucks in air and reaches forward to brace himself against the wall, and I glance up to see his gaze fixed on me, hectic color on his face.

"So hot," he breathes, and if I needed any more encouragement to blow his mind, that would be it.

It's gotta be fast, but it's gonna be good.

I work him with my tongue for a moment, then bob forward, taking him into my throat—which makes him swear—then easing back until he's almost all the way out and my tongue is just toying with the head. His hips jerk in an arrested thrust, and I take pity and get down to the serious business of sucking cock.

"God," he moans, and I pinch his thigh—harder than it looks, no pun intended—to remind him to be quiet. Slapping one hand over his mouth, he stifles the delicious sounds of pleasure, and then his breath catches and his hand drops to tangle in my hair. Jaw clenching, tendons in his neck standing out, he comes.

I swallow as much as I can and fumble in my pocket for a tissue to catch the rest. Even if he's buying these pants, we can't risk cum stains on them.

He collapses back against the cubicle wall, panting hard, and I stand.

"Why don't you try on that jacket while I find some ties to go with those shirts?"

THREE
JORDAN

If I'd known suit shopping on my own could be that much fun, I'd have bought a new suit a long time ago. I'm still grinning when I get back to my dorm with my new shirts, shoes, and ties. I never would have thought I'd need more than one tie —I only have one neck, after all—but now that I think of it, Uncle Luke and Grant have a bunch of ties. Blaise suggested three, and picked ones I could wear with any of the shirts.

Blaise... Man, that was unexpected. Fun, though. And it answers a question I've had for a while.

My roommate woke up and left sometime while I was shopping, so I toss the shopping bag onto my desk, then throw myself onto my bed with my phone. It's my preferred location for making calls.

Mila answers on the third ring. "Jordy, why aren't you sleeping off a hangover? Don't waste the college experience."

"Jordan," I correct, for the millionth time. "And believe me, I'm not." It took four aspirin, a Red Bull, a hot shower, sunglasses, and the promise of a bacon sandwich to get me out of the dorm this morning. Though, gotta admit, the BJ totally cured my hangover. "Aren't you supposed to be the responsible older sibling?"

Her laugh makes me smile. Mila and I are super close, even though there's nearly four years between us. That's why I'm calling her now—I can talk to her about anything.

"Seriously, though," she says when she's stopped chuckling. "Why are you calling me?"

"I don't know why everyone acts like I never call. You and I talk all the time."

"Via text," she reminds me. "And sometimes it takes you a day to reply to me. You only call when something's going on or you need something."

Guilt tugs at me. Maybe I need to call more regularly. I can add it to my class schedule so I don't forget. "I'll try to call mo—"

"I mean, I won't say don't, but also, you don't have to. We all know what college is like, Jordy. Just enjoy it and let us guilt trip you about the calling thing."

I snort. "Yeah, okay."

"If you still don't call after graduation, *then* I'll get pissed off." There's a teasing note to her voice that makes me grin. "Now... do you need something?"

"No. Yes." I change my answer. "But not from you. You don't have the right perspective."

"I'm intrigued. Is this a guy thing? Want me to get Jamie?" She and her high-school boyfriend broke up when he went to college, but they were back together only a few months later when he came home for the holidays. After that, they made long-distance work for the rest of the year, and Mila picked a school only an hour away from his. They moved in together after she graduated.

"Nah, it's a bisexual thing." I wait.

She barely skips a beat before yelling, "Jamie! Jordy's having his big coming out moment!"

"For fuck's sake, Mila, are you trying to deafen me? And it's *Jordan*. I haven't been called Jordy since I was twelve."

"You'll always be Jordy to me. Mostly because it bugs you."

Are all sisters this big a pain in the ass? "Wait, what do you mean, my big coming out moment?"

"Oh, please, Jamie and I figured you were probably bi or pan."

They did? I mean, I thought so, too, but I wasn't sure, and I definitely never talked to anyone about it.

"Did you say Jordan's coming out?" I hear Jamie ask in the background. "You owe me twenty."

"Are you *betting* on me being queer?" I demand indignantly.

"Shush, Jamie. We weren't betting, exactly. We just…"

"Were betting," I finish. "Shame on you both. Tell Jamie that twenty's mine for this betrayal."

"What's he saying?" Jamie demands. "Put it on speaker." A second later, he adds, "Jordan? Congratulations!"

Aw. That's nice. Not that I figured he and Mila wouldn't be supportive, but still. "You owe me twenty."

He sighs, immediately understanding why. "Dammit. It wasn't actually a bet, though. More like a…"

"Bet?"

"A relationship disagreement."

"Involving my preferences? Weird, dude."

"Forget that," Mila interrupts impatiently. "Tell us everything."

"Yeah, no. I want to know why you thought I was bi or pan."

"Which is it, by the way?" Jamie asks. "For… reasons."

"Another bet?"

Neither of them answers.

"I'm not sure," I admit. "Before now, I kind of thought I might be interested in more than just women, but I wasn't sure.

I'd never been attracted to a real person who wasn't female, so—"

"Wait, stop," Mila says. "What?"

I replay what I said and try to work out which part confused her. "Huh?"

"You've never been attracted to a *real person*," she repeats. "What does that mean?"

"Who wasn't a woman," I remind her, because that bit's important. Obviously I've been attracted to my girlfriends over the years.

"Yeah, but aside from women, who were you attracted to that wasn't real? Is this an anime thing? I don't remember you being into anime."

"No, I mean like celebrities. People I'll never meet in real life. Everyone thinks Henry Cavill is hot, right?"

There's a little silence.

"Wait, not everyone does?"

"I do," Mila assures me. "But I don't think it's universal."

"Jamie?"

"Weeeeeell," my straight almost-brother-in-law says. "I can objectively see that he's attractive, but I'm not attracted to him."

Oh. "Not at all?" I check. "Like... there's not even a tiny tingle?"

Mila makes a choking sound.

"Sorry." Jamie sounds genuinely regretful. "I've never seen a guy, in real life, celebrity, or animation, who gave me any kind of tingle."

Maybe I should have talked to someone about this a lot sooner and saved myself wondering. "Oh. So... I might be pan, then." I can think of a few nonbinary and trans celebrities and content creators that I find attractive, but I wasn't sure if it was the celebrity element. Because they're not "real."

"You don't have to know all the answers now," Mila reminds

me. "But you do have to tell me what brought all this on, because I'm dying to know. Spill. Or you won't get a birthday present."

"You're so mean," I tease, and she growls. "Okay, fine. I went to buy a new suit—"

"Why?" Jamie interrupts.

"Because the school says I have to wear one on game day." He knows that. Jamie's an assistant baseball coach at a sports academy that prepares talented teenagers for the big leagues. He knows most of the D1 schools' rules back to front.

"I'm going to kill you," my loving sister threatens.

"No, I meant why did you need another one?" Jamie says at the same time.

"Who the fuck cares?" Mila exclaims.

"I ripped mine," I tell Jamie, ignoring Mila. "Uncle Luke said to get a new one. So I went today, and the guy at the store was fucking hot. All trendy, and kinda artsy."

"How did you not realize you were attracted to men?" Jamie wonders. "Ow! Mila, what the fuck?"

"Stop interrupting him, or I swear to god, there will be pain," she threatens. "Jordy, speak."

I stay silent for ten seconds, just so she knows she's not the boss of me.

"Jordan, maybe finish the story," Jamie suggests. "Her face is going kind of purple."

"So anyway, the guy at the store, Blaise, was hot, and he saw me without a shirt and obviously wanted me, because why wouldn't he, and then he blew me."

There's another little silence. "I feel like you might have missed a few steps," Mila says.

"He blew me in the fitting room?"

She sighs. "Okay, fine. I guess I didn't want any graphic details anyway."

"Like I'd tell you. Ew." She's my sister, after all, no matter how close we are.

"So... how do you feel about it now?"

I grin so wide, my face might split. "Great. Can't wait to do it again."

"Get blown? Yeah, all you guys are like that."

"No details," I remind her, because gross. Then I sit up. "But that's the thing I need help with that you can't help me with." I pause. Did that sentence make sense?

"Getting blown? Yeah, I absolutely cannot and will not help you with that. What is *wrong* with you?"

What? Oh, blech! "Okay, a) that's disgusting; b) not what I meant; and c) I don't need any help getting blown."

"Aw, did you hear that? Jordy knows his ABCs," Mila says—I'm guessing to Jamie.

"You can't see me, but I'm flipping you off right now." I try not to sound like I'm laughing, but I totally am.

"Seriously, though," she continues, "what do you need help with?"

"What if I'm cool with getting a BJ but freak out if I have to give one?" I don't want to be sexually selfish.

"Yeah, I can't help with that. Are dicks hot to you? Like... I think dicks are hot."

"How many have you had contact with?" Jamie asks. "Also, thank you."

Mila scoffs. "I don't have to have been up close and personal to know I find dicks hot. There's pictures online, you know. And we watch porn."

"TMI, guys." Oh my god, what the fuck? I don't need to know that my sister and her boyfriend watch porn together.

Although... maybe I should watch some porn and focus on the dicks?

"Jordy?"

"Yeah?"

"Are dicks hot?"

"I don't know!" My exasperation is tangible. "I don't find mine hot. I mean, it's not ugly, but I'm not exactly turned on by my own cock." I don't think. The way it's starting to perk up in my jeans is a little confusing.

"What about other dicks?"

"This conversation is so weird," Jamie mumbles.

"I'm not all that familiar with other dicks, Mila."

"How is that even possible? Don't you jocks get naked in the locker room all the time?"

"We don't look!" Jamie and I exclaim at the same time.

"You don't? That seems like a wasted opportunity. Also, I feel so betrayed. Porn lied to me."

"Okay, you're being creepy now. Those are my teammates, and I'm not going to stare at them."

"Yeah, but how is it possible to never see anything? Do you all just close your eyes?"

Why is she obsessed with this? "I mean, I see stuff, but I don't look. If that makes sense."

"Not really, but I'm getting bored with this."

"Maybe I should watch some gay porn."

"You absolutely should. But also, have you considered going back to the store for a tie or something and telling the guy you want to return the favor? Did he know he was your first guy?"

I remember the smug expression on Blaise's face. "Yeah."

"Then he probably won't get too upset if you freak out."

"Or," Jamie suggests, "and hear me out, this is a wild idea... You could go to the LGBTQIA+ Association on campus and see if there's anyone you can talk to who might have similar experience."

"Oh," I say. "Yeah. I didn't think of that."

"That... would be the sensible solution," Mila adds.

There's a little pause, and then Jamie sighs. "You're going back to the store, aren't you?"

"Not *today*. But the suit's getting altered, so I have to go pick it up on Wednesday. Who knows what could happen?"

I do. I know. Because when I see Blaise again, I'm totally offering to suck him off.

FOUR
JORDAN

I'M STUPID NERVOUS AS I APPROACH THE MENSWEAR STORE on Wednesday afternoon. It surprises me—I haven't been nervous about sex or dating for years. Though if Uncle Luke asks, I totally didn't start having sex until my senior year of high school, and I definitely did not have sex in our pool that one time. But if, in some alternate universe, I had, I would have learned that pool sex is a great way to slip, nearly crack your head open, and almost drown when the girl you're with panics and drags you under even though you're only in four feet of water. It gets less sexy when that happens. On the plus side, once you've been through that, actual sex itself is a breeze.

So I don't know why I'm so nervous. I mean, it's just a blowjob, right? Mouth on dick, suck and pump, cum everywhere. Easy.

Except I'll be the one giving it, which I've never done before. Never touched another man's cock before. Never even really looked at one, if I'm being honest with myself. Not *looked*, looked.

Okay, maybe I do know why I'm nervous.

The nerves ramp all the way up when I walk into the store

and don't see Blaise. What I do see is an older guy talking to a woman with a toddler in a stroller. They're looking at a shirt while the kid snoozes. Maybe Blaise isn't even working today. If he is… can I really suck him off with other people here? A kid? That's kind of gross. I mean, it's not like they'd be watching or anything, but what if Blaise is loud when he comes? Or I could gag—that happens during BJs. The kid could hear something that would scar them for life. Worse, because they're asleep, it would be like an unconscious thing, and they wouldn't even know what traumatized them, so they couldn't work through it in therapy. They'll end up forty, unemployed, unable to talk to other people or sustain a healthy relationship, all because of trauma they don't even know they have.

"Someone will be with you in just a moment, sir," the salesguy calls to me with a professional smile before turning back to the woman. Does that mean Blaise is here after all? But I don't know if I want to go through with this now. I mean, I do, but maybe not here in the store. I could suggest meeting up later?

Before I can make a decision, a woman about my age walks out of the fitting room area, spots me, and smiles, heading in my direction. I guess Blaise isn't here after all.

Shoving down my disappointment—there will be other chances, right? And maybe Jamie was right and I shouldn't jump into this mouth-first—I smile politely back at her.

"Hi! Is there anything I can help you find?"

"Uh, I'm actually here to pick up a suit that was being altered?"

Her smile changes subtly, losing some of its enthusiasm. "Of course! What was the name?"

"Jordan Marks."

Recognition lights her expression. "Blaise is just pressing it now. I'll go get him."

She walks away, leaving me swimming in nerves again. Blaise *is* here. Shit. Now what do I do?

As though in response, the older salesman walks the woman and her stroller to the register and begins processing the sale. The kid's gonna leave. Maybe—

But there will still be two other people here, and I'm not sure Blaise is gonna want to risk his job for a BJ from a novice.

Okay. Revised plan it is: ask him to meet up later. If I can, hint that good things will happen. I have to be clear it's not a date, though—he seems nice and all, but I'm not sure if I'm ready to date men, and I don't want to give him the wrong impression. FU is liberal and has had queer athletes in the past —Peyton Miller is the most famous example—but there's a whole PR circus involved with Division 1 athletes coming out, and I barely know him. Before I commit myself—and my date—to all that hoopla, I'd need to know him better.

Right now, I know I'm attracted to men, but not sure if I can handle a stick, so to speak. I should clear that up before anything else.

Blaise walks out from the back and smiles at me, a little knowing, a little smug, and I nearly swallow my tongue. My cock goes to half-mast as the memory of his lips wrapped around it fills my brain.

Definitely attracted to men, and I want to learn how to handle a stick.

"Hi, Jordan," he says, his voice completely professional. "I've just finished pressing your suit, and it looks great. Let me grab a garment bag for you and you'll be good to go."

"I don't need to try it on?" Crap. If I can't talk to him more privately, this is going to be a lot harder. No pun intended.

He pauses. "You can if you'd like to."

Now that he's given me the opening, I hesitate. "I don't want to be any trouble..." The guy's trying to do his job, after all.

"No trouble." His smile is friendly. "Come through to the fitting rooms, and I'll get you set up."

I follow him, my eyes dropping to his ass before I jerk them back up. Jesus, what's wrong with me? I never blatantly checked out guys before. Has admitting I'm into men opened up a lecherous side of me?

Or is it just because Blaise and I have already done more than I ever did with any other man, and I'm hoping we'll do more?

Blaise goes through a door marked Staff Only, and I wait near the giant ottoman. I wonder where stores even get stuff like that, and can the general public buy them? There isn't room in my dorm, but one day, it'd be cool to have—it looks big enough to stretch out and take a nap on.

"Where can I buy one of those?" I ask Blaise when he comes back, holding my suit.

"The suit? You already bought it."

I shake my head and point to the ottoman. "No, that."

His lips twitch. "I don't know where that one came from. But I think there's a furniture place in town that has similar ones, over on Short Street."

Filing that away for future reference, I nod. "Thanks. You ever tempted to nap on it? Or... do other stuff?" My face gets hot. They're stupid questions—he *works* here, for fuck's sake.

To my surprise, he grins. "Tempted, yes, but there's a security camera just above that mirror." He nods to the giant mirror at the end of the room, and I try not to panic. The cubicle curtain was *open* the other day when he blew me. How much can that camera see?

Math isn't my strong point, but the thought of that footage being sent to my coach or the NCAA—or worse, ESPN—has me calculating trajectories so hard, I'm pretty sure my brain starts smoking.

Blaise must see my panic, because he shakes his head and lowers his voice. "Relax—it can't see anything inside that end cubicle, even with the curtain open. The angle's all wrong."

I try not to sag in relief. "Thanks," I croak. "It, uh, would be kind of a circus if—"

"I get it. 'College Athlete is a Sex Addict' is just the kind of click-baity news headline you never want to see."

"Exactly." I breathe a little easier. "But, uh... it occurred to me that I should probably return the favor." Definitely not here, though. I've just discovered that public sex is *not* for me.

Well... not under these conditions, anyway.

Heat flashes in his eyes, and one brow quirks. "Oh? That's something you'd be interested in?"

"I can't promise any kind of expertise. Just lots of enthusiasm," I warn him, but if anything, that just makes his gaze spark hotter. "Um... somewhere else, though." I glance up at the camera, and he laughs.

"Yeah, I kind of need this job, so it definitely wouldn't happen when my manager could walk in. But my shift's done in fifteen minutes, and my roommate's not home until tomorrow..."

I take the hanger from him. "I'm going to try this on and go get a pretzel. My dad always taught me to eat dinner before dessert."

I park my car on the street outside Blaise's place and wipe my sweaty palms on my jeans. I'm so ready to do this.

He's parked in a carport and is waiting for me, so I jump out and try to look cool as I hurry to join him. There's a frown on his face, and my stomach sinks.

"Where's your suit?"

I blink. "In the car?" I didn't realize I'd need it for this. Does he want to do some kind of workplace role-play? I'm not sure if I can act and suck cock at the same time.

"Yeah, but I can't see it hanging." He squints toward my car.

"It's on the back seat. I laid it out and everything," I assure him, trying to impress him with how I didn't just dump it in the footwell. Not saying that was my first instinct or anything.

He doesn't look impressed, but he nods and turns toward the building. I make a mental note to ask Uncle Luke if I did something wrong by not hanging it. Where would I even hang it in the car? If suits have rules, then you should get a copy of them when you buy one.

We go up a flight of stairs, though I saw a tiny elevator tucked in the corner, and into the apartment on the right.

"Whoa, this is nice." I fail at not sounding surprised. After he said he needed his job, and knowing what retail pays, I was expecting something... not this.

"Yeah, I got lucky. My roommate's family is rich, and he's away a lot for work, so he wanted someone who could be here to keep an eye on the place. I only pay utilities."

"Sweet." My dads asked me if I wanted to move off campus this year, but honestly, I like the dorms. Still, they wouldn't have set me up in a place this nice—Uncle Luke tries to walk a line between making sure we have everything and keeping us humble. "So, uh..." Well, this is awkward.

The smug smile from before is back on his face, and he steps up close to me. "Just so you know, I won't be mad if you change your mind. But if you still want to do this, I promise to be gentle."

I don't know why that makes me so hot, but I just got the best shivery feeling.

"I want to do this," I assure him. "I, uh... full disclosure, I've never, uh, I mean—"

"I know you've never done this before. I was there Sunday, remember?" he says dryly, and I chuckle.

"Ha, no, I mean obviously I liked having a man suck me off, but I don't know..." I trail off. There's no way to say this without sounding like an asshole.

He seems to get it, though. "You don't know if you're going to like doing the sucking? That's fine. Some guys don't. It doesn't mean you're not attracted to men."

"Can I see your dick?" I blurt, and he grins.

"Whoa, straight to business, huh?"

I bury my face in my hands, and he laughs and grabs my wrist, tugging it down. "Come on. Let's sit on the couch, and you can see anything you want."

I follow him like a puppy, and when he raises a brow and offers to get naked, I'm only too happy to accept. I even take my shirt off in solidarity.

"Keeping the pants on?" he asks, and I grimace.

"I think I might need the restriction." I've been half hard since he left the store after his shift and winked at me, and if this is anywhere near as good as Sunday was, I need to keep my pants on to help me maintain control.

"Suit yourself." Buck naked, he gracefully sits on the couch, and I drop down beside him, my eyes tracing over his body. He's around my height but a little leaner, more lithe, and his skin is a few shades darker—like he has an all-over tan. His body hair is sparse, the same dark color that's on his head.

And his cock...

For the first time ever, I deliberately look at another man's penis.

And swallow hard. Dicks are hot.

I'm not a good judge of cock size, but if I was guessing, I'd say his is a little longer than mine, and thicker. Or maybe it just looks that way because I'm planning to put it in my mouth. It's standing at attention, flushed dark and seeping a tiny drop of precum, and god, I want to taste that.

But... "Not to sound like a cheesy porn movie, but are we sure that will fit? I kind of need my jaw intact."

He smirks. "It'll fit. But start slow—you don't have to be a champion cocksucker your first time."

Forcing my gaze away from my late-afternoon snack, I snort. "Dude, I'm an athlete. We don't like second place."

Arching a brow, he says, "That's big talk from a guy who hasn't even touched my *arm* yet."

Immediately, I put my hand on his arm, and he laughs. But it actually makes things easier—it's a first step. Like putting on my glove for a game. So I take the second step, moving my hand from the safe area of his arm to the more intimate expanse of his chest. Guys don't touch other guys' chests platonically. This is new for me.

I like it.

I like the way his skin feels under my callused palm. I like the little shiver he gives. I *love* the way his nipple goes hard when I touch it, and I slide my fingers back and forth over it, teasing, until he groans.

So I lean down and lick it.

"Tease," he accuses as I lick again, then give it a gentle little bite.

"It's not teasing if I intend to follow through," I retort, then slide off the couch and kneel between his legs. His dick is right in front of me, but I ignore it for now, returning my attention to his delicious nipples. It's only fair the other one gets the same attention, right?

I've been complimented in the past on my attention to detail in this area, and it's nice to know the skill is transferable to men. I play with his nipples until he's all squirmy, then decide it's time for the main event.

I lick a trail over his stomach, pausing to nuzzle his belly button, then... stop.

Fuck. I have no idea how to do this.

"It's still okay if you want to stop," he says softly, and I glance up to see him watching me.

"I don't. But maybe you could... guide me?"

His gaze darkens. "Verbally or physically?"

Oh wow, I hadn't thought of that, but man, my dick just got so hard. "Both. You steer." I pick up his hands from where they're lying on either side of him and put them on my head. "Show me how to pleasure you."

He shudders hard, his eyes falling closed, and a little more precum seeps from his cock.

"Can I lick that off?" I ask. He opens his eyes to see what I mean, then nods.

"Do it. Tongue only." He guides my head lower, and I stick out my tongue and lap up the liquid. The sharp saltiness is... not good, exactly, but I want more. I want to suck it out of him. "Good boy."

"That shouldn't be as hot as it is," I mutter, and he huffs.

"I'm with you on that. Ready for more?"

Fuck yeah. "Yes."

"Open your mouth and relax your jaw. We're going to start slow. Let me direct."

I do as he says, and he guides my mouth over his cock—but just a bit. Just enough for the head to press between my lips. It feels so strange, but I also want more. I lick him, stroking my tongue over the hard flesh within my reach, and he groans.

"You're a fucking natural. Keep doing that—I'm going to feed you more."

My jaw stretches around him as he slides me down onto his dick, and god, I knew he was big, but he feels enormous. He fills my mouth, and yet Blaise keeps going, pushing my head lower.

It's kind of uncomfortable, but also... I love it. I use my tongue as much as I can, like he told me, and when he stops and strokes my hair, I glance up at his face.

"You look amazing, stuffed full of my cock."

The praise makes my dick throb, and I give myself a little squeeze through my pants. He sees what I'm doing and says, "Jack yourself if you want."

What a good idea.

His hands grip my head again, and as I start jerking myself off, he draws me backward, off him. I make a noise of protest, and he shakes his head. "Relax. I'll give it back."

He does. Over and over, he feeds me his dick and then takes it away, while I lick and suck at whatever I can and frantically stroke myself, until everything starts to feel hazy. I'm going to come soon—I know it—and I want him to, as well. So this time when he eases his cock into my mouth, I ignore the restriction of his hands and lunge forward, taking everything—and promptly gag.

"Oh, *fuck*," he cries, and I take that as encouragement, backing off a little but still working him on my own schedule. "Jesus, Jordan, that's... Fuck, I'm gonna come!"

So am I. As the tingles race up my spine and my muscles start to stiffen, I pull off him—don't want to accidentally bite. And then orgasm rushes me, hard and fast, and I'm sure I hear him yell, but I don't know what. Fluid spatters across my chest.

When I can see again, Blaise is a panting heap on the couch, his cum decorating my body like a badge of honor.

I grin, struggling to get my breath back. "I guess I can handle a stick."

FIVE
BLAISE

Trying to breathe like I'm not dying, I wonder if Jordan's up for learning other new things. Because, yeah, he definitely didn't have any expertise, but I think I have a newly discovered kink for sex with novices. It's superhot.

He stands and wipes his mouth with the back of his hand, and something about it—or maybe it's his puffy lips or the glazed pleasure in his eyes—makes my cock twitch again.

"So... was that okay? I mean, you came, which is a good sign, but... any notes?"

I huff a laugh. "It was more than okay, and sure, practice makes perfect, but enthusiasm helped. A lot."

He smiles cockily. "That's my secret to life. Do everything enthusiastically, and people either don't realize you suck, or they feel bad for you and try to help."

Ah, to be that confident. Though it's not really that bad of a life motto to have. "To be fair, you did suck. It's just that's what I wanted."

It takes him a second to get the (admittedly terrible) joke, and then he cackles. "So, uh, is there anywhere I can wash up?

I'm kind of gross right now." He grimaces, and remorse floods me.

"I'm so sorry. I should have asked if you were okay with... that." I wave toward his chest, then bite my lip. God, he looks hot wearing my cum.

His cocky grin flashes. "I am seriously fine with it. But I also came in my pants, so... can I clean up?"

"Sure. Down the hall, first door on the right. If you want a real shower, that's fine—towels under the sink."

"Thanks." He turns away, then hesitates and turns back. "Uh, so... you said practice makes perfect, right? Any chance you're volunteering for me to practice on?" His cocky little smirk almost masks the insecurity lurking in his eyes.

"You want to give me BJs until you perfect your technique? Oh no, how will I cope?" I ask, deadpan, and he laughs again.

"I know it's a sacrifice. You're a real American hero." He saunters off down the hall while I snicker over that. Getting head for America? Sign me up.

I use Drey's bathroom to clean up—he won't care—and hear Jordan in the shower as I pass the bathroom on the way back to the living room. I'm a little surprised that he didn't just use a washcloth—I figured jocks weren't that fussy about stuff like that. I guess I shouldn't stereotype.

Plus, dried cum itches.

In the kitchen, I get the water pitcher from the fridge and fill a glass, then drain it. Gotta replace those fluids.

I take my time with the second glass, sipping while I wonder how this is going to work. I hope Jordan means he literally wants to practice gay sex with me, and not that he wants anything more. Not that I'm opposed to dating or even having a boyfriend, and sure, he's hot and seems like a great guy, but I haven't heard anything about a queer player on the baseball team at Franklin, and I have enough friends still taking classes that I probably would. That's the thing about rainbow mafia friendship groups—when someone in sports comes out or is openly queer, we talk about it. Only one of my friends even *likes* sports, but we still talk about queer athletes. And we'd have gone to a baseball game at FU by now if one of the players was out, because the community stands strong when we support each other.

So it's very unlikely Jordan went home on Sunday and openly proclaimed he was queer, which means any dating would either need to be behind closed doors or invite a publicity circus. Which... no thanks. I don't want to be a household name in college sports circles. The only people I want talking about me are in the entertainment and design world... and one day, maybe on the awards circuit.

I hear the bathroom door open and footsteps padding out, but they stop too soon. Curious, I lean over the counter and catch a glimpse of him standing in the doorway to my room, mouth agape. He's seen my Hector costume. Most people react like that—it's why I keep it on the dress form instead of packing it away or taking it apart like I do for most of my "for fun" costumes.

Pulling back, I wait for him to regain his wits and come to join me. He glances around the living room, then spots me in the kitchen alcove. "Hey."

"Want some water?" I lift my glass in demonstration, and he nods.

"Yeah, that would be great. Thanks."

I get a glass and pour him some, and for a moment we both sip in silence. Then he clears his throat. "Ah, so, I couldn't help but see into one of the bedrooms."

"My bedroom," I correct. "Unless you were opening doors."

He shakes his head fast. "No, the door was open. Sorry if I wasn't supposed to look."

"Nah, it's fine. Door was open, and I've got nothing to hide."

There's another little silence, and I wait for him to ask. He will. Everyone who sees Hector does.

"So... that costume was for Hector from the *Space Reivers* live-action remake, right?" he says, surprising me. Not everyone gets it right away—mostly they ask me what it is and if I'm going to a costume party.

"Good guess. Most people don't pick that."

He shrugs. "Well, it's not exactly the same as what Hector wears," he says, surprising me again. The only people who've ever picked up on that are my friends in the same industry, because we all scrutinize costumes like other people do with sports statistics. "Where did you get it?"

I smile. "I made it."

His mouth drops open again. "Get out! You *made* that? Fuck, you're insanely talented."

"Thanks." I preen a little. That's always nice to hear.

"Why'd you make it a bit different? Supplies or something?"

"No." I shake my head. "I made it when the movie was first announced, before the costuming was decided on. I like to do that sometimes, with remakes or adaptations—pick a character and design the costume I think would work best." I shrug. "Sometimes they're incredibly different, because I have no idea what the studio's vision for the movie is, or even who the costume designers will be that early on. But this one came really close. How'd you spot the differences, by the way? Only two other people ever have."

He opens his mouth, hesitates, then says, "I really love that movie. I have an, um, emotional connection to it, I guess. Well, to the animated version, but that transferred over."

I want to ask about that, but he seems uncomfortable, so I

don't. Probably worried I'll judge him for loving a kids' movie. Which of course I wouldn't—kids' movies are the best for tongue-in-cheek jokes aimed at adults. Plus, they get some great costuming opportunities.

"So you just made it for funsies? That seems like a lot of work."

"No. Yes," I correct. "It was a lot of work, and I guess I did make it for fun, since it's never going to be used unless I go to a dress-up party. But that's what I do—what I want to do, anyway. I'm trying to get into wardrobe and costume design."

"That's cool. Uh, seems like a tough industry to break into."

I put my empty glass in the sink. "Yeah, not the easiest. Right now I'm building my portfolio with local stuff and saving to apply for an internship at Joy Inc."

Something changes in his face, but I can't put my finger on it. He's not going to judge me for wanting to work at Joy Inc., is he? That would be hypocritical, since he just said he has an emotional connection to one of their movies.

"Oh? I didn't know internships cost money to apply to."

"They don't. This one doesn't, anyway. But it's unpaid, so I'd need to be able to support myself living in LA for a year, which..." I grimace.

"Yeah," he says sympathetically. "You're not the first person I've heard mention that. It sucks that the internship is unpaid, though. You'd think Joy Inc. made enough in profits to pay one measly minimum wage salary."

Aww, he's cute. "Most internships are unpaid. Or paid so badly that they barely cover coffee. It's not ideal, but instead of raging about it, I'm going to get this internship—eventually—and maybe one day I'll be in a position to do something about it." Or at least to insist that any interns working with me get paid.

The outrage on his face turns to determination. "That's a good plan, but I'm going to rage against it instead."

I laugh. What does he think the rage of a college student will do? "I appreciate the solidarity, since ball players don't usually have to intern." Do they? Don't they all get huge deals when they're scouted at their college games? That's what movies and TV have taught me.

He shakes his head and puts his glass in the sink beside mine. "I'm not going to be a professional ball player, and I'll probably have to intern somewhere." A slightly guilty expression crosses his face, though I have no idea why. "Or at least get summer jobs as a lackey in my field."

"What's your field going to be?" I'm genuinely curious. I thought most college athletes aspired to go pro.

"Events management."

My brows shoot up. That's not anywhere close to what I was expecting. Jordan notices my surprise and chuckles.

"You thought I was going to say sports management or physical therapy, didn't you?"

"Or agent," I agree. "There was also the chance that you'd opt for phys ed teacher."

"Not gonna lie, I thought about all those when I was still in high school," he admits. "It would be a way to still connect with my sport, you know? But a friend of my dads' works in event management, and this one time on 'take your kid to work day,' I ended up shadowing him for a couple hours. There were so many details he had to think about, so much scheduling, but it was also really creative. And at the end, the result was that a lot of people had a fun time." He waves a hand. "I talked to him about it, and shadowed him a few more times after that, and it feels like a good fit for me."

Seeing the way his face has gone all happy and intense, I can't help but agree. "You might also get the chance to still be connected to your sport," I point out. "Teams use event managers, don't they?"

He winks. "That may have occurred to me too."

A new thought strikes, and I realize why he looked guilty when he talked about needing an internship. "And your dads' friend, will he let you get some experience working with him?" He's got a connection. Most of the kids with money do.

Jordan nods sheepishly. "Yeah. Toby—that's his name—already said if I keep my grades at the right level, he'll keep a spot in their summer program open for me. I didn't do it last year because they don't take freshmen, but I'm on track this year."

"That's great. You totally shouldn't feel bad about that," I assure him. "If he was holding the place even if you failed everything, I might judge you, though."

He shudders. "Dude, no. My dads would say no, even if he wanted to. Uncle Luke told me before I started college that it was fine if I struggled with classes, but if I wasn't even trying, he'd confiscate my stuff. I've got some pretty cool collectibles."

"Your dads would let him take your stuff?"

For a second, he looks startled. "Oh—sorry. I forget sometimes that people don't..." He shakes his head. "Uncle Luke *is* my dad. He adopted me and my sister when our parents died."

Foot, meet mouth. "Sorry," I say awkwardly. He seems fine talking about it, but...

"Nah, it's fine. I mean, it's not, but I don't mind talking about it. I was only five, and I don't remember a lot about my parents. And Uncle Luke really is my uncle, kinda. He was married to my mom's brother at the time. Then Uncle Matt split, and he adopted us."

Whoa. That's some crazy movie shit right there. "Uh... can I ask about your other dad? I'm guessing it's not... Matt."

"Nope." He shakes his head. "I still talk to Uncle Matt sometimes, but not a lot. When I was eleven, Uncle Luke started working with Grant—they knew each other in college but hadn't seen each other since. Anyway, they ended up together, and two years ago they got married. He was my dad before that, though," he adds thoughtfully. "I'm lucky to have had two sets of parents who love me."

I'm literally speechless. His dad's life is the plot of a Hallmark movie.

SIX
JORDAN

"Lunch," I say firmly the next day, cutting into Polly's waffling diatribe about our stats professor. Sure, the guy's a douchecanoe, but he can complain about it while I eat.

He stares at me blankly, proving he's been so lost in his own rant that he'd forgotten I was even here. "What?"

"Lunch. Let's get something to eat, and you can keep whining."

"I'm not whining! I'm just—"

"Whining?" Calla, one of our classmates, asks as she pauses beside us. She's cool, and we've hung out a few times. I've seen her at our ball games occasionally—you get to recognize the regulars when the crowd isn't capacity. And I think she has a thing for Polly, but he swears she's a lesbian. I'm trying to teach him that just because he saw her making out with another girl doesn't mean she's a lesbian, but for some reason, he won't accept that. He's normally cool about that stuff, so I think he likes her but doesn't want to get his hopes up.

Polly pouts. "*Not* whining."

"He's whining," I tell Calla. "Wanna come to lunch with us? I'm starving."

"Sure. Dining hall?"

"It's closest."

We set off in that direction, Polly trailing behind, still muttering about how he's not whining, and of course it's chaos when we get there.

"Ten minutes ago, when class actually ended, it probably wasn't this bad," I observe, taking in the line.

"Too bad Polly was busy whining," Calla agrees.

"I wasn't whining!" Pol shouts, loud enough for people to hear and turn around. A micro-silence falls, all eyes on us, and Polly's face gets red. "Well, I wasn't," he mumbles.

I clap him on the shoulder. "Sure, you weren't."

We join the line as the noise begins again, and Calla says, "Okay, Polly... you have until we sit down to rant, and then you're done. Go."

"Why are you like this?" he asks her.

"You're wasting precious time," she sings, moving forward with the line.

"How come you're not annoyed too?" Pol bursts out. "You're both in the same class as me. You've seen how he is."

Calla shrugs. "Yeah, but there's nothing we can do about it. He's an asshole, but not any more than everyone else. You gotta learn to go with the flow in class and then spread a rumor that he has herpes or something. Maybe you should take up yoga."

I snort-laugh, and Polly glares at her. "I already do Pilates, fuck you very much, and why are you even taking this class, anyway? You're an arts major."

"Yoga and Pilates are different. Do both. And since I plan to run my own business someday, this class is an investment in my future. There will come a time when my understanding of statistics will enhance my business so much that I can sit back and sip champagne on a pile of diamonds, and I'll think fondly of Professor Douchebag Brooks and the fact that he'll probably still be slogging away teaching whiners who hate him."

Polly and I stare at her, and she smiles. "What? I have dreams, too, you know."

"A pile of diamonds sounds uncomfortable," I observe. "Are they huge diamonds or thousands of tiny little ones?"

"Does it matter? They're diamonds, and they're mine." She frowns. "Probably lab ones, though. I don't want to support the exploitation of children in Africa."

Polly throws up his hands and stalks forward to order his food. I grin at Calla. "I think you're wearing him down." It's the first time I've hinted that I think she's into him.

"It's a long game," she agrees.

I really like her. "Just so you know, you've got an ally on the inside." I hold out my fist, and she bumps it. The rings on every one of her fingers make it a little uncomfortable, but the artsy vibe reminds me of something. "Hey, you're doing design, aren't you? Like fashion and stuff?"

She rolls her eyes. "Yeah, fashion and stuff."

What else do I call it? I file that question away for later. "I was talking to someone, kind of a friend, who does designing for, like, costumes for movies. Well, he's trying to do that. He said the internship he wants to apply for is unpaid and he needs to save up for living expenses first."

"I'll have the chicken sandwich, please. And chips and a soda," Calla tells the server, then looks at me expectantly. "Is there a question?"

Uh... is there? "I guess I was hoping he was wrong? And that you'd know of some paid internships he could apply for? Because he's really good, and he graduated last year." That was something else he told me before I left yesterday.

"He's not wrong. Sorry, Jordan. Internships are mostly unpaid. There are a couple that might offer a really small stipend, but he'd still need the money to cover living expenses first, because it's seriously not enough to support a whole person."

"Shit."

"It's not my fault, man," the server tells me, an offended look on his face.

"Sorry. I wasn't swearing at you, I promise. Uh... I'll have what she had." Because I haven't even looked at what's on offer, and I don't want to make him wait after I already sort of swore at him.

But seriously, unpaid internships? That sucks so hard. What I really hate is that my dad—both of them, I guess—works for a company that doesn't pay interns. Do they know that? Grant technically works for Joy Universe, not Joy Inc., and neither of them are based in LA or more than peripherally connected to the studio, but still. They're execs for the company.

I grab my tray, and Calla and I head toward where Polly's already staked out some seats at a table. "Who's your friend? Maybe I know him. The design school here at FU is small and incestuous, even if it is mighty."

"Blaise," I say, then realize I don't know his surname. It doesn't matter, though, because she blinks in recognition.

"*Blaise?* About so tall"—she holds a hand up near the top of my head—"dark hair and eyes, great style, thinks the Met Gala started out as a great thing but is now way overhyped?"

"Uhhhh... I don't know about that last thing, but otherwise, yeah? So you do know him?"

"He's one of my besties," she announces confidently as we sit. "How did *you* meet him?"

"How did you meet who?" Polly asks, stabbing his fork into some kind of casserole that frankly looks unidentifiable.

"My friend Blaise," she tells him. "Unless the world has turned upside-down, you wouldn't know him."

Polly looks insulted. "I know people."

"Design people?"

"I know you," he points out.

"Uh-huh. And who else?"

"I'm really starting to not like you."

She blows him a kiss, then turns back to me. "Talk."

"It's not that interesting." Not the parts I'm willing to tell her, anyway. "I ripped my game day suit, and Uncle Luke told me just to get a new one since apparently I wasn't supposed to have had that one for so long. So I went to the mall and Blaise sold me a suit."

"How long did you have the old one?" Polly asks curiously.

I shrug. "I got it for homecoming junior year."

Calla shudders. "Oh, honey, no."

"What's wrong with having a suit for nearly four years?" I can't help being defensive. I don't know what the problem is here.

"It's not the four years part, it's the part where you were, what, sixteen then? And now you're twenty. Teenagers change fast."

"I'm not twenty until March," I mutter, like that makes a huge difference.

Calla pats my hand. "It's a good thing Blaise was there to take care of you."

She has no idea how true that is.

Uncle Luke calls me just as my last class of the day is letting out, and panic flashes through me. He doesn't call. When I left for college, he told me he understood that I'd be busy with my new life so he wouldn't be calling. He does send messages to remind me that I have family who worries about me, though.

"Uncle Luke? Is everything okay?"

There's a pause. "Oh, kid, I'm sorry. Yeah, everything's fine. I didn't mean to scare you."

I breathe easier. "Nah. Okay, yeah, for a second I was a tiny bit apprehensive."

"Well, I'm sorry about that. I just wanted to see if you'd had any luck finding a suit."

I start walking toward my dorm. I've got practice in twenty minutes, so I can't delay. "I went to the mall on Sunday and got one, like you said. And some shirts and stuff. It needed to be altered, but I picked it up yesterday."

"Good. That's great news." He sounds relieved, and I wonder if I should be offended by his lack of faith in me. "Send me some pictures later."

I miss a step. "What?"

"I want to make sure you don't look like a hobo."

"I can't even with you, Uncle Luke. I'm not taking a photo like you made me for prom."

"Fine. Did you at least charge it to the credit card like I told you?"

"Duh. I didn't even look at the prices." That's kind of true. I didn't look at the tags, but I know how much the total was because Blaise told me before I handed over the card.

Uncle Luke makes a choking sound. "Okay. I guess if the transaction went through, it couldn't have been too terrifying. I hope," he adds in a mutter. "Anyway, I know you have practice today, so I'll let you go."

"Actually," I say as I reach the dorm. One of the guys from the first floor is coming out and holds the door for me, and I give him a smile and an up-nod. "I wanted to talk to you about something."

"Shoot."

"Why doesn't Joy Inc. pay interns?"

Uncle Luke takes a second to digest that, and I hit the stairs. "That was not what I was expecting you to say. Uh... I didn't know they didn't. I haven't worked with an intern while I was there."

"I was talking to the guy who sold me the suit, and he said he wants to apply for a costume design internship, but he needs to save up for living expenses first. That's not cool."

"It's not," he agrees. "You didn't tell him—"

"That my dads are Joy executives *and* I have honorary uncles who work in theater and have connections? No. Of course I didn't." I like Blaise, and not just because he got me off and wants to do it again. I think we could be friends. And it's not like any of my connections could solve his problem—he needs money. Once he's ready to apply, I might ask Uncle Luke to put a good word in with whoever handles that stuff. We'll see.

"I don't know what to tell you, Jordan. I can ask some questions, because I agree that it's not okay to expect someone to work for free. But it's not my department, and ultimately, whoever *is* in charge would need to get the budget for it signed off by the CFO."

"Who you don't like," I finish as I let myself into my room. Uncle Luke had a really great working relationship with the previous CEO and CFO, but they're both in their eighties now and retired a couple of years ago. He says the new ones are good enough, but their vision and approach are a little different.

"It's not that I don't like him," he begins as I put the phone on speaker and toss it on the bed. "It's just—"

"Yeah, yeah, I know. Anyway, I just wanted to see if you knew, and register my opinion." I pull my sweatshirt over my head.

"Noted, and I'll take an action item," he replies. "Any other news while I've got you on the phone?"

"Not really. I'm heading to practice in a few minutes. Our

game this weekend is an away one, so I'll be off campus almost the whole time. Oh, and I worked out that I'm either bi or pan."

"What?"

My roommate walks in, and I flip him a wave. "Gotta go, Uncle Luke. Talk later."

"Wait, you can't—"

I end the call. Even if I wasn't in a hurry, now wouldn't be the time to talk about this. I'll definitely hear about it later, though.

SEVEN
BLAISE

I'M LATE, THANKS TO ONE OF MY FAVORITE CLIENTS coming in five minutes before closing. Silas—or as I privately think of him, the hot grouch—is a professor at Franklin and completely clueless when it comes to clothes. He basically tells me what he needs and lets me pick what I want. I try to dress him to match his conservative vibe, and I must be succeeding, because one time, he thanked me for picking clothes that didn't make him feel like he was wearing a costume. Tonight he wanted to get the jump on his spring wardrobe, so I'm not mad about staying late and making a fat commission. Drinks are on him.

But the store closes at nine on Fridays, so Shenanigans is already busy by the time I roll in close to ten. There's a text on my phone telling me my friends are in one of the back booths, so I weave through the crowds to find them.

"Finally!" Butch cheers, lifting her glass in salute. "We thought you'd ditched us."

"Customer," I explain, sliding in beside Harold (No last name. It's his thing.). "He's paying for the next round." They all cheer this time, even Phil, and Calla slides a glass and the pitcher across the table to me. "So what'd I miss?"

"Harold told his client she has bad taste," Butch says. Her name is actually Belinda, but she used to find herself saying, "Yes, I'm butch, get over it," so much that it was just easier to call herself that. Now she introduces herself with "Hi, I'm Butch." She also says it works like magic on dating sites.

"I didn't tell her she has bad taste," Harold corrects. "I said she has *no* taste."

I wince. "Because that's so much better. What did your boss say?" Harold's an interior designer and works for a big local firm. It's a cherry job, but he and his boss (who is *not* a designer) find themselves at odds a lot.

He shrugs. "Unhappy, blah blah, need to grovel, blah blah. You know what these corporate philistines are like. The other designers all agreed with me. She wanted a green velvet couch—"

"You love those," Calla interrupts, surprised.

"Let me finish. With orange shag carpet and purple satin drapes."

We all suck in deep breaths.

"Wow. Psychedelic," Butch comments.

"Like an acid trip," I add. "But still, I bet the other designers wouldn't have told her she has no taste."

He pulls a face. "Maybe. They did say something about gently steering her away from those choices or talking her into muted patterns where those colors work together."

"Was your boss mad? Or will apologizing to the client fix it?" Calla asks.

"I have to crawl, he said. But someone in the moving crew dropped an eighteen-thousand-dollar custom hand-blown vase about an hour earlier, so he was distracted by that."

We pause to take that in. "Yep. That'd distract me too," I agree.

"Imagine putting that on an insurance claim." Butch holds up her hands as if she can see it written. "The claims adjuster might have a coronary."

Laughter echoes around the table. Even Phil, the quietest member of our group, joins in. We're pretty sure he's some kind of neurospicy, not just regular shy, but we haven't asked. He doesn't talk much and often blushes when he does. We took him under our wing last year—he hangs out with us, and we don't make him join in if he doesn't want to.

When he does talk, he usually has great insights. And he's an incredibly talented designer. Calla's mentioned to me that she's thinking of asking him if he wants to go into partnership with her after they graduate. She'll handle all the business stuff and do the garment construction, and he can design and make the patterns. I think it's a fabulous idea.

I order another couple of pitchers as the conversation switches to Butch's family, who think if only she'd give up art, she'd no longer be a lesbian. "So I told Mom I'm not giving up art or vag, and if she's got a problem with it, she can give up quilting and stop being hetero."

Harold sprays beer across the table.

"Gross," I say as Phil passes him some napkins. "Also, be careful. This is a nice shirt." I turn back to Butch. "Um, does she not realize you get the artsy genes from her, the seven-times winner of the state quilting association Best Quilt award?"

"Right?" she exclaims. "Art and queer aren't synonymous." She shakes her head. "Now my sister's gonna call me and tell me to be nice to Mom, and why can't I *pretend* to be straight to make things easier with the family?"

"Is this the sister whose husband insists she needs to cook potatoes as a side for at least four meals per week? And bought a new recliner for himself with the money she'd earmarked for a family vacation?" Harold asks.

Butch nods, smirking. "Yep."

Calla snorts. "Her life would be a lot better if she told her husband she was leaving him to be a lesbian."

I laugh and take another sip from my glass, glancing around the bar. It's completely packed now, the noise level extreme. I love it. There's so much color and personality and fun at moments like this. I see some people I know from classes last year and wave. Then someone moves, and my eye falls on a table of loud, must-be-center-of-the-universe-at-all-times jocks.

More specifically, on Jordan. He's standing, waving a glass around as he tells a story, and his friends are split between laughter and jeering. There's a huge grin on his face, and honestly, I've never been more attracted to a jock in my life. Except for when they do those shirtless charity calendars that I always buy, even though I've never used a paper calendar.

We made tentative plans on Wednesday to meet up next week, since apparently he can't this weekend. That's a shame, because it's the only weekend this month that I'm not working.

The sound of Calla banging her hand on the table gets my attention, and I turn to look at her. "Was it too hard to say, 'Hey, Blaise'?"

"I said that, but you were too busy daydreaming."

"I wasn't—"

"You were," Harold cuts in. "We looked to see what you were staring at, and Calla recognized someone called Jordan and said you had news."

I blink. She can't mean...? No. There's no way she could know. Not unless Jordan told her, and somehow that doesn't fit. Especially since there's no reason for her to even know Jordan personally. Though she probably knows *of* him, since she's the sports lover of the group. "I do?" I raise my brows at her, playing it cool.

"I heard that you sold a suit to Jordan Marks, that you're kind of friends now, and you told him your life story."

I breathe a little easier. "Where'd you hear that?"

"From Jordan. He's in my stats class."

"Who's Jordan Marks?" Harold leans forward, his avid gaze darting between me and Calla. He's a gossip whore.

"He plays baseball," I tell him, then look back at Calla. "And I did not tell him my life story."

She smirks. "Yet somehow he knows all about the Joy Inc. internship. Yesterday he got so upset about it being unpaid that he swore at the server in the dining room."

My jaw drops. "He *swore* at a server?" Not something I thought he'd do, and totally not cool.

She seesaws a hand. "Not *at*, at, but he swore at the exact moment the server was waiting to take his order. He apologized. Anyway, that's not the point. Since when do you get all deep and meaningful with your customers?"

"Is talking about an internship with a student actually deep and meaningful?" Butch wonders.

I shake my head. "No."

"Yes," Calla argues. We look to Harold to break the tie.

"Ehhhh, it depends. Were you already talking about internships, jobs, or work of any kind?"

"Who even remembers? I guess so—I was saying how I wanted to break into wardrobe and costume design, and how tough it was. The internship just came up."

Harold grimaces at Calla. "Sorry, sweetie. That seems like a legit segue."

"Is it, though?" she counters. "Why were you talking about being a designer while you were selling him a suit? He doesn't seem the type to want to go custom."

I roll my eyes. "You're really reaching now. I didn't bring it up; he saw Hector and—"

The group gasp cuts me off, and belatedly I realize what I've done.

"He saw Hector?" Butch breathes.

"He was at your apartment?" Calla shrieks. Luckily, the place is so loud, nobody notices.

"Yeah, this changes my ruling," Harold points out. "Why was he at your place... in your bedroom?"

Even Phil leans forward, elbows propped on the table.

"It's not like that," I insist, even though it totally is. I scramble for a believable lie, because I am *not* going to out Jordan. Not even to my best friends who I could trust not to gossip about it to anyone else.

"How is it then?" Calla demands. They're all staring at me, and I'm pretty sure I just broke out in a sweat.

"It's like he told you—we're kind of friends now. He bought the suit on Sunday, came to pick it up at the end of my shift on Wednesday. We were talking, I had to clock out, and we decided to hang out. That's it." I wait to see if they'll buy it.

Phil slowly shakes his head, and Butch says, "That's weak, Blaise. So weak, if it was beer, we'd call it piss water."

I lift my glass to salute her. "Cheers."

"Why'd you have to go to your place to hang out?" Harold asks.

"Where else would we go?"

Calla scoffs. "You were literally at the mall. The mall. Also known as the place people go to hang out. Or you could have come, you know, *here*. A bar where people also hang out, much like we're doing now. Or—"

"Yeah, okay, I get it. There are other places we could have hung out. But we went to my place, and that's all."

"It doesn't explain why he was in your bedroom, though," Butch says, drawing out "bedroom."

"He wasn't," I reply smugly, glad that this, at least, is completely true. "The door was open, and he used the bathroom." To shower, but they don't need that little tidbit.

It shuts them up for about fifteen seconds, then Harold shakes his head. "I don't know. It still seems suspicious to me."

"Me too," Calla agrees, eyes narrowed.

Butch turns to her. "What do we know about this baseball player, other than that he plays baseball and is in your stats class?"

"You're not going to ask me, his kind-of friend?" I demand, irrationally annoyed.

"He's good at baseball, but not obnoxious about it," Calla begins. "He's detail-oriented too—the one who makes the list for group projects. And he pulls his weight. But he gets bored really easily during class and doodles instead of taking notes, then begs them from his friends."

"Are his doodles any good?" Harold asks, and I pay close attention to her answer. Hey, we're in the arts. We care about that stuff.

Calla shakes her head. "Nope. No talent whatsoever. One time I had to ask him why his stick figure had no elbows."

I cringe. "It's a stick figure. How hard can elbows be?"

She shrugs. "Whatever, he's a nice guy. He'll be a good *friend*."

I frown. "Calla Lily—"

"Ooooh, Blaise is real-naming you," Butch says. "This must be important."

It's true that we don't usually use her full name. People start jeering when they hear that her whole first name is Calla Lily. Especially because her surname is Gardner.

"I'm just saying... even implying something more happened could have a big impact on Jordan if someone overhears you."

Grudgingly, she nods. "Fair enough. No more jokes or innuendoes... when we're in public."

That's the best offer I'll get. "Thank you."

"*But* since you have a friend on the team now, you have to come to a ballgame with me."

Fuck. Really? "You're kidding, right?"

She shakes her head. "Nope. Gotta support your friend."

"I doubt me being there would—"

"I'll come too," Harold announces. "A friend of Blaise's is a friend of mine."

"And me," Butch adds. "I've always thought we should support school sports more." We all look at her like she's crazy, but she ignores us, turning to Phil. "You coming?"

He nods emphatically, cheeks pink. For once I think it's excitement and not social anxiety.

"Excellent," Calla declares. "The team's away this weekend, but I'll get tickets for next Saturday."

I leap on the excuse. "I'm working."

"But you're not working this weekend," Harold helpfully points out. "See if someone wants to switch for Saturday."

Sighing, I give in. "Fine. But that means you're all coming to the open-air cinema at the beach with me next week. I heard the 'reality' show production the senior performing arts class is doing will be filming there, and I want to see some behind-the-scenes stuff."

"I saw them filming in the dining hall the other day," Calla says. "I love that they included a queer couple in the cast, and Chase and Amos have *chemistry*. I wanna see what's happening behind the scenes too." She smirks and wriggles her brows, and I roll my eyes.

But yeah. That too.

"What's showing at the cinema?" Butch asks.

"*Jaws*."

EIGHT
JORDAN

Coach is on a tear at Tuesday's practice, and we all know why. At the hotel on Saturday, two of our players sneaked out after curfew to go to a party a couple of girls told them about. That would have been enough to get them in trouble, but the party they went to got raided by the cops, who found illegal drugs and plenty of minors… including the one who was sucking Hannaway off. He got arrested.

As if that wasn't bad enough, it somehow made it to social media and then the sports news headlines. The preseason friendly on Sunday sold out, but the crowd wasn't welcoming, even though the two players involved were suspended pending review. Hannaway's going to be kicked off the team—the breathalyzer and then blood test showed he had an obscenely high blood alcohol level, and he's only twenty. He'll lose his athletic scholarship and might have to drop out of school. He's also potentially facing charges for having sex with a minor, which is probably his bigger problem.

Timmins was also stupid-drunk, but he's twenty-one, and since he wasn't in possession of any drugs and wasn't caught dick-out with a minor, he didn't get arrested. He's still in trouble for breaking curfew and getting drunk the night before a game, but his suspension would probably just have been for a week if not for the media circus. Now, I don't think he'll be allowed to play again until the news dies down and will probably miss the season opener—his last one, since he's a senior.

So yeah, practice is closed because there's fucking reporters hoping to grab a sound bite from one of us, and Coach is so mad, we're all afraid to speak. He has been since he came pounding on all our doors Saturday night, checking if anyone else was out before he went to see what was going on with Hannaway. Fun fact I just learned: Franklin U won't bail you out if you get arrested, so Coach called Hannaway's parents to either send the money or come and deal with it themselves. They're locals, so they opted to come and tear their son a new one in person, and since Coach basically said he didn't want to see him, they took him home for a few days while they manage the fallout. I'm glad—it was awkward enough having Timmins moping around, hungover, all day Sunday.

The only good thing to happen since Saturday night—because of course we lost the game Sunday, and I got a barrage of texts from friends and family when the news broke, plus another call from Uncle Luke—was the text I got from Blaise this morning, asking when we can meet up. I've never answered a message so fast in my life, and I'm going straight there when I'm done here... if that ever happens. It feels like Coach is taking his rage out on the rest of us.

By the time we finally hit the locker room, I'm aching, dripping sweat despite the cold day, and glad Hannaway isn't here for me to give my opinion to. Spoiler alert: it wouldn't foster the spirit of teamwork.

A shower revives me, and I make sure to be thorough, since I'm hoping Blaise will want to get up close and personal with my parts. I'm mostly dressed and wondering whether texting him to ask if he wants anything from the McDonald's drive-through would be weird—I mean, I'm stopping there anyway and we're friends, it's not like I'm asking him on a date or anything, but I've never actually brought food over for a hookup before—when Coach comes in.

"Listen up! You all here?" The room falls silent, and his gaze skims over us, doing a mental headcount. "It's been a rough few days, and I wish I could say it's over, but it's not. I just heard that Hannaway's been charged, which means Franklin and this team specifically are going to come under heavy scrutiny. I know you've all seen the media outside and that some of you have been contacted directly for information. I'm going to make this very clear: The school's media liaison will be the only point of contact for any media inquiries. Do not stroll out there and give your own fucking press conference. If a reporter contacts you, your only response should be 'no comment, talk to the media liaison.' Do not post about this on social media. Do not write emails about it, or text messages. I don't want to see screenshots online of your opinion. If your friends ask what's going on, tell them you know as much as they do and *do not* give an opinion, I don't care how long you've known them. We have a legal team and a PR team to deal with this shit; your job is to focus on the game. And your education," he tacks on as an afterthought. "Is that understood?"

There's a little silence while we digest all that, and he glowers. "Is that *understood*?"

"Yes, Coach," we chorus, but it's ragged.

"Coach?" Boyle half raises his hand, then lets it drop. "How long is this going to last?"

Coach sighs, and for the first time he looks more tired and stressed than angry. "Too long. But if we all stay focused on the game, no trouble, no scandals, hopefully the press will lose interest in us and annoy someone else. So nobody else had better get their attention with non-baseball stuff. Unless it's because you rescued orphans from a burning building or something." He pauses. "No, not even that. No media attention, period, unless it's because we're playing a winning game."

There's a half-hearted murmur of agreement, but I feel like my breath is frozen in my chest. It's not that I want to come out—I'm still getting used to what it means to acknowledge this about myself—but the feeling of *not* being able to because of the potential media circus is... awful.

I grew up in a liberal family, surrounded by people who were openly queer or active allies. We had a couple of minor skirmishes when I was younger with people who found out my parent was gay and didn't want their kids to play with me, which sucked, but generally, the idea of queer being something bad or that needs to be hidden isn't one that's been part of my life.

I know that's not everyone's experience—Uncle Luke was kicked out of home as a teenager and hasn't had contact with his parents since—but it's been mine. It never occurred to me that if I did work out I was attracted to men, I would have to hide that. My desire to keep things under the radar was because I didn't want to deal with the media if I didn't feel it was a hundred percent worth it. Not because I *can't*. This is an eye-opening feeling, and I don't like it.

Coach leaves, and Polly leans over. "I heard the media is camped outside Hannaway's house," he murmurs. "And they tried to follow his parents to their jobs."

"Christ," Laringo hisses. "Why'd he have to be such a dumbass?"

There's a general murmur of agreement, though a few of the guys look like they want to argue. I get it—we've all gotten drunk before, even though we're underage. And it's not like we all ask to see a girl's ID before we hook up—though you can bet your ass I'm gonna from now on. But Hannaway threw his team under the bus, and seriously, who gets *that* drunk the night before a game? My limit's zero if I'm playing the next day, because *there is no fucking I in team.*

So yeah, if we gotta deal with the fallout from his shit, then I'm going to call him a dumbass and not feel like we need to rally around him.

But given all the media attention on us right now, how dangerous is it for me to be going to Blaise's place for sex?

After agonizing over it all the way to McDonald's, I decide that me hanging out at a friend's place isn't the same as coming out—and given I've never even been that close to Hannaway, it's unlikely any reporters will be following me to notice anyway. And in the spirit of "friends do nice things for their friends," I texted Blaise and asked if he wanted anything to eat. He's getting a Big Mac meal.

He opens the door as I walk up the stairs and smiles at me. "I saw you pull up. Did you get my fries?"

"And the rest." I pass him the drinks tray but hang on to the food as I walk past him into the apartment. It's weird, because I've only been here once, but I'm comfortable here. "Did you just get home from work?" He's still wearing his suit pants and shirt, though the jacket and tie are gone.

"Yeah, I was changing when I saw you and the need for fried potato took over my entire being. Dump everything on the counter, and I'll be back in a second." He puts the drinks down and then disappears into his room. I take the food out of the bags, perch on a stool, and try not to drool at the scent of my fries while I politely wait for him to come back. He's right: fried potato makes everything better.

When he comes back out, he's in sweatpants and an old FU Kings tee. It gives me a funny feeling, seeing the same logo I wear at every game on his chest. "Cool T-shirt."

He smirks. "Thanks. I bought it when Peyton Miller came out. Gotta support that football team, you know?"

"I'd be offended, but him being a student here was the deciding factor for me picking this school." It mattered to me that the school rallied around Peyton when he kissed his boyfriend at a game. I didn't think I was queer then, but I didn't want to be part of a system that wouldn't support the community. "That doesn't mean I'm not gonna pretend you bought it for the baseball team."

He laughs and slides onto the stool beside me. "Whatever makes you happy. You could've started eating."

"Habit. Uncle Luke has a thing about waiting for everyone to get their food before eating." I rip into my sandwich with gusto, and for a few seconds, the only sounds are of eating.

"So," I say when the second sandwich is gone and I'm mopping up ketchup with fries, "how's your week going?"

Blaise side-eyes me over his own fries. "Probably better than yours."

He knows, then. A tiny frisson of fear skates down my spine. What if he plans to sell his story to the media? He needs money, and I bet some of the seedier sites would love to break a story about another FU Kings ball player right now.

But... Calla said he was one of her besties, and I've heard her talk about how crappy it is to out people. I'm sure she wouldn't be such good friends with someone who'd do that. And even if she would, it's kind of late for me to worry. Blaise and I have hooked up twice already. If he wants something to sell to the media, he's got it.

So I swallow my fries and say, "I can't talk about it. But probably."

He nods. "I don't need to hear about it, to be honest. It's taken over my socials, and I don't even follow any baseball stuff, so I can't imagine how much worse it is for you. I just wanted to put it out there that I've seen it, and this can be a stress-free zone."

I wish I'd bought him extra fries. "If I wasn't already here to suck your dick, I would be now."

His laugh is genuine. "Wanna try something new?"

A tiny bit of trepidation creeps in. "Like?" I'm not sure if I'm ready for anal.

"Ever sixty-nined?"

NINE
BLAISE

"How does this work, exactly?" Harold asks Calla as we find our seats and settle in. It's not too bad a day for the end of January, clear skies and only the lightest breeze, so I'm not too mad about sitting out in the fresh air for the afternoon. Plus, it'll be cool to see Jordan in his element.

"Well, Harold," she begins, straight-faced, "we sit in these seats here and watch what the players are doing there." She points to the... field thing. "It's also considered part of the experience to have a hot dog or two."

"I like hot dogs," Butch chimes in. "When do we get the hot dogs?"

I study the... game area. "Hey, all those little path thingies are laid out to form a diamond!"

"Ooh, where? I like diamonds," Harold announces, leaning forward. He pulls a face. "Not so much with the dirt diamonds, though."

Calla ignores all that and tells me, "It's called a baseball diamond, so gold star for noticing."

"I noticed too," Harold whines. "Where's my gold star?

Anyway, you never answered my question: How does baseball work?"

A woman in front of us turns around. "Did I just hear one of you ask how baseball works?" She's wearing a team jersey and cap, her long brown hair pulled into a ponytail of loose waves. The jersey has been tailored to fit her body perfectly, and she's paired it with dark jeans embellished down the outside leg with gold and purple diamantes, and gorgeous dark brown heeled boots. Her makeup is flawless, with eyeshadow in FU Kings purple and gold, red lipstick somehow not clashing, and her long nails are done to match in purple with gold decals. If I wanted to design a costume for "fashion influencer who's a baseball super fan," I'd go with something like this.

"Your look is incredible," I tell her, and she grins.

"Thanks. A girl's gotta support the team, but that doesn't mean she can't be fabulous."

"Did you do those jeans yourself?" Because if not, I need to know who did.

"Yup! I looked around for a pair but couldn't find exactly what I needed."

"You're talented," Butch tells her. "These guys are designers, and if they're impressed, that means you're impressive." She gives a little half smile. "I'm Butch."

Our new friend looks her slowly up and down and then smiles back, her lips curling suggestively. "Oh yes, you are. Xera." She holds out a hand to Butch. "You're not a designer, Butch? How do I impress you?"

Butch winks. "I'm an artist, but I'm still impressed. Do you know a lot about baseball? Because aside from Calla, we're all hopeless and could use some help."

Harold leans over to me and whispers, "Is this how lesbians hook up? They talk to each other first?"

Everyone else hears, of course, because "quiet" isn't a setting Harold has. "Don't you talk to your hookups, Harold?" Calla asks. Butch is shooting death rays with her eyes.

He shrugs. "I mean... only if I have to."

"I want to go on record here that Harold isn't representative of all gay men," I put in. I know what he means, though. Sometimes, in the clubs, with the music pounding and so many people pressed up around you, it's easier just to use facial expressions and gestures to get the point across.

"Since we're going on record," Xera says, "I'm not a lesbian. I'm pan."

"Should we go round the group and give names and orientations?" Calla wonders, and I snort.

"I think it's safe to say we're all some kind of queer. Nice to meet you, Xera. Great name, by the way. I'm Blaise, and the rest of them are Harold, Calla, and Phil. You've met Butch." I wait to see if she says something about the fact that so far, Phil's been so quiet, it's like he's not even here, but she just flashes her killer smile at everyone.

"I'm gonna have so much fun helping Calla teach you all baseball. Also, the name thing? My mom got it from a book. Don't call me Xerox and we'll get along fine."

"Was it a good character, at least?" Harold asks, and Xera shrugs.

"Some kind of tree spirit? I don't know. My brother read it once and said it's not embarrassing, so I didn't bother. He got a normal name, though, which is so unfair."

"Rude," Butch agrees. "Do you want to sit with us? Or do you have friends joining you?"

Xera laughs. "My friends would *die* if I asked them to come here. I go to San Diego State, and they call me a traitor for supporting the Kings." She climbs over the back of her seat, and we make room for her. It's not like the stadium's sold out—not even close.

"Why do you support the Kings, then?" Calla asks.

"My brother's on the team." She half turns to show Calla the name on the back of her jersey. It says BOYLE in big, sparkly gold letters that I'm pretty sure aren't the ones that came with the shirt.

"Marty Boyle's your brother?" Calla exclaims. "Wow, you won the gene lottery in your family." She cringes, but Xera bursts out laughing. "I'm so sorry, my filter died outside of warranty."

Xera waves a hand. "Don't worry about it. I've been telling my baby bro that he's an ugly fucker since we were little."

"He's not ugly, exactly," Calla begins, trying to dig her way out of the hole, but Xera's moved on.

"Anyway, little bro might be a pain and butt-ugly, but he worked damn hard to get on the team, and we're proud of that, so I come every home game to support him. What about you guys? Calla drag you all here?"

"Kind of," Butch says. "We're here because she and Blaise have a friend on the team and we're nosy."

"Nosy's good. Who is it? I bet I know him—I hang out with the guys after games all the time."

"Jordan Marks," Calla announces while I try to look only mildly interested in the conversation. Jordan and I hooked up twice this week—Tuesday night, when he brought me McDonald's, and then again yesterday morning. I had the closing shift at work, and he apparently doesn't have classes Friday morning. It was a great way to start my day.

"Oh, sure. Marks is great. He's the one who explained to Marty what pan means. The guys always ask him when they've got questions around LGBTQIA+ stuff, because they figure having gay dads makes him an expert."

"He's got gay dads?" Butch asks, just as Harold says,
"Say what?"

Even Phil looks interested.

Calla shrugs. "He's mentioned it, but I don't know details. Blaise is more his friend than I am." She shoots me a wicked grin.

"His gay uncle adopted him and his sister when they were orphaned," I say, leaving out the bit about the other uncle who left them. It's complicated, and more than anyone needs to know. "Then he got married, so Jordan has two dads."

"That's sweet." Harold puts a hand on his heart. "If one of my siblings tried to die to escape their monsters, I'd drag them back from the claws of death and reanimate them like zombies if I had to."

That sounds harsh, but I've heard all about Harold's niblings. Monsters is a kind description. Plus, his siblings are so bad that death probably wouldn't want them, anyway.

Xera, unfazed, grins at him. "You're going to be such an amazing parent one day." She sounds completely genuine, and I relax into my seat. She's going to fit in just fine.

"I don't get it, though. It looks the same." I squint at the field, trying to make it all make sense.

It does not.

Calla threw up her hands forty minutes ago and is now watching the game and sulking into her popcorn. Harold, surprisingly, only needed to be told the rules once before he became some kind of baseball expert. Butch and Phil got the hang of it by the end of the first inning. But it seems that I'm a complete and total baseball dummy, because no matter how hard I try, I cannot see the difference between a ball and a strike. It seems completely arbitrary to me.

"You'd see it if we were up close," Xera consoles me. She's got endless patience, and she didn't laugh—much—when I accidentally cheered for a foul. "We'll ask Marty and Jordan to demonstrate later—they'll be thrilled to show off."

Xera's assumed that we're all tagging along with her when she meets the team after the game, and the others have fallen in with the idea with excessive enthusiasm. I'm a little uncomfortable putting Jordan in that situation without warning, so when nobody was paying attention before, I sent him a text with a heads-up and asked him to say the word if he wanted me to beg off. I might need to fake Ebola to escape Calla's clutches, but hey, I'm a costume designer—I can find a way to pull it off on the fly.

Marty steps up to bat. I know it's him because of the very helpful nametag on his back. That's been a godsend, frankly, because they're all wearing caps or helmets, and while our seats are pretty good, it's still tough to see their faces... not that I'd know any of them except Jordan anyway.

"My mom told him if he hits a homerun in the preseason and at least two during the season, she'll pay for him to move off campus next year," Xera says, her eyes glued to the field.

"Has he gotten the preseason one yet?" I ask.

"Nope." She pops the *p* as Marty settles his shoulders and the pitcher winds up. "So today's pretty much his last chance not to blow it all."

These stakes are interesting, so I watch closer. The ball whizzes past Marty, and the umpire calls a ball.

"It looked like a strike to me," I complain.

"Too high," Xera explains absently. She's in her baseball fan zone now. On her other side, Butch smiles indulgently.

I let my gaze drift over the crowd. I know it's only preseason, but given how nice a day it is, I'm surprised there aren't more people here. Tickets didn't cost that much, and even though I know shit about the game, it's been fun. Maybe—

A loud *thwack* fills the air, and Xera is on her feet, screaming and jumping up and down. I look down at the field and see the Kings cheering as Marty jogs slowly around the bases. "He got the homerun?" I guess.

"You bet he did!" Xera shrieks.

What the hell. My friends and I get to our feet and start screaming and jumping too. Calla and Harold come up with a chant.

"Marty hit a homer
'coz he's gonna go far!"

I wince. That's... not good. And definitely doesn't rhyme. But none of us are writers, and I join in anyway, ignoring all the weird looks and snickering aimed our way. We're arts students. Fitting in is for other people.

"Marty hit a homer
'coz he's gonna go far!"

Down on the field, where the Kings are clustered around the dugout, slapping Marty's back and head, one of them glances our way, then does a double take. It's Jordan, and he's clearly not expecting to see me here. I probably should have mentioned it this week, but we were otherwise occupied.

He stares for a second, then breaks out in a slow grin before slapping Marty and pointing our way. Xera's brother waves at her while Jordan grabs another guy and nods toward us.

"Who's that?" Harold asks.

"Polly," Calla says. "Brad Polling. He's in the same class as me and Jordan. I'm wearing him down, a little bit at a time." She blows him a kiss, and even from here I can see the way his face flushes and his eyes widen.

Jordan grins at me, and then the players turn back to the

game, but my mind is made up. We're definitely going to Shenanigans tonight.

And I'm going to learn the difference between a ball and a strike if it kills me.

TEN
JORDAN

OF ALL THE PEOPLE FOR XERA TO BEFRIEND AT A GAME, she had to find Blaise and Calla. Mostly I don't believe in fate, but then when people meet in weird coincidences like this, I wonder if there might be something there after all.

I wasn't that surprised to see Blaise in the crowd. Okay, I was surprised, because he never mentioned it and doesn't really seem to be into ball. But I wasn't shocked, because I know he's friends with Calla and she comes to our games all the time. It makes sense that now that she knows I know Blaise, she'd drag him along. I don't know who all those other people were, but knowing Xera as I do, they'll all be at Shenanigans.

Usually those of us who are going straight there instead of heading home to change first leave the stadium together, go to Laringo's car, and dump our jackets and ties on the back seat. Coach and the athletics department say we have to arrive and depart in our suits—nobody says we need to still be wearing all the pieces when we leave the parking lot. Or at least, if we do, nobody's pulled us up on it yet. Today, though, the parking lot has journalists in it, hoping to take advantage of our good mood after winning and sneak in some questions about Hannaway, maybe get something quotable. I know, because they've been outside practice all week, and the only difference today is that there are more of them.

So instead of walking to the bar from the stadium, we pile into cars, leave the press behind us, and drive to Reiner's place. His cousin's a professor at FU, so he's living in the apartment over the garage at her house, and they have off-street parking where the cars will be fine overnight... plus it's easy walking distance to Shenanigans.

Even with that win stacked on top of the game win, the mood is a little low as we walk. Nobody likes having to walk past reporters who don't even want to talk about our game, and the stadium was a little sparse today, even for one of our preseason games. I was hoping people would turn up out of morbid curiosity, see how fun it is, and decide to buy season tickets.

I've always been an optimist.

Laringo breaks the silence. "Tonight's the night I'm gonna score with Boyle's hot sister."

We all jeer in response, even though we know he's not serious. Xera's too cool for any of us to talk about her that way, and even if she wasn't, she'd rip his nuts off if she found out. Besides, Laringo's hit on her about thirty times already with no luck.

"I'm staying out of Xera's way, but I hope she brings her friends with her," Reiner adds. "Anybody know who they are?"

"The blond is Calla," I say immediately. "She's got a thing for Polly."

"She doesn't! She's into girls," he argues, and I sigh.

"Pol, trust me. She's got a thing for you."

"But—"

"Xera's into girls *and* guys *and* nonbinary people... basically, she's attracted to people, not their genders," Boyle says, and it has the rhythm of something he's memorized. I'd know, since

I'm the one who explained it to him. "Unless your girl Calla says she's only into girls, you shouldn't assume. Or she might pinch you," he adds under his breath, and I snort.

"What about the rest? The girl with pink hair?" Reiner presses.

I shake my head. "Don't know. The tall guy next to Xera is Calla's friend Blaise, but I've never met the others. Boyle?"

He shrugs. "I bet Xera brings them all along. They looked like they were having fun."

Polly shakes off his confusion and laughs, slinging his arm around Boyle's shoulders. "You mean because they think your homer means you're going to 'go far'?"

"Obvs they're super smart as well." Boyle smirks as he pushes open the door to the bar, and we follow him in.

It's still early, so it's not that busy, but it's also Saturday, so there are already people here getting a start on the night. We head toward our favorite table in the back, and after only a few steps, shrieks break out.

"Xera's here," Laringo says happily.

"Dude, you've got, like, zero chance with her," I tell him in a low voice. He's a nice guy, and nobody wants to see the balance of the group thrown off.

He shrugs. "I know. But a guy can dream. Plus she's hot, so it's nice looking at her."

I guess my sister was right when she said college guys aren't complicated. Jamie and I got kind of offended, but...

We get to the table, and Xera throws herself into Boyle's arms, jumping up and down and yelling, "You're on the way!" If I didn't already know what their mom promised, I'd think she was getting a little too excited over a preseason game. "Only two more," she tells him. "Do *not* fuck this up."

I look past them and see that she did bring the others, though Blaise isn't with them. I hope he didn't skip because of me. We're friends, after all, and drinks in a group is totally something we can do.

Calla winks at me, then tells Polling, "That last pitch was a disgrace. Did you check out early or something?"

He sputters, face going red, even though he said the same thing in the locker room earlier. "It was *one* bad pitch!"

She pats his arm and leads him to a chair. "One's all it takes."

"But we won!"

"Next time, you might not. Do you need life coaching? I can help you get in the right mindset, you know."

He looks hopelessly over at me, but I just grin.

"You were right about Polly," Reiner says. "Pink hair is mine."

I look closer at the woman with short pink hair talking to the blond guy. She's... butch. It looks good on her, but I didn't think Reiner went for that. His last girlfriend was the princess type. I blink as she lifts a hand to swipe her bangs back and I catch sight of the small lesbian flag tattooed on her inner forearm. "Uh, Reiner—"

But he's already sliding into the empty chair beside her. I grab a seat on the other side of the table and fold my arms, ready for the entertainment.

"Hi, I'm Ben and I think you're—"

"Butch?" she interrupts. "Because I am. Also a lesbian."

I resist the urge to applaud as Reiner's mouth opens and closes like a fish's. "Cool," he says weakly. To give him credit, he doesn't walk away. "Uh... baseball fan?"

She rolls her eyes but then smiles. "I wasn't before, but today was fun."

Someone sits beside me, and I glance over to see Baise's now-familiar smile. "What's got you so enthralled?" he asks, and I nod across the table.

"Watching your friend shoot down my teammate."

"Always a good time," he agrees. "This happens all the time. We can't work out why the straight guys go nuts for Butch. It's not like she encourages them."

I blink. Did he...? "Did you call her Butch? As in, name, not adjective."

He smirks. "Introduce yourself to her."

I'm totally being set up, but I lean across the table and wait for Reiner to stop talking. "Hey, sorry to interrupt. Blaise is going to go up and order a round on me—you're both drinking, right?"

"You bet," Reiner says.

"Yeah, me too. Thanks," the woman adds.

"No problem. I'm Jordan, by the way."

"Calla and Blaise's friend? Nice to meet you. I'm Butch."

It's only the fact that I knew something was coming that lets me keep a straight face. Reiner, on the other hand, isn't so lucky. "That's your *name*?" he asks. "No way."

Yeah, I'm going to leave them to it. Turning to Blaise, I say, "So, wanna order a round? I'm paying." I got cash at the ATM this morning just for this purpose. The bartenders here are cool, but if you're underage, you don't get a wristband, and they do *not* sell alcohol to anyone under twenty-one. I can't even use a fake ID, since the staff knows I'm on the ball team and check the players' ages. It's a fucking conspiracy.

But as long as we don't get obviously drunk in the bar, they look the other way when we're at a table crowded with beer pitchers.

Blaise stands. "Come on. You can help me carry." He raises his voice slightly, enough for our group to hear but not for the bar staff. "First round's on Jordan!"

There's a low cheer, and we make our way toward the bar. With it being so early, we don't have to wait long.

"What'll it be?" Perry asks. He smirks at me like he thinks I'm going to try to order a beer.

Please. I'm not stupid.

"Three pitchers of beer," Blaise says.

I put on my innocent face and add, "And two of soda. And..." I turn around to count heads. Huh, I didn't see that red-haired guy before. "...thirteen glasses." The others can get their own when they arrive.

As soon as he turns away to start getting our order, I slip Blaise the cash.

When we get back to our table, we get a hero's welcome. Beer does that.

"Calla mentioned you were one of her besties, but she didn't say you were coming today." I sip my drink. I won't be having a lot tonight—with so many eyes still on us, getting plastered would be a stupid thing to do. I can just imagine Coach's reaction if there are pictures of us sloppy drunk online tomorrow. "Neither did you." I just saw him yesterday, when he introduced me to the fine art of frottage. Never did I think dry-humping could be so hot... or so wet.

A sheepish expression crosses his face as he drinks from his glass. "To be honest, I was kind of hoping Calla would let me out of it. Sports aren't usually my thing."

I push aside the pang of disappointment. Sure, it'd be cool if he liked the same stuff I do, but not all my friends are into baseball. Different hobbies and personalities make groups interesting. "At least the weather was good today," I offer, looking for a silver lining. "Sometimes it's not, especially in the preseason."

"Yeah, that probably helped, but I had fun," he says, surprising me. "I'm not gonna be a rabid fan, but the occasional game wouldn't be too bad. Well," he adds, "if I can work out the difference between a ball and a strike."

"Yes!" Xera shouts, surprising everyone. We turn to look at

her and see she's pointing at us. "Marty, you and Jordan have to show Blaise how a strike and a ball are different."

Boyle screws up his face. "What, in here? They'll kick us out. And I don't have a ball."

She smacks the back of his head. "Why are you so stupid? Use a napkin. He doesn't have to actually hit it."

Rubbing his head, Boyle says, "Sometimes you make me wish I'd picked an East Coast school." But he obediently gets up and grabs a couple of napkins, crumpling them into a ball.

"Hang on, I should do this," Polly objects. "I'm the pitcher."

"Before we start throwing things," I interject, "does Blaise know what the strike zone is?" I'm asking Xera, and Blaise clears his throat.

"I'm right here."

"I told him, but..." She shrugs.

"It's between shoulders and hips, right?" Blaise asks.

Every single ball player at the table groans.

"Not right, then," he mutters.

I stand up. "Let's start with that. The strike zone starts halfway between a player's shoulders and the top of our pants" —I put my hand at the correct point on me—"and goes all the way down to just below our kneecaps."

"But then what stops a pitcher from aiming at your nads and taking you out of the game?"

Polly chokes on his beer. Turning Blaise into a baseball expert is going to take a while.

ELEVEN

BLAISE

THE DING OF A TEXT INTERRUPTS THE DRAMA ON *THE Gilded Age*. It's fine—I've seen these episodes before. I'm rewatching and making notes on the costumes. I hit Pause at just the right moment to capture a screenshot of Bertha's ensemble, and grab my phone.

JORDAN:
You awake?

I glance at the time. Shit, it's after midnight already. Good thing I don't have the opening shift at work tomorrow.

BLAISE:
Yep. What's up?

JORDAN:
Can I come over? Not a booty call

JORDAN:
Tho I wouldn't say no if that was on offer

Chuckling, I type:

> Sure, come over.

Then I stand and stretch. He probably wants to talk more about his newfound bisexuality. I'm good with that—and with anything else that might happen once he gets here. While I'm waiting for him, I finish the notes for Bertha's costume, then go to the bathroom. The knock comes just as I'm done.

"Hey." Holding the door wide, I step back for him to walk past, taking him in. His hair is standing on end, and he's wearing what I think might be his pajamas with a sweatshirt on top. "You okay?"

He flops onto the couch, making himself at home, and I find it strangely endearing. We don't really know each other that well—except carnally—but I like that he's so comfortable in my space. "You mean because I so obviously can't sleep and dragged myself out of bed to come here in the middle of the night? Sure, I'm fine." He's smiling, so I'm going to take the statement at face value.

"Great. Want a soda?"

He shakes his head, and I join him on the couch. "So what's up? If it really is a booty call, I don't have a problem with that."

"Nah." He grins. "But my early class was cancelled, so let's do that next. I wanted to talk to you last night, but there wasn't a chance for any privacy."

That's true. I had a way better time than I expected to, both at the game and hanging out with the team after, but it was chaotic and hectic, and I ended up giving Phil a ride home around one-ish.

"Well, it doesn't get more private than this." I wave to the empty apartment.

"Is... I mean, obviously you guessed that I didn't tell anyone about... us. What we're doing. Our friendship. Ugh." He closes his eyes in frustration. "Obviously I told them we were friends. But not..." He makes a lewd gesture, and I snort.

"Yeah, I got that. I did the same, by the way. I didn't think you were out, and that's something you should be able to do on your own terms. I told my friends that I sold you a suit and we're friends now." I hesitate. "They're a little suspicious, especially Calla, but my official story stands, and none of them would spread any rumors or anything."

He nods, and the relief on his face is clear. "Thanks. It's not that I'm ashamed or anything—"

I hold up a hand. "I'm going to stop you there. I don't think you're ashamed, but even if you were, that's not my business. This is your decision to make when you're ready to make it. We're friends, and we fuck, but you don't owe me anything beyond that."

"God, you sound like my dads and their friends," he mutters. "Should I be creeped out by that?"

"Depends. Are they hot?"

The grossed-out look on his face makes me cackle.

"Dude, they're my *dads*. And my honorary uncles. That's... just no."

"I'll imagine them with poor hygiene and bad style, then," I tease. "Totally a no. But they sound smart."

He shrugs. "They are, but what I meant was, they're all very vocal about choices and respect when it comes to orientation, gender identity, coming out, and relationships—just like you." Jordan's smile is warm and almost conspiratorial, like he's invited me to be part of something a little special, and I push aside the bitter pang that I never had family like that myself. "Anyway, I wasn't sure where I landed on the identity line, but that wasn't traumatic or difficult for me—I just needed time to work it out, you know? I'm not ashamed to be attracted to more than women, and I'm definitely going to be open about it." He winces. "But while I'm playing college ball, that most likely means media attention. And I don't want that, not for me, and not for anyone in my life."

"I don't want that either," I reply honestly. I understand exactly where he's coming from. "If you told me you wanted to come out publicly, as in announcements and all that, we'd still be friends, but the fucking would probably stop. We're not in that place, and I wouldn't go through all that hoopla for anyone except a serious boyfriend."

His face lights up. "Exactly! That's how I feel. And since I don't plan to go pro, I don't see a reason to make any announcements right now. I might come out to my closest friends and some of my teammates, but it's gonna be low-key. No big declarations."

"Sounds smart to me."

"My sister and her boyfriend already know, kinda. I called her after the BJ at the store. But they don't know you and they'd never tell anyone anyway. And I told Uncle Luke I'd figured out I was bi or whatever, but then I ended the call and we haven't had a chance to talk since."

The bitterness is back, teasing the edges of my awareness. "It's great that you can talk to your family about this stuff."

The corners of his mouth turn down. "You don't?"

"No." I shake my head. "Not anymore. Not ever, really." I intend to stop there, but he's watching me with such an earnest, supportive expression that instead I find myself spilling my guts. "My mom was okay with me being gay. Mostly. She didn't really understand, but she loved me and we just didn't talk about it. Dad..." I shake my head again. "Even when I was too little to understand what gay meant and that I'd like boys 'that way' instead of girls, he was disappointed by me. He didn't understand me and my interests. My parents divorced when I was ten, and I lived with Mom full-time, with occasional weekends at Dad's place. Then Mom got sick." It still hurts to talk about, even after three years. "She died at the beginning of my sophomore year here."

Jordan squeezes my hand. "I'm so sorry. That sucks so hard."

Blinking, because yeah, he'd know, I muster a smile. "It does. Then Dad decided to prove what an asshole he is by going after her estate."

His face goes hard. "What? Did she leave a will?"

"Yep, everything got left to me, including her half of the house. I don't know why they didn't sell it during the divorce, but instead Mom paid him rent for his half and we kept living there. Anyway, she didn't have much, but he tried to contest the will. Said I shouldn't be able to inherit any of it because I'm gay."

My friends had either one of two reactions to this news. Either they were too shocked to speak, or they started yelling with rage. Interestingly, Jordan does both.

He leaps to his feet, hands on hips, and shouts, "What? He — But— Are you... URGHH!"

I nod, curling my legs up. "That's pretty much how I felt. It's fine, though. The judge called him a bigot, and I got the estate. I sold Mom's share of the house back to Dad, and the money mostly paid for college. I only needed a part-time job to help with expenses. That was pretty much the end of my relationship with my dad, though. And with Mom gone too..." I shrug. "I have a few cousins I don't hate too much, but none of them really get me. Mom was an only child, and her parents died when I was little. Dad's sisters and parents think like he does. So my friends are my family now."

"You've got great friends, so that's something." He sits again and pats my knee. "I'm so sorry. My grandparents all died before I was old enough to remember them, and my dad was an only child, but even after my parents died, I had Uncle Luke... and Uncle Matt, but he wasn't so good with the talking about feelings. And then later, when we moved to Georgia and I gained half a dozen or so honorary uncles... It feels like there was always someone I could talk to. For a few years, we had these housekeepers, Jus and Jas, and they—"

"Wait." I hold up a hand to stop him. "I'm going to need more. Jus and Jas? Were their parents on acid?"

He grins. "Justin and Jasmine. They're twins, and they wanted to job share so they'd have time to work on their art too. You'd like them both."

"Because I'm a designer?"

"No, because they're awesome. Though the design thing would probably help." He hesitates. "Jas had some of her work go viral on Insta after a European princess posted a pic of it in her house."

I sit up abruptly. "Are you talking about Jasmine Henson? *She* was your housekeeper?" Her glass sculptures are indescribably beautiful.

He nods sheepishly. "Yeah."

"Butch is going to freak when she hears. Wait... that means Jus is Justin Henson, the painter."

"Well, they are twins. So yeah."

I shake my head. "I won't tell Butch. She'd rupture my eardrums with her screams. She made us all go with her to Justin's show at Quint Gallery two years ago. I can't believe two successful artists used to clean your house."

"And take me to ball practice," he adds. "They're the best. Seriously. When I said there was always someone I could talk to, I meant it." He hesitates again. "I know we haven't been friends long, and you have some pretty great friends already, but if you ever need another ear, I'm here, man. Or if you need, like, an adult, I can hook you up. All the ones in my life are cool, even if Uncle Luke tried to limit my Pop-Tart intake."

I'm simultaneously touched and befuddled. "He tried to limit your Pop-Tart intake? How does he even know how many you're having?"

"Oh, not now. Now I eat as many as I want, though sometimes I pay for it in the gym. But when I was a kid, he was always going on about how I couldn't eat a whole box at a time."

A whole *box*? Just thinking about all that sugar makes me queasy, and we art students live on junk food. "He might have had a point. That many Pop-Tarts would probably lead to death." I eye him. "You're not doing that now, are you?"

His gaze slides away. "That's not important."

So he is. Holy crap, he must work out like a demon to stay in the shape he's in. "I promise to get rid of the evidence when you fall into a diabetic coma."

Jordan's laugh lights him up, and a trickle of happiness runs through me. "Nah, I'm not ashamed. My dads know I have a sugar problem."

As our chuckles settle, I shift positions and lean up against his side. "Thanks for the offer. To listen, I mean. And to hook me up with an older man."

"That so does not sound like what I offered."

"It so is, almost word for word. You baby bisexuals make the best wingmen."

"Yeah, before this gets any weirder, I'm just going on record that I didn't offer to 'hook you up' with anyone in a sexual sense. Except me. We can sex all you want."

"I don't think sex works that way. The word, not the... sex." I let my eyes drift closed. I can't remember ever being this comfortable with a fuck buddy.

"Sex the word and sex the sex work however you want them to. That's the beauty of it." He curls into me, resting his head on mine. "You mind if I grab a quick catnap before I head home? I'm kinda sleepy now, and sleepy driving is dead driving."

I don't bother to open my eyes. "You bet. Wake me before you leave, and I'll blow you."

It's the last thought I have until morning.

TWELVE
JORDAN

> **MILA:**
> Whatever you said to Uncle Luke to make him paranoid, fix it. He keeps asking me if you've talked to me about anything important lately.
>
> **JORDAN:**
> Uhhh. Sorry? I kind of mentioned liking men and then hung up. That was a couple of weeks ago.
>
> **MILA:**
> I am going to kill you.
>
> **JORDAN:**
> I'll call him! I promise.

I SENT THAT TEXT THREE DAYS AGO, AND I NEED TO FOLLOW up soon. Uncle Luke and Mila talk a couple of times a week, and if he asks her again... Well, let's just say my sister can be super creative when it comes to revenge.

So on this rainy Thursday morning, I decide to blow off my first class of the day and stay snuggled in bed instead... and call my dad.

"Jordan? Is everything okay?"

"Yep. Can't a guy call his dad randomly?"

"We've been over this," he reminds me. "Also, aren't you supposed to be in class?"

"Maybe. But I figured talking to you about the big things happening in my life was more important."

He pauses for a second, then says, "Hold on." He covers the microphone, but I hear his voice talking to someone else before he adds, "Okay, I'm back and ready to talk."

Shit, I forgot he'd be at work. "You don't have a meeting or anything, do you?"

"No, I was just about to grab some lunch with Toby. He'll bring me back some sandwiches."

Guilt is a knife that stabs me through the heart. "You should go; this can totally w—"

"If you're about to say this can wait, and 'this' is what I think it is, then you're wrong. I'm here, I'm listening, and I will damn well enjoy the roast beef sandwich when Toby brings it back. Plus Grant should be out of his meeting by then, so he can eat with me. It's a win all around."

"Well, when you put it that way…"

"I do. Now talk."

I grin and pull the covers up a little more as the wind blows rain against the windows. "You know how I bought a new suit?"

He sighs. "Yes, Jordan. I know."

"Well, the guy who sold it to me is insanely attractive. And before then, I'd never been attracted to a man I'd met in my actual life, just to, like, Ryan Gosling and George Springer—"

"Who?"

I roll my eyes. "He plays for the Blue Jays."

"Sure. So you're saying you found celebrities attractive but figured it might just be their celebrity power?"

"Yes!" I knew Uncle Luke would get me. "That's exactly

right. Though apparently straight guys aren't attracted even to famous men. Who knew?"

"Straight guys," he says deadpan. "And probably most other people. Okay, you're attracted to celebrities of both sexes—"

"All genders, actually," I correct. "I think I'm probably pansexual. Though I did some reading online, and a lot of people say 'bi' even though they're also attracted to nonbinary and trans people. I haven't decided on a label yet."

"You don't have to," he assures me. "If anyone tells you otherwise, refer them to me."

Aw. "I can stick up for myself now, Uncle Luke."

Another sigh. "I know, kid. Just sometimes I like to feel like you still need me."

I sit up, letting the covers fall away. "I *do*. Who did I call when I ripped my suit? Trust me, Uncle Luke, I'm always going to need you."

"You're such a good kid," he says fondly. "Dopey sometimes, but good." I want to argue, but he doesn't give me the chance. "Getting back to what you said earlier, though... tell me about the insanely attractive guy who sold you the suit."

"Blaise?" I smile.

"Uh-huh," Uncle Luke murmurs. "That's what I thought."

"What? No. It's not like that," I protest immediately. "We're friends. I mean, sure, realizing I was attracted to him helped me understand myself better, and he's been, like, mentoring me in the whole liking-men thing, but we're not dating or anything."

"Jordan—" There's a tiny pause. "Never mind. You're an adult now. Technically. Just... bear with me for a second and listen, okay?"

"Oh-kaaaaay?"

"Condoms are just as necessary for anal sex as they are for vaginal sex, and I know the team requires semi-annual physicals, but you also need to be getting tested regularly for STIs."

"Oh my god." I never thought I'd have to sit through "the talk" again. Whyyyyyy???

"I don't know if you already did this once you turned eighteen, but if you didn't you should talk to a doctor about going on PrEP. I know I've mentioned it before—it's not just for gay men. *But*," he continues, because yes, I'm getting "the talk" *again*, "remember that HIV isn't the only thing you can catch. Condoms really are important unless and until you're in a committed, monogamous relationship. And even then, some couples still use them."

"Uncle Luuuuuuuuuke," I whine. Though I hadn't thought about PrEP. When I was only seeing women, I was always super careful about using condoms *and* asking if they were on birth control, and PrEP seemed like overkill. But maybe I should? Blaise and I haven't had anal yet, but I want to, and if I end up liking it as much as I've liked everything else, I'm going to want to do it often.

"I'm done, I swear. Except don't be afraid to tell your partner if something is uncomfortable, lube is a lifesaver, and make sure you know how to find a prostate. Okay, now I'm done. Unless you have any questions?"

I do, but even as close as we are, I'm not asking him to answer them. "I'm good, thanks."

He lets out a breath. "Great. Duty done. Now... is there anything you need from me? Have you thought about whether you want to tell people about this, or just let them find out naturally...?"

I love that he doesn't even consider the possibility that I might want to keep it secret, and I hate that I need to tell him that's what I'm doing.

"For now, I'm not telling anybody," I hedge, easing into the subject carefully. "Mila and Jamie know, of course, and I'm sure you've told Grant."

"Actually, no. I didn't know if you wanted me to."

I love my dad so much. "Thank you. I do want you to, though. And it's fine if you talk about this with the uncles. Um, Blaise knows, obviously." I don't bother to explain why that's obvious. We both know Uncle Luke figured it out. "But I don't want the attention that would come with an NCAA athlete coming out, and since I don't have a boyfriend I want to publicly claim or anything, I don't see any reason to."

"I think that's sensible," Uncle Luke says slowly. "Especially given you don't plan to be a baseball player forever. Making a big public announcement would put you, your team, and probably a lot of your friends in the spotlight. But... when you said you weren't telling anybody, did you mean *anybody*? What about your friends? And some of your teammates? You said Boyle's sister was queer, so it's unlikely he'll be homophobic."

I hesitate. "Boyle would be cool," I begin, "and so would Polly and most of the others. FU is a liberal school, and even if someone wasn't okay with it, they'd probably keep their opinions to themselves." Mostly, anyway. "I'm just not sure I want it to be out there just yet. You know how it goes—if I come out to the team, that's dozens of people who know, and people talk. With Hannaway's fuckup, there are a lot of eyes and ears on us right now, and I don't want them picking up on this and running with it. Coach was pretty firm about only wanting us in headlines for our win record, and I agree with him."

He doesn't say anything for a minute, and I know he's struggling with this. He's never not been out, not from the moment he told his mom he was gay and she kicked him out. He believes strongly in everyone's right to be their authentic self, but I know he also respects everyone's right to set their own narrative. Right now, those two beliefs are warring in him.

"I'll support whatever you decide to do, you know that," he says finally. "I do think you might find it hard to not share this part of yourself with the people you spend the most time with—those who you trust with it, anyway. Especially if it's something you plan to explore, which it sounds like you do. So just think about that."

I turn my head and stare toward the rain-splattered window. I hate that he's right and that it would make things harder. "I will."

"And if you do decide you want to come out, but your coach is still harping on about not making headlines, let me know."

My smile is involuntary. "Uncle Luke to the rescue?"

"If I have to." He chuckles. "Your season opener is this weekend, isn't it?"

The change of subject is kind of a relief. "Yeah. It's a home game, and we're pretty well set up for it."

"You'll kick ass. Grant and I are going to be in LA toward the end of February, and we thought we might extend it over a weekend and come down to see you and come to one of your games. You're playing at home the last weekend in February, aren't you?"

I mentally flip through the season schedule and realize I have no idea. It's almost definite that he does, though. "I think so. Did you check the schedule?"

"Grant did. I'll send you an email to confirm once we get the details locked in. Plan to have breakfast with us on the Sunday."

"Yeah, of course. And dinner on the Saturday."

"That's not necessary. I know you like to go out with the team."

I roll my eyes. We talked about this last year. "Jeez, it's not like you're here all the time. I think I can miss one night out to see my dads. Or I'll just go out later."

"We can work it out when the time comes. I love you, kid. Stop skipping classes."

Laughing, I reply, "Love you, too, and I'm not making any promises," then end the call.

When I get to the locker room for practice that afternoon, the guys are clustered around Reiner's locker, yelling encouragement and trash talk about... something. I dump my bag and go to see, but just as I get there, they groan in disappointment.

"What's up?" I ask.

"Timmins's brother sent him this game app he's developing, and so far nobody's been able to get past level two," Laringo says.

"Reiner didn't even get past level one," Boyle adds, smirking, and Reiner flips him off.

"This thing's impossible," he complains, passing the phone —Timmins's, I'm guessing—to me when I hold out my hand.

I glance down at the screen. It looks like a basic tile-matching game, the kind that exists in a billion different versions. "None of you got past level two? What kind of athletes are you?"

"Dude, you haven't even played it yet," Polly points out.

Scoffing, I say, "I will, and I'm gonna smoke level two. Then you can all bow down and worship me."

"Oooohhhhh, listen to Marks talking smack." Laringo smirks. "I bet you'll fail level two just like the rest of us."

"Hell, I bet he'll fail level one," Reiner snipes.

"You're on. What do I get if I win?" I've been playing these games instead of studying for the past eight years. This is going to be a cakewalk.

"Drinks on us all night after the game Saturday," Polly suggests, and we all agree.

"And if he loses?" Boyle asks. "It's gotta be something epic."

"Drinks on him for all of us?" Reiner suggests, but Boyle vetoes that.

"He'll just use his dad's credit card like last time. There's nothing epic about that."

I hide my wince. The lecture I got from Uncle Luke after last time was pretty damn epic. Not to mention, he made me pay all that money back, with interest, over the summer.

"What, then?" Polly asks.

Laringo's face lights up in a wicked grin. "He's gotta dye his hair purple—school colors."

Pfft. "Done," I declare. Please. My hair grows superfast, but even if it didn't, I know from my friend Cara that bright colors fade a lot when you wash your hair in hot water. That dye will be gone in a couple of weeks, max.

"*Not* done," Coach growls from behind us, and we jump and spin around. "Why the hell is Marks dying his hair purple?"

We look at each other. He doesn't usually care about shit like this. "Uh," Polly starts, then explains.

Coach sighs, shakes his head, then says, "No bright hair colors. Nothing that will stand out in a crowd. We're trying *not* to get attention, remember? Get to regionals, and the whole team can dye their hair purple, me included. Until then, pick something else."

The guys look at each other, and I really hope they don't go back to the idea of me paying for everyone's drinks Saturday night.

"What about ear piercing?" Boyle asks Coach, who huffs.

"They're not my ears. Marks?"

I think about it. I'm pretty sure piercing holes close over if you don't have anything in them. I seem to remember Uncle Luke assuring Mila of that when she got her lip pierced and then decided she hated it. And she doesn't have a hole there anymore, so...

"As long as I can take the earring things out for games and practice." I don't like the idea of having anything on my ears when I'm wearing a batting helmet.

"Deal!" Reiner crows. He's way too excited for something this normal.

They all crowd around me—including Coach—as I start the game.

Two minutes later, they're all crowing and high-fiving at my defeat.

Fucking level one.

THIRTEEN
BLAISE

Leaning against the wall beside Target, I wait for Jordan to show up. He sent me a text this morning saying he'd lost a bet and did I want to come with him to pay up during my lunch break. Nothing interesting ever happens on a Monday, so I told him what time to meet me, and now I'm waiting.

"Hey!" He's grinning wide as he walks up to me. "Sorry I'm late."

"You're not really. I've only been here a minute. Tell me about this bet."

"Yeah, but you gotta walk with me. I've got an appointment."

Intriguing. I fall into step beside him.

"Congrats on your win Saturday, by the way." Calla texted me after the game to demand I join them for celebrations at Shenanigans when I finished work, but I begged off.

"Thanks. It was a good way to start the season. Hey, Calla said you got a design job?"

"A commission," I correct. "A group of friends going to some kind of book convention who want to cosplay their favorite characters. They decided to be extra and hire someone to design and make their costumes." It's not going to get the attention of any studios, but it *is* something I can add to my portfolio. And it pays well.

"Still awesome, dude. What book?"

I shrug. "I don't remember the title. Apparently it's a series. I had the first meeting with them Saturday, and we talked about the characters' aesthetics and sketched some initial ideas." He stops in front of Studs, and I do a double take. "Really? The bet is that you have to buy jewelry?"

"The bet is that I have to get my ears pierced," he corrects. "Come on."

This is going to be... interesting.

Five minutes later, he's staring at the array of stud earrings on offer, mouth pursed. I watch with amusement and wish it wouldn't be totally weird for me to video this.

"None of these plain ones," he says decisively. "The guys thought this would be a big deal, so I'm gonna lean into it. What have you got that's big and sparkly?"

"For a new piercing?" the technician, Jenn, asks. "The six-millimeter cubic zirconia is probably your best bet. That's this one. Unless you want a colored stone?"

We look at the pair she's pointing to. They're... big. "Can you even wear something that size under your helmet?" I ask, trying to be practical. The helmet he wears while batting comes down over his ears. "Won't it be uncomfortable?"

Jordan shrugs. "I'll take them out when I play."

"Uh, you need to leave them in while your ears heal," Jenn interjects. "For around six weeks, usually."

"Need to leave them in or the holes will close? Or need to leave them in or my ears will fall off if I don't?"

Jenn looks at me as though to ask if he's serious, and I shrug. "The holes will close. And for the first week, there's a chance of infection if you're not looking after them properly."

Jordan nods. "New plan. I'll get something slightly smaller and hope they don't annoy me too much."

"Maybe the four millimeter?" Jenn suggests, indicating another pair. "And you can tape them if you're worried about them catching on anything. Medical paper tape is really good for that."

"Ooh, I can tape them? Scratch the new plan. I want the big ones."

"Maybe you should think this through," I suggest. "The last thing you need is infected ears."

He laughs. "I might be a dumb jock, but I know how to follow instructions. Jenn's going to tell me everything I need to do, and if they start to get infected anyway, I'll go to campus medical. Worst-case, I gotta take them out."

"You're not a dumb jock," I protest half-heartedly, because I still don't know what the bet was, exactly, and maybe he's piercing his ears for a stupid reason. Still… it's not a tattoo. The holes will heal if he hates them that much.

I am way too invested in this.

"Are you ready?" Jenn asks brightly, and Jordan grins.

"You betcha. Stab me through the ears so we can go get lunch. I'm in a burrito kind of mood."

I hadn't thought about what we were going to eat, but burritos do sound good. Or maybe enchiladas.

Right after the nice technician stabs Jordan through the ears.

"So the whole reason you did this is because you couldn't pass a game level on the first try?" I repeat. I'd say that was ridiculous, but I get it. When I first learned how to use a sewing machine, invisible zips confounded me. My first attempt was abysmal, yet I was convinced it would be so easy.

And it is. *Now*.

"Yep." Jordan bites into his burrito and makes a humming sound. "Mexican food is so much better in California than it is in Georgia."

I pause before taking a bite of my own burrito. "Is that where you're from? How come you don't have an accent?"

He chews and swallows, then says, "I'm from here originally—well, LA. We moved to Georgia when I was eleven for Uncle Luke's work."

"What does he do?" I don't think it's come up.

"Business consultant."

That's one of those things that sounds so made up, and my opinion must be reflected on my face, because he bursts out laughing. "He basically reviews policies and procedures for big corporations and makes sure things are working properly. The job he does now has him working with individual departments to sort out the kinks and set up workflows that fit the team so they can be more effective. When he first started out, he worked for a nonprofit that helped small businesses get set up and through the first five years of operations."

"So, like... management and organization?"

Jordan shrugs. "Pretty much. He uses a lot of corporate speak too. When Mila and I wanted something we were pretty sure he'd say no to, we'd use all his jargon to ask."

I almost choke on a mouthful of pulled pork. "Like?"

"One time Mila told him she had a team-building opportunity that clashed with her regular schedule and she needed his help to optimize her commitments to take advantage of all benefits."

Trying to work out what that means gives me a headache. "Translation?"

"She got invited to a party but wouldn't be home before curfew and needed him to make an exception."

Laughter takes me by surprise. "Seriously? And did he go for it?"

"They negotiated. He pushed her curfew back an hour, I think."

I shake my head. "My dad's a lawyer, but he's more the yelling kind than the negotiating kind. And Mom was pretty easygoing about things like curfews."

"Sometimes I wished Uncle Luke was more easygoing. Like, he wasn't super strict, and if I had a reason to ask for an exception, he'd usually agree, but he worries. A lot. He used to think he was failing at being a parent to us." He cuts himself off self-consciously. "I don't know why I told you that. It's not something I talk about."

"We're friends," I remind him, though an annoying little voice at the back of my head reminds me that the only friends of mine who know about my dad's asshattery are the ones who were there during it... and not even all of those. "I don't talk about my parents to everyone either," I add honestly.

"Yeah. I guess."

"For what it's worth, I don't think your dad failed as a parent at all. You're pretty great."

His grin flashes, and the way he tips his head makes his new bling catch the light. "I mean, a lot of that is just the natural me."

"Of course it is. Your innate awesomeness."

"That should be my catchphrase: Innately Awesome." He gives me two thumbs up. "Good job."

"I'll add 'coming up with catchphrases' to the list of services I offer clients."

Laughing, he says, "Speaking of clients... tell me about this commission. What do the costumes look like?"

I hesitate, because most non-arts people get bored when I start going into that kind of detail, but he asked, so I launch into an overview of what I have planned, and then, when he listens intently and asks intelligent questions, I delve into more detail.

Until the alarm on my phone beeps. "Shit. I have to get back to work." I already wrangled a longer lunch break than usual by promising to stay after closing and merchandise the new stock that came in.

"And I should probably go to class. You know, if I want to pass and all that shit."

"Always a good idea."

"Thanks for coming with me. Hey, I never asked... what do you think?" He turns his head from side to side so I can see the studs in his ears.

"Stunning," I say dryly, but the truth is, they do suit him. I've never really thought of piercings as "hot" before, but I have this insane urge to lick his, suck them into my mouth.

I won't, though. At least... not until they're healed. "I do still think the smaller stones would have been a good idea," I add. "But these look good on you." They're pretty substantial, and I get the feeling that in sunlight, they'll be blinding.

"I like them more than I thought I would," he admits. "Maybe I'll keep them."

There's something oddly endearing about that. "If you do, I'll get you a pair of earrings for every game you win this season," I say impulsively and instantly want to take it back. We don't have that kind of relationship.

His face lights up, though, and I can't bring myself to say "haha, just kidding." "You're on," he declares. "Just you wait, this is going to be my best season ever, and the rest of the team will rise to meet my standard."

FOURTEEN
JORDAN

Maybe getting my ears pierced unlocked a secret superpower in me, or maybe I'm a whore for jewelry and Blaise's promise was the incentive I needed, but my game over the next few weeks is on fire. Coach actually smiles at me. Twice!

And just like I boasted to Blaise, the rest of the team can't stand the idea of me being better than them, so they lift their game to match. We're gelling like we never have before, and considering what a close-knit team we are, that's really saying something. Whatever it is, we win the first four games of the season, two of them so easily that I wonder if we have a secret benefactor paying off the other teams. That's not something I'd ever say out loud, though.

I decided to keep my piercings—I tape them for games, since that's more comfortable under a batting helmet. Plus, the stones catch the light a *lot*, and as much as I like being the center of attention, the last thing I need is to get in trouble with an umpire because I'm too distracting.

Speaking of distracting people…

I FaceTime my sister.

"Jordy, I'm in the middle of *what did you do to your ears oh my god!*" she shrieks, then bursts out laughing. I knew she'd react that way. "Jamie, come and see this!"

"Hi to you too, sis."

"Don't talk to me while I'm blinded by your pimp bling." She snorts at her own joke. "Holy crap, Jordy, are those real piercings or are you pranking me?"

Jamie's face appears in view before I can answer. "Hi, Jordan. What are we— Oh." He grins as I move my head to catch the light. "They look surprisingly good on you."

"Thanks, bro. See, Mila? That's how you support family."

"You don't need my support to wear jewelry," she points out. "They do look good, even if I wasn't expecting to see them. Are they real?"

"Yep. I lost a bet." I scowl. Stupid game. As soon as that app gets released, I'm downloading it and kicking the shit out of level one—*and* level two.

"Of course you did. Did the terms also say you had to have the biggest studs available? I mean, there are bigger ones out there, but not by much."

"Nah, that was all me. Blaise tried to convince me to get the smaller ones, but go big or go home, right?"

Mila blinks, and then she and Jamie exchange glances.

"Blaise... as in blowjob Blaise?"

I cringe. "Rude, Mila."

"Sorry. I meant, Blaise, as in the guy who sold you a suit and gave you a blowjob?"

I nod. "That's him."

"So... you've seen him again?" Jamie asks, trying to be casual but failing.

"We're friends. And he's letting me practice gay sex with him. You know, fuck buddies."

Mila makes a doubting face. "That's not exactly fuck buddies, if he's coming with you to get your ears pierced."

"How would you know?" She's dated one other guy besides Jamie, and I'm pretty sure they never fucked.

Jamie laughs. "Yeah, babe, how would you know?" he teases, and she elbows him.

"I have friends who had fuck buddies. They never went shopping together."

I shrug. "Well, we're friends who fuck then. I dunno. Does everything need to fit in a box?"

"Of course not," Jamie assures me. "It's good that you're making more friends outside the team. Congrats on the killer season so far, by the way. I've been watching your games, and you're playing like magic."

"Don't jinx me," I warn. "Blaise said he'd buy me a pair of earrings for every game we won."

They exchange another glance. "Did he?" Mila asks. "That's nice of him. Are you guys hanging out a lot?"

"Well, sure. His friend Calla loves ball and just started dating Polly, so she brings him to games when he's not working. And we have dinner and sex a few times a week. Plus he's doing these costumes for people going to a convention, and sometimes I help him with that."

Mila puts her face in her hands.

"What?" I ask.

"She's being dramatic," Jamie says. "So Blaise likes baseball?"

"I think he's starting to. He'd never been to a game before he met me, but he says he's been having fun."

"Uh-huh. And do he and his friends come hang out with the team after games?"

"Sure, when we're playing at home. Boyle's sister and Blaise's friend Butch are dating now too."

"Your friendship group is way too incestuous," Mila says, the words muffled by her hands. Because she's still being dramatic.

"Tell us about helping him with the costumes," Jamie prompts, ignoring her. "I didn't know you were into that stuff."

I lean back in my desk chair. "I'm not, but it's kind of fun. Mostly I do grunt work—cut out pattern pieces and hold pins and iron seams open. Did you know you have to iron seams open when you're making clothes?"

"I did not."

"But one of the costumes needs horns, and Blaise couldn't find any that fit the concept that didn't cost a bomb, so next week we're making them with wire and papier-mâché."

"Sounds fun."

"Yeah. It's better than just watching TV while we hang out, though we do that too sometimes. We decided to start that vintage show everyone used to love—*Friends*."

Mila's hands come down, and she stares at me. "How can you be this stupid?"

I blink. "What?"

"Jordy, you're dating him!"

"Don't call me Jordy," I say automatically, my brain in a tailspin. "And what the fuck are you talking about?"

"It does sound like you're boyfriends, dude," Jamie says apologetically. "You hang out all the time just watching TV, help him with his work, he comes to your games... he offered to buy you jewelry."

"No, that's..." *Click, click, click* go the puzzle pieces. "Oh my god."

"Yeah."

"I think I have a secret boyfriend." So secret that neither of us even knew about it.

"Congratulations?" Mila offers. "He sounds great."

I smile, the issue of what to do next seeming less urgent all of a sudden. "He really is. His dad is a total asshole, and his mom died, so he's basically on his own, but his friends are so supportive. He's got goals and he's so determined to meet them—it makes me want to try harder, you know?"

"Wow. I can't believe you didn't know you were together."

In retrospect... neither can I.

Now that I've discovered I have a secret boyfriend, I need to work out what I'm going to do about it. I still don't want to do the whole big coming out thing—and I think Coach would murder me if I tried. The media is mostly focused on our winning streak at the moment, but Hannaway's name does still come up, and that's probably going to continue until he's tried—or whatever happens in cases like this. I should find that out. Regardless, I don't want my name mentioned unless it's connected to my game and my stats, so that's a problem I'm going to need to solve... and discuss with Blaise.

About that... does Blaise know? Like, this whole time, has he known we're boyfriends and just thought I wanted it kept a secret? Because I'm not sure how I feel about that. It would mean that we're really shitty communicators, for one thing, but also that he thinks I'm basically making him go back in the closet. Or that I'm ashamed of being with him?

The other option is that he's just as oblivious as I am and also doesn't realize we're secret boyfriends. Which is scary, because what if he doesn't want to be my boyfriend, and once I tell him that's what we are, he decides to end things between us? I don't want that. I actually want more, if I'm being honest. I like the idea of hanging out with him more often and kissing him more. I've been... not *avoiding* kisses, because that would be stupid, but sometimes I've wanted to kiss him and haven't because it seemed too intimate for friends.

I want to be intimate with him. What happens if he doesn't want that too?

I don't know exactly, but I know it's not a situation I can just leave the way it is.

Which is why I'm on the street outside his apartment, waiting for him to get home from work. I texted him earlier and asked if I could come over, and even though he's never said no when I ask him that, this time I held my breath waiting for a reply. I was irrationally afraid that he was going to tell me he had a date or something. I guess knowing I'm in a secret relationship has made me paranoid.

A car turns the corner ahead, the headlights preventing me from seeing If It's Blaise's as it gets closer. Then it's close enough to blind me, and I look away—just as it turns into the forecourt of Blaise's building. Yes!

He parks in his spot, and I get out of my car and walk over to meet him.

"Hi," he says, smiling brightly at me as he slams his car door. The overhead fluorescents mean I can see every inch of him, and I'm reminded of how sexy he is. Men in suits—even famous ones—never really did it for me, but something about Blaise in his work clothes makes me wonder why suits aren't legally mandated for all men.

Of course, he looks a lot better in his suit than I do in mine. I don't know how he does it.

"Hey." I shove my hands in my pockets, suddenly nervous, and his smile fades.

"Everything okay? I thought you were working on your Communications paper tonight."

"I am. I mean, I was." Not all that hard, though. I was too distracted after I talked to Mila and Jamie. "But I, uh, need to talk to you about something."

He looks dead serious now, likely in response to me sounding like I'm about to go to my own funeral, and it changes his face. I hadn't really thought about how... *happy* is the wrong word. Animated, maybe? His face is always so friendly and open, even when he's talking about something that's painful, and to see it close down in this solemn way makes me feel shitty. "It's not bad," I add. "I think. Just... Could we go upstairs?" The late winter evening is chilly.

Nodding, he leads the way, and when we're inside, I look around and wonder how I ever thought we were just friends. That's my hoodie on one of the kitchen stools and my Stats textbook on the coffee table. I don't leave my stuff scattered like that at my other friends' places.

Folding my arms across my stomach, I turn to face him.

"Jordan, you gotta tell me what this is about. Because you said it isn't bad, but you look like your dog just died." His face falls. "Oh, shit. Did—"

"Nobody died," I assure him. "I don't have a dog." He did, though, when he was little. A yellow lab called Sunny. I have no idea if any of my other friends had childhood pets.

"Then what is it? Did you meet someone and want to end us? Do you have Chlamydia? What?"

I blink. Why did his mind go straight to an STI? Oh my god, does he think I'm fucking other people? Is he? "Nothing like that. Uh... so I was talking to my sister before."

"Mila." He nods. "Did she and Jamie decide if they're going to start looking for a new place, or wait another year?"

How did I not know? Seriously. How?

"It didn't come up. Anyway, it was a video call, because I wanted to show her..." I lift a hand to my ear. "And somehow we started talking about you. And..." I falter, and he walks over and puts his hands on my shoulders.

"Jordan. Seriously. Just say it."

"Did you know we're secret boyfriends?"

FIFTEEN
BLAISE

Did you know we're secret boyfriends?

The words echo through my head as I stare at him with my mouth open. What? No, seriously... what?

He looks back at me steadily, if nervously, and I realize he means it.

"Uh... excuse me?"

Relief crosses his face, and he nods vigorously. "That was my reaction! I'm so glad it wasn't just me. But Mila pointed it out, and—"

"Your sister told you that we're boyfriends?" How would she even know?

"Yeah. And Jamie. Though after they said it, I realized they were right. Then I started wondering if you knew, and maybe I'd been disrespecting you this whole time. But turns out, we're both dense."

I'm still back on his sister and her boyfriend telling him that we're dating. "Can I get you to back up a little? Why did Mila... I mean, how did this even come up?"

He shrugs and walks over to collapse on the couch, making

himself comfortable the way he always does, and it strikes me that he spends a lot of time here. Like... a *lot*. Which I like more than I probably should for a friend.

"I video called her to show her the ear studs, because I wanted to see her react, and I mentioned that you'd come with me... and it kind of snowballed from there. She and Jamie were asking things like how much time we spend together and what we do—*not* the sex stuff," he adds hastily, seeing my face, "though they know we have sex. Anyway, there was a whole bunch of questions, and then Mila called me a dumbass and told me we were dating."

"But—"

He holds up a hand. "My first thought was that she had to be wrong, but when I thought about it... I think we are."

I take a deep breath. "We agreed this was just going to be a casual thing. You don't want a boyfriend." I don't know that I do either. I'm really focused on my career goals at the moment. A boyfriend would split my focus and take a lot of time.

Though having Jordan's help and company while I work on the cosplay costumes has been really ni—

Wait.

Wait.

Fuck. I think he's right. I mentally tick off all the things we do together and compare the list to the things I did with past boyfriends, and yeah... we're dating. You could even say we're pretty serious.

I drop onto the couch beside him and lean back, needing the support. "Wow."

Jordan pats my shoulder, then curls into my side and leans his head on it. I automatically lift my arm to wrap it around him. "Yep."

For a little while, we just sit there. Then he straightens. "So... what do we do now?"

Oh, god. "Uh... I know you didn't want a boyfriend—"

"It's not that," he interrupts, his earnest gaze locked on mine. "I just don't want the attention associated with being an out ball player. Especially because there are so few already. But I'm good with having a boyfriend. You, specifically." He smiles shyly, and it's so unlike him that my heart melts.

"Yeah. I'm good with being your boyfriend." The thought of "breaking up" with him, not seeing him all the time and being able to talk to him... touch him... makes me feel physically sick. I'm so ashamed of myself for not working this out sooner. But... I brace myself. "The thing is, while I get you not wanting to come out publicly, and I don't want to be part of that kind of attention either, I'm not okay with being in a secret relationship." I stop. "Not now that I know about it, anyway."

He nods. "That's fair enough. I didn't think you would be, and honestly, neither am I. It feels... skeezy."

The weight of this dilemma seems crushing. "So where does that leave us?"

"Compromise?" he suggests. "We tell the people closest to us, who know us the best and who we can trust not to sell an exclusive to the press. Not that they'd get much money for it," he adds.

"Another collegiate ball player being queer would make headlines, even if you're not on a College World Series team," I defend automatically, and he leans over to kiss my cheek.

"Aww. Look at you, knowing what the College World Series is. I'm gonna make a baseball fan of you yet."

I grab the front of his hoodie and pull him in for a proper kiss. We've kissed before, but this time feels different. It's our first kiss knowing that we're boyfriends, and that makes me so fucking horny... yet also so sentimental.

"This is nice," Jordan murmurs against my lips when I finally ease back. "Let's do more of this."

Reluctantly, I let him go and pull away, huffing a laugh. "In a minute. First let's work out what the fuck we're doing with our lives."

He pulls a face. "Fine. What do you think of the compromise idea?"

"I like it," I admit. It would mean that with our friends, we can be together—though no obvious PDA if we don't want the wider world to know. "But it would still mean you coming out. And your closest friends are on the team with you. Is that going to be a problem?"

"No." He shakes his head firmly. "My family already knows, and you know Boyle and Polly will be cool about it. I might tell Coach too—just so if it does accidentally get out, he's not taken by surprise. The other guys on the team, I'll just see how things go. They all know my dads are gay and that I'm a fierce LGBTQIA+ ally anyway, and nobody's ever said anything hateful before now."

"Are you sure?" I don't want to push him into outing himself, even if it makes things more complicated for us.

His smile is gentle and... loving? "Yeah, babe. I'm sure."

The thrill that goes through me at the endearment would be embarrassing if I didn't like it so much.

"Then I guess we're officially telling our friends that we're together."

"Great!" He grins. "That means I can bring my boyfriend to dinner with my dads on Saturday."

Uh... what?

Jordan suggested that since Calla was my friend first and I'm closer to her, I should be the one to tell her and my other friends that we're officially together, while he tells Polly and Boyle.

That means outing him, of course, but he earnestly gave me permission to do so. It was so adorable that I had to kiss him, and then we decided we'd had enough talking and "consummated" our newly recognized relationship with a celebratory sixty-nine.

Which is why my friends are all in my apartment on a Thursday night, stuffing themselves with the charcuterie platter and dips I got from the deli—not to mention the fancy bread from the bakery—to soften them up. Not that I think they'll react badly, but there are going to be a *lot* of questions and teasing, and I'm hoping that rich food and carbs will make their brains so slow they don't think of many. If it works, it'll be totally worth the expense.

Ditto the snobby craft beer and thirty-dollar bottle of wine. Though I couldn't bring myself to buy expensive vodka, so they've got the rotgut there.

"Are you dying?" Butch asks point-blank, smearing brie onto a round of bread and topping it with prosciutto. "Because if you are, we're going to stick by you. All this"—she waves the bread at the array on the coffee table—"isn't necessary."

"Appreciated, though," Harold says with his mouth full. He swallows. "Oooh, you got the stuffed peppers."

I ignore him and answer Butch. "I'm not dying. Not that I know of, anyway. But I do have news."

"Bad news?" Calla puts her wineglass down. Another benefit of having a rich roommate is that his mom stocked the place like we're wealthy socialites. Otherwise, we'd be drinking wine out of cheap tumblers from the grocery store. Gotta admit, I'm going to miss living this comfortably when I go to LA for the internship.

"Not bad news. Good news. *Happy* news."

"You got the internship!" Harold jumps up. "That's great! But I didn't think you had enough money yet."

"I don't, and no. I haven't applied yet. Sit down and let me tell this. It'll go a lot faster without the interruptions."

Harold flips me off, sits down, and reaches for another goat-cheese-stuffed pepper.

"Okay, so... Jordan and I are dating."

They all watch me expectantly. "And?" Butch asks when I don't continue.

My brows draw together. "What do you mean, 'and'? Isn't that enough?"

Calla snorts. "Blaise, we already knew that. We just figured you were keeping it secret because Jordan's not out."

What? I look around at all their faces. Phil nods sympathetically and sips his beer.

"There's no way you could have known," I protest.

"Honey, baby, sweetie... we did." Harold leans over to pat my arm. "Xera knows too. She was the one who said it out loud first."

"What about her brother?" If Boyle knows already, I need to give Jordan a heads-up. It's not a bad thing, but I don't want him blindsided like this.

Butch scoffs. "Xera wouldn't out anyone, Blaise. And Marty... well, he's sweet, but she says it took him a year of watching *Drag Race* with her to realize that RuPaul in a suit and RuPaul in drag were the same person. So I doubt he's guessed."

I give that a second of incredulity before letting it go. "Well, anyway... we're official now. Jordan's still not coming out publicly, but he's going to tell some of his friends and then see where things go from there. We want the people closest to us to know."

Calla puts a hand to her chest. "That's so sweet. What do you mean, you're official now? Haven't you been together this whole time?"

I scratch my head. Damn her for picking up on that. "That depends on what you mean by 'whole time.'"

They exchange glances and then all lean forward. It's creepy, and I lean back. "Well," Harold begins, "we assumed you hooked up, like, in the first week you met, then by the time we all went to that first game, you were dating."

In retrospect, I can see why they would think that. "You're close. We, uh, well I guess we hooked up the day we met. Then when he came to pick up the suit, we got to talking and hit it off. But we've been just casually seeing each other since then. Until now." They don't need to know that's because we're both dumbasses.

"Hooked up on the day you met but didn't get to talking until days later?" Butch repeats, grinning. "Blaise Warner, were you a naughty boy at work?"

I can't help it. I blush.

Calla crows. "Someone's breaking company policy!"

"It's not like that," I protest, even though it was. "He's special." I feel guilty saying it, because at the time, he was just a sexy, sweet stranger with a smile that made me tingly and an air of helplessness that made me want to protect him.

Huh. Maybe he *was* special, even then. Even if I didn't realize it. After all, my dumbassedness has been clearly established already.

But, just to get it on record, I add, "He's the only one I've ever... broken company policy with. And we only did it once."

"How gross would it be if I asked for details?" Harold wonders aloud.

"Very," the rest of us say in unison—even Phil.

Harold rolls his eyes. "Fine. But just so you know, without the actual details, I'm totally going to be picturing a porno movie."

"With your friends' faces? Also gross," Calla tells him, and he shakes his head.

"Oh, hell no. I'm replacing Blaise with someone else. Jordan's staying, though. I don't know him well enough yet for him to be an exception to 'never have sex daydreams about friends' rule."

Yeah, I might leave that out when I call Jordan later and tell him how tonight went.

SIXTEEN
JORDAN

Blaise told his friends about us last night, and according to him, they'd already guessed. I don't think my friends are as smart as that about queer stuff or relationships in general, though. Even though I'm confident they're going to be cool about this, I'm still sweating bullets right now.

The Rockies and Diamondbacks are playing tonight, and even though it's still only Spring Training and we won't be watching live, we all love ball enough that neither Polly nor Boyle thought it was weird for me to invite them over to watch the game in my dorm room. My roommate's gone out—because it's Friday night. Duh—and I'm the only one of us with a TV in his room. It was my Christmas present from my dads freshman year, and even though it's pretty small, the room's not big, so it works fine.

I wait until we're well into the second inning of what's turning out to be a really mediocre game. Boyle, for reasons only he understands, is stretched out on the floor, his neck craned at the most awkward angle known to man. Polly and I are sitting on my bed, backs against the wall, feet dangling over the side. We have soda, popcorn, and Twizzlers, and the path to the door is clear if one of them needs to get away and take some time to process. This is going to be fine.

"So," I say abruptly. "Blaise is my boyfriend."

Polly chokes on his soda. I guess my timing could have been better. I thump him on the back while Boyle rolls onto his side and stares at me with his mouth open.

When Polly can finally breathe again, he wheezes, "Bro. A little warning?"

"Sorry." I grimace. "But... yeah."

"Since when are you into dudes?" Boyle demands. "You never said before."

Neither of them seems mad about it, and that bolsters my confidence. "It turns out, always. Before it was just men I'd never met, like Nolan Arenado." I nod toward the screen, where my number-one MLB crush is currently up at bat.

"But now it's not?" Polly looks confused. "I don't get it—when did you and Blaise start dating?"

"And why did you never tell us you were queer?" Boyle sits up. "Did you think we'd be bigots?" He sounds hurt, and I shake my head.

"No way. I knew you both would be fine with it." I push aside the pang of guilt as I remember how nervous I just was. "But like I said, I wasn't even sure until I met Blaise and realized it wasn't just a famous people thing, you know? And then I was getting used to the idea, and we were fooling around... I don't want to, like, *come out*, come out. Coach would shit a unicorn about the media attention."

"He so would," Polly mutters, and Boyle shudders.

"He'd shit a bigger one if it was a surprise," he warns.

I shrug. "I'll probably tell him. Maybe. For now, Blaise and I have only just decided to make it official, so we're telling our friends, but we don't want it to be a thing. As far as everyone else knows, I've dated women but never said anything about my orientation."

"Well, I like Blaise, and I'm happy if you're happy," Boyle declares. "Does Xera know? Because if she knew before I did, we're gonna have a problem, man. I know she and Butch are all loved up and Butch is Blaise's friend, but you and me are bros."

Wincing, I tell him, "She didn't *know*, but Blaise told his friends last night, and apparently they'd already guessed. Including Xera." Which made me feel like a prize idiot.

He screws up his face in thought. "I guess that's okay," he concedes finally. "She's always had, like, radar for relationships. It's not your fault she guessed."

Gee, thanks. I look at Polly, who still seems a bit shell-shocked.

"Who else knows? You said Blaise's friends."

"My sister and her boyfriend. And my dads know I'm queer, but I haven't told them about Blaise yet. I thought he could have dinner with us tomorrow night."

"Whoa," Boyle mutters. "So he's a *boyfriend* boyfriend. Wait, your dads are coming here?"

Polly's eyes go wide. "It's not just to meet Blaise, is it? You're not going to propose or anything, are you, because if you are, I need more than just soda right now."

I sock him in the arm. "No, you moron. Jesus, we've only known each other six weeks. My dads had meetings or something in LA this week, and they're coming down to see me before they go back." I was kind of relieved when they got held up this afternoon and told me they wouldn't get in until late—it gave me this chance to talk to the guys. "I'm going to have breakfast with them tomorrow and tell them about him then."

"What about the rest of the team?" Polly asks, a frown creasing his brow. "You said you'd maybe tell Coach, but what about them?"

That's something I've been trying not to think too much about since Blaise brought it up the other night. "I don't know," I admit. "I want to. Team unity, right? But that's a lot of people who'll know, and they're cool, but..."

"Not all of them are *that* cool," Boyle finishes. "There's a few who avoid Xera. Maybe they just don't like her, but maybe they don't like that she's not hetero." He shrugs.

"C'mon," Polly protests, but it's weak. "We know these guys."

"That doesn't mean accidents don't happen. We knew Hannaway, and he did something stupid that ended up being really stupid." They know I don't mean he deliberately hooked up with a minor—just that when you're drunk, your judgment is off. Even if all my teammates are genuinely okay with me dating a man, that doesn't mean one won't accidentally let it slip to the wrong person. And then bam, I'm an out collegiate athlete and ESPN will be televising our games for the wrong reasons.

It's not a risk I'm ready to take yet.

Uncle Luke looks up from his menu, sees me, and breaks into a broad grin that I can't help returning. Thankfully, he doesn't call out across the room or any of the other potentially embarrassing things I've seen my friends' parents do. Instead, he and Grant wait until I reach the table before standing up to give me giant bear hugs, as if it's been a year since they saw me and not two months.

Man, I've missed them.

When we're all sitting, Grant says, "You look good, Jordan. Winning clearly agrees with you."

"Don't jinx it," I warn him. That's the last thing I need right now.

"Um, excuse me, are we just not going to talk about the elephant in the room?" Uncle Luke demands, surprising me. I didn't think he'd make a big deal of me being queer, not after our talk about it, and he doesn't know about Blaise yet... does he? Maybe Mila told him?

"What elephant?" Grant asks, and Uncle Luke reaches out to tug my earlobe.

"The one that's blinding me right now. Honestly, Jordan, have you never heard of subtlety?"

I laugh as Grant mutters, "I didn't even see those."

"I would have gotten bigger ones if they had them," I admit. "I lost a bet. But it's fine, because I like them." Plus, next week Blaise and I are going shopping to pick out the first three pairs of earrings he owes me. I'm thinking biiiiig bling and maybe some colored stones.

Our server comes over just then, and we order. I love the breakfasts here at Food Café, but I don't eat here that often because usually I'm grabbing stuff on my way somewhere else, and the dining hall or the food trucks are more convenient and faster.

"So," Grant begins, sitting back, "I heard your news. Thank you for trusting me with it."

Aw. "Please. Like I don't trust you with everything in my life. There's no way I wouldn't have told you this." I stop, because I actually *didn't* tell him. "I mean, I would have told you myself, except I'm too lazy to make an extra phone call, and I knew Uncle Luke would want to angst over it anyway, so..." I shrug. "Two birds, one stone."

"I didn't angst over it," Uncle Luke protests. "What does that even mean, anyway?"

"I love you, but you did," Grant tells him. "Worrying about your kids is an automatic reaction for you. But clearly Jordan's fine." He sweeps a hand in my direction. "He's happy, he's expanding his personal style, he's excelling in his sport. This is a kid we only have to worry about a normal amount." He lifts his water glass in salute to me before taking a sip.

"Thank you." I grin and wait for him to put his glass down. I learned my lesson from Polly last night—no more talking while people are drinking.

"I guess that's true," Uncle Luke concedes. "You gave me fewer gray hairs than your sister did." Considering he's only just started graying around the temples, I roll my eyes. But I'll definitely be telling Mila he said she's the problem child. "So, we have news. I wasn't going to say anything until tonight, but I'd rather get it out of the way."

Uh-oh. "Are you sick?" Panic spirals dizzyingly through me. I can't lose Uncle Luke. I just can't.

"No, sorry, it's not that. I'm fine, Grant's fine, everyone's fine." He reaches out to pat my arm as I sag in my chair.

"Jesus, Uncle Luke, don't scare me like that." I gulp down my water, still feeling a little shaky.

"You suck at this," Grant says affectionately, then turns to me. "We're happy about this, but your uncle is a little worried about how you and Mila are going to take it."

"If you're happy, I'm happy," I declare, then add, "Unless you're divorcing."

"We're not," they say in unison, then smile at each other.

"Not happening," Grant tacks on. "No, I've been offered a job at a company here in California, and you know Joy wants Luke to move back to head office here, so—"

"You're leaving Joyville." I'm surprised by how much my stomach sinks. I knew this would happen eventually, but it's harder than I expected it to be.

"Yes." Uncle Luke watches me closely, and I muster a smile.

"Like I said, if you're happy, I'm happy."

"Really?" Grant eyes me. "Because we know how much you love it there."

"But I don't live there anymore," I point out. "And a big reason for me loving it so much was my family being there and the life we had. I love you guys the most."

Uncle Luke looks up at the ceiling and sniffles a little, while Grant clears his throat and smiles at me. "We love you too, Jordan. You know you'll always have a room in our house, no matter where we all end up, right?"

I snort. "Grant, you're my dads. That's a given. Now, in a minute I'm going to ask you about your new job, but first I have news too."

"Oh?" The worried look is back on Uncle Luke's face.

"Yeah, but don't worry. You'll like it."

"Hit us with it, then," Grant invites.

"My boyfriend and I told our closest friends about us."

Our server comes back at that moment with our food, which is just as well, since I've shocked my dads into silence.

"Bon appétit!"

SEVENTEEN
BLAISE

"Would you relax?" Jordan says, half laughing, as we walk toward the restaurant and I straighten my shirt for the third time. "They're going to love you."

"Yeah, you keep saying that," I mutter. I'm not convinced. From what he's said about his dads, they're both the business type, execs, and his stepdad at least is into sports. That's not a demographic that usually appreciates my aesthetic as a costume designer.

On the other hand, they're Jordan's dads, and he's fucking awesome. Plus, his uncle adopted two kids and never let them feel unwanted, even when it cost him his first marriage. So... maybe I'm getting all worked up over nothing.

The restaurant they picked is a nice one, way nicer than anything I can afford, and I'm glad I called and checked the dress code. Jordan was less than helpful when I asked him—just shrugged and said he was planning to wear jeans.

He is *not* wearing jeans. I put a stop to that plan.

We pause outside the double glass doors, and I take a deep breath and straighten my shoulders. "I might need a minute."

Jordan looks at his smartwatch. "Okay, but we're already running a tiny bit late, so—"

I push open the door and march inside before he can finish. There's no way I want to keep his dads waiting. He was delayed getting cleaned up after the game, because he played so fucking amazingly that the college and local sports media wanted to interview him on the field. Then apparently a scout was at the game and wanted to talk to Polly, so half the team waited around to see how it went. Don't get me wrong—I'm bursting with pride over how Jordan's playing, and nobody screamed louder than me when he hit the homer today (though Calla and Xera gave me a run for my money). I never thought I'd love a sport, but being with Jordan is converting me to the church of baseball.

Or maybe it's just Jordan's altar I worship at.

The host smiles at me. "Good evening. Do you have a reservation?"

"Yeah. We're meeting some people..." Shit. Is Jordan's uncle's surname the same as his? And what if it's under Grant's name?

Luckily, Jordan steps up to my side and says, "I can see them over there."

The host glances in that direction. "Oh, they said they were waiting for two more. Come right this way."

As we get closer, it's easy to see where we're going. There's only one table with two men sitting at it in this part of the room. I study them while I have the chance—both appear to be tall, both dark-haired, both dressed similarly to us in dress pants and shirts open at the collar. If I had to guess ages from here, I'd say late forties, which is younger than I expected. They're both fit-looking and wear their clothes well.

And they're both fucking hot. Like... seriously. If I was into older guys, this would be when my brain started with the sugar daddy fantasies.

We reach the table, and they both look up, then stand with big smiles. Their expressions are curious but friendly, and that makes me feel a bit better.

"Your server will be with you in a moment," the host informs us, then leaves.

"This is Blaise," Jordan announces. "And these are my dads."

Helpful, Jordan. Very helpful.

The slightly shorter of the two huffs and rolls his eyes. "If I hadn't raised him myself, I'd say wolves did it." He extends a hand to me. "I'm Jordan's uncle, Luke Durrant. This is my husband, Grant Davis."

"Blaise Warner," I offer, shaking first his hand, then Grant's. "It's so nice to meet you, Mr. Durrant. Jordan talks about you both all the time."

"Please call me Luke. And if he was complaining about the Pop-Tarts, I don't feel any guilt about it whatsoever."

I laugh as we all sit, my tension draining away. "That might have come up. Plus, I've seen how many he eats, and I don't blame you. He's not allowed to bring them to my place anymore."

"Wow," Jordan says to nobody, "bonding over your mutual betrayal of me."

"Looking after your health isn't betrayal, kid," Grant tells him. "Great game today, by the way."

"Yes, congratulations," Luke adds. "You made it worth our effort to come." He grins in a way that tells me he'd have thought it was worth the effort even if they'd lost miserably and it was all Jordan's fault.

"I'm having a good season," Jordan concedes modestly, then with a wicked sideways glance at me, "Blaise is giving me incentive. For every game we win, he's made some very attractive promises to me."

My face gets hot, and I sputter. "Oh my god, don't make it sound like that!"

His dads are laughing, though. "You're such a shit," Grant says affectionately before turning to me. "What is it? Are you letting him have Pop-Tarts?"

I snort. "No. He has enough already. I don't know how all his teeth haven't fallen out from the sugar overload." Part of me can't believe I'm saying that, being so casual so soon after meeting them, but it just feels… natural? It's an odd sensation to me. I'm not used to having father-figure men I'm so comfortable with. "I said I'd buy him a new pair of earrings for every win."

Luke laughs so hard, I worry he might hurt himself. "Oh my god, he's going to ask for bigger ones. They'll be able to see him from space."

"That's the dream," Jordan agrees cheerfully, winking at me.

Our server comes to take our drink order and give us the specials, and I turn my attention to the menu. Everything looks amazing, but the prices make me a little dizzy. What's the etiquette for ordering when your boyfriend's dads, who you just met, are paying for dinner? I mean, I could offer to pay my own, but that would be a little awkward, and I can't offer to pay the whole check—the hit to my savings would be too hard. Should I just order the cheapest thing on the menu?

Or would that be insulting? Like saying I think they can't afford more?

I wish I'd talked to Jordan about this before we arrived… though he probably wouldn't be much help. I don't think he even thinks about budgets and where his money comes from.

Better to play it safe and order light. I can always say I had a hot dog at the game, or something.

"The roasted Mediterranean veggie salad looks so good," I muse. It's not the cheapest of the salads, but I don't want to be obvious. "I wonder if they'll do that in an entrée size?"

"It does look good," Grant agrees. "I think I'll have that to start, and then the prime rib." He grins at me over his menu. "That and dessert should cover most of the food groups."

I grin back, but my stomach sinks a little. Will anyone believe that a salad has made me too full for dessert? Jordan won't—he's seen me eat.

Luke catches my eye. "Are you a vegetarian?" he asks, and Jordan snorts but doesn't look up from his menu.

"If you'd seen him fight me over Korean barbecue, you wouldn't be asking that."

"It's not my fault you eat like a vacuum cleaner," I argue. "I have to defend my territory, or I won't have anything to eat." Too late, I realize that's not going to help my story of a hot dog a few hours ago making me so full I can only manage a salad. Maybe I can say I had chili cheese fries too?

"He's always been like that," Luke says fondly. "Like that kids' book about the caterpillar."

"We're still waiting for him to become a butterfly," Grant adds.

"Wow, so much hate tonight." Jordan pretends to wipe away a tear. "Just for that, I'm ordering the lobster salad, the prime rib, two sides, *and* two desserts." He purses his lips. "Maybe I'll get another entrée too, ask them to box it up for me to take home for lunch tomorrow."

Luke laughs. "Meet us for brunch like we planned, and we'll make sure you're sufficiently full. You too, Blaise, if you're free."

My smile this time is completely natural. "That's so nice of you, but I'm working tomorrow. I swapped with a coworker to have Saturdays off when Jordan's playing at home, but that means I'm basically working every Sunday until the end of time." It also means a hit to my commission, since Saturday is one of our busy days, but even before we made it official, it was something I wanted to do. My goals are still on track—and what's the point of working so hard for something if you don't enjoy life along the way?

Jordan puts down his menu and looks at me. "You did? Really?"

"You didn't notice?" Grant asks dryly.

"We're only a few weeks into the season," Jordan defends. "And he doesn't work every weekend. That's so cool, though." The look he gives me is so happy and sweet that my heart melts.

"Someone's gotta cheer you on." It's awkward, but I don't know what else to say. He bumps my shoulder with his, the closest we'll get to PDA in public, but under the table, his foot twines around my ankle.

"Well, if you can't join us for brunch, I insist on feeding you up tonight," Luke announces. "I remember what dining hall food is like. Feel free to borrow Jordan's plan and order multiples of everything to take home with you." His eyes lock with mine, and I don't know what Jordan told him about me, but I get the feeling he knows I don't have a lot of money and wants to treat me.

Normally, that would make me feel awkward, maybe a little offended. But just like my earlier feeling of comfort and ease, this gives me a good vibe too. It's nice to have someone care the way my mom would—the way my dad *should*. Still...

"I actually graduated last year," I offer. "But since Ramen doesn't give me the same joy as just looking at this menu does, I might have to eat enough tonight to get me through the rest of the weekend."

They laugh, and I relax a little more. I don't know why I was so nervous. Jordan was right—his dads are great.

The server comes back with our drinks and to take our order, and I get the salad to start and the chicken special, plus I agree to share one of Jordan's sides with him (because he does, in fact, order two).

Then I sip my soda—no way was I ordering alcohol my first dinner with Jordan's parents—and congratulate myself on navigating what could have been a sticky situation.

"So, Blaise, you graduated last year? And you're working at the menswear store now, right?" Grant asks. His tone is curious and friendly, but the question still makes my gut freeze. Is this when the judging begins?

"Yes—temporarily, anyway. There's an internship I want to apply for, but it's unpaid and..." I shrug. "The cost of living in LA isn't something I could cover with a weekend job alone." Not to mention I don't know exactly what demands on my time the internship will have. What if the occasional weekend is required? Sure, I plan to keep costs down by finding somewhere cheap with a whole lot of roommates, but they're not going to let me stay if I can't cover my share of the rent because I had to skip some paying shifts unexpectedly.

"That's right," Luke says. "Jordan mentioned a while back that he had a friend saving for an internship. You're the costume designer."

EIGHTEEN
JORDAN

Blaise suddenly looks like a deer caught in headlights, and I have no idea why, but I'm spurred to rescue him. "He's an *amazing* costume designer. You should see some of his stuff, Uncle Luke—it's so good! He's doing cosplay outfits for some people going to a book convention at the moment. I read the character descriptions in the book, and I swear, he's brought them to life." Uncle Luke is smiling faintly, and Grant's got his analytical face on, but Blaise is still quiet and a little green.

So I press my knee against his and keep talking. "And he did a costume for Hector from *Space Reivers* that's so freaking awesome—I like it better than the one he wore in the movie."

"It's different?" Grant asks. He's currently the director of Joy Universe, and the live-action movie was made in the studios on-site there not long after he took the promotion. He didn't have any direct interaction with it—the studios are separate from the parks—but he still had to stay across the project overall. And of course he got me access for some set visits. There's gotta be *some* perks to being the stepkid of a JU exec.

"Yeah, he made it when the movie was first announced, so

he didn't know what the actual costume was going to look like." I turn to Blaise. "Do you have pictures on your phone?"

He hesitates. "Jordan, I don't think your dads—"

"If you do, I'd love to see them," Grant cuts in.

"Me too," Uncle Luke adds. "Jordan was obsessed with that movie, even before the remake. When he was little, he used to pretend to *be* a space pirate. Only he didn't have a laser blaster thingy, so he used the remote control. It was annoying when we were trying to watch TV and the channel would suddenly change, or the volume would zoom up to deafening."

"Thanks for sharing that," I say, deadpan. Uncle Luke's usually so cool that I forget he *does* do embarrassing parent things like this sometimes.

But at least Blaise is smiling now. "You must have been so cute," he teases. "Are there pictures?"

"Hundreds," Uncle Luke assures him. "Give me your email before we go, and I'll send you some."

"Speaking of pictures...," Grant prompts, and Blaise pulls out his phone and starts scrolling.

"Hector. Um, sure, I have some I took when I was making it, and then my friend took a few of me wearing it for me to add to my portfolio... Here." He passes his phone across the table to Grant.

My stepdad takes it, glances at the screen, and his eyes immediately widen. "You made this? When the movie was first announced... so you were, what, a freshman?"

Blaise nods. "Yeah. I ended up using it for a project that year for my intro to design class."

Uncle Luke leans in to see and blinks. "Wow. I know Jordan said you were good, but I was expecting him to have rose-tinted glasses."

Now my boyfriend's cheeks are turning pink. "Thank you. I

can see the problems with it, things I might do differently now, but it's still one of my favorite projects."

"We can see why. Is it okay for me to scroll?" Grant asks.

"Sure. There's a few more from the side and back views."

They scroll through the pics, and I elbow Blaise and shoot him a grin, bursting with pride. He smiles back at me, but I can tell he doesn't understand what this means. Probably because I haven't told him all that much about where my dads work and who my honorary uncles are.

This is huge, though.

The dads will go home and tell Dimi and Jason about Blaise's mad skills. Jason used to be a Broadway director—he works exclusively at JU now, but he's still touted as one of the all-time best directors Broadway has ever seen, and he knows *everybody*. Plus, Uncle Luke works for Joy Inc. directly, not JU—he's got connections in the design and wardrobe departments, because he works with them on processes and efficiency. Blaise might already have a leg up for getting this internship because the guy who runs it likes his work, but once he has the money, I can pretty much guarantee he's going to get it, thanks to my family.

And if he decides he wants to try something different instead... well, we can help with that too.

I just have to find a way to tell him that doesn't make it sound like I think he needs the help. Maybe it would be better if I stayed in the background on this? Like a puppet master, pulling all the strings behind the scenes.

Heh. I like the idea of my dads and uncles being puppets.

"Could you send these to us?" Uncle Luke asks, on cue. "I have a friend who'd love to see them."

Ding ding ding. Step one, complete.

"Sure." Blaise shrugs. "You can just text them to yourself, if you want."

Grant does, and a second later hands Blaise's phone back. "When you're ready to apply for that internship, I have every confidence you'll get it," he says. "They'd be idiots not to take you."

"That's so nice of you to say." Blaise grins. "Let's hope you're right. My savings are going pretty well—I started before I even finished my sophomore year. I'm hoping that maybe I'll be close enough to put my application in come April, for the July intake."

"That soon? That's great!" I don't know why I thought it would take longer.

He lightly raps his knuckles on the tablecloth. "Touch wood, anyway. It's not for sure, and I'd probably have to take on some side work next year as well, to cover the gaps. But if not this time, then definitely next year, and in the meantime, I can continue working locally to build my portfolio."

My dads exchange an approving look. They like work ethic. Then Grant lifts his glass.

"Let's toast to hard work paying off, then."

I wave my dads off after brunch and consider how to spend the rest of this sunny almost-spring Sunday. I could study, but we all know that's not going to happen. What I really want to do is go see Blaise, but he's at work and even if me hanging out in the store all day wouldn't be weird, he actually has to *work*. I'd be a distraction. I'll call him later.

Instead, I wander toward the beach. It's too cold to swim, and I'm not a surfer, but the sun is nice enough to sit in the sand and make the most of living in SC. Back home—which I guess won't be home when my dads move in a couple months—the beach is a two-hour drive away, minimum. I hadn't realized how soothing I find the ocean until I moved here.

A lot of other students have had the same idea, and it takes me a minute to find a relatively clear spot and flop down. The sun glitters off the deep blue of the waves, and a few seagulls caw overhead. Nearby, someone's playing music, but it's not obnoxiously loud. There's a low hum of chatter, the occasional peal of laughter. It's nice.

I can smell the enticing aroma of coffee from the Bean Necessities coffee cart, and something else from the food trucks that would make my stomach growl if I hadn't just eaten. If I'm still here in a couple of hours, that's going to be my next stop. Meanwhile, I'm just going to sit here and be Zen. Let nature speak to me. Be at one with my thoughts.

Yeah, that's not as easy as it sounds. My thoughts are clear enough, but it's hard to be Zen when I know I need to tell Coach I'm queer and seeing someone. If Blaise and I weren't together, it wouldn't be necessary, but no matter how low-key and non-PDA we are, there's always a chance that someone will work it out. I don't need Coach being taken by surprise on two fronts if that happens.

I just really don't want to have that conversation with him.

It's not that I think he'll be homophobic. I've talked openly about my dads with the team, and he's talked *to* them—when I started last year, Grant called to offer discounted JU passes for everyone associated with the team, and Coach helped him set that up. He's got firm rules about use of homophobic language in the locker room too.

But he's under a *lot* of pressure right now, with the Hannaway thing. The athletic department and the PR department are still in serious damage control mode, and the other sports teams are giving us serious side-eyes and cold shoulders, so I can only imagine what their coaches are being like to him. I don't think me telling him about another possible thing that might attract the media spotlight is going to be a fun experience for either of us.

"Jordan?"

I glance up at a familiar face: Harrison, the guy from my stats class last semester who pretended he was going to hook up with me to make the guy he really wanted jealous, because said guy and his identical twin had been playing swapsies and never told him. Or something like that. I'm still not entirely clear on the details. But he's with the twin he wanted now, so it all turned out.

"Hey, what's up?"

He sits beside me. "I was just about to ask you the same thing. You look very pensive."

I shrug. "Just thinking. I gotta tell my coach something that's probably going to add to the shitpile of stress he's under right now, and I don't wanna."

Harrison pulls a face, his red hair all fiery in the sunlight. "Yeah, I heard about what happened."

"You and everyone else at this school... and in SoCal... and who follows college baseball or hates jocks."

"I can't help with that, obviously, but is there something else I can do? I'm a good listener, and Benny's going to be in line at the coffee cart for a while."

I glance over my shoulder in the direction of the cart, and sure enough, the line is long. Austin, the cute guy who works at Bean Necessities, has his work cut out for him.

Harrison *would* be a good person to talk this through with—until he started dating this guy, he was straight.

"Okay, so... this goes in a vault, right? And it's all hypothetical," I add.

His eyes widen, and he glances around, then nods solemnly. "I swear."

"You used to be straight, yeah? Or at least you thought you were," I amend, because I'm not sure how he wants to approach the concept of his pansexuality. "When you thought you were straight, did you think male celebrities were hot? But that it wasn't a reflection of your preferences, because they weren't real people?"

He looks a little confused. "I don't think I ever really thought about it?"

Moving on, then. "So let's say that a member of the… swim team had recently discovered they were bisexual."

Harrison's mouth forms an O, and then he nods. "Sure. It happens."

"And there's no existential crisis because they've got queer family members and don't have any problem accepting that part of themselves."

"Great news."

"But they don't ever plan to try out for the Olympics or anything, so they don't see the point in making a big 'I'm a queer athlete' announcement when they actually just want to live their life in peace. And their new partner also doesn't want that kind of attention. And someone else on the swim team was recently caught up in a scandal—let's say doping—and there's a lot of media attention and pressure on them at the moment already."

"Well… that's definitely a sticky wicket."

I blink. It's a what? You know what, never mind. "What would be the best way to tell the swim coach that they're bi so that if it somehow came out, he'd be prepared? Or would it be better to just not say anything and hope for the best?" I'm hoping he'll vote for option two, but I know that even if he does, I need to tell Coach. My friends think so. My dads think so. Even Blaise thinks it would be smart.

Harrison winces. "No, sorry, y—I mean, the swimmer

should talk to their coach. And maybe it won't ever need to be discussed again, but at least that way all bases are covered."

I chuckle. "Pun intended?"

He looks blank. "Sorry?"

Okay, so he's not really a baseball fan. "Never mind. Any suggestions for the swimmer?"

"Open and straightforward is the way to go. 'I don't think this will ever be a problem, but I thought the responsible thing was to let you know. I'm bisexual, I'm dating someone, and though we don't plan to make this public, sometimes secrets come out.'" He frowns. "The coach isn't bigoted, is he?"

I shake my head. "Nope."

"Then that's the best bet."

A shadow falls over us, and we look up at the scowling face of Harrison's boyfriend. I can't resist poking the bear a tiny bit. "Which twin are you?"

Harrison scrambles to his feet. "And on that note, I think I'm ready for a walk. Come on, Benny. Jordan..." He gives me an encouraging smile. "Good luck to the swimmer."

They walk away, and I hear the twin—Benny—mutter, "Who the fuck is the swimmer?"

Time for me to go and find Coach.

NINETEEN
JORDAN

I find Coach in the video room, watching tapes of yesterday's game. It was a pretty sure bet he'd be there, since that's what he likes to do every Sunday. His wife's a nurse who deliberately works weekend shifts, since he's busy every Saturday and a lot of Sundays anyway, so he does a lot of stuff on his free Sundays and takes off another day during the week to spend time with her. It's sweet.

He must have radar or something, though, because even though I'm quiet, I've barely stopped in the doorway before he turns around and says, "If you're about to tell me you got arrested last night, you'd better start running."

"Me? I had dinner with my dads last night," I protest. "If I'd gotten arrested—which I never have anyway—you'd already know, because their yelling would have been heard by the whole county."

Snorting, he hits Pause on the tape. "What can I do for you, Marks? If your dads want to take the team to JU for spring break, I gotta say no. I don't want the media calling the team spoiled rich kids again."

I hadn't heard that one, and it makes me wince. Though I

guess it's true, for me at least. It's not like we have a mansion and private plane, but I've never had to worry about things like college loans or anything. I had a part-time job in high school, but that was because Uncle Luke thought it would be good for me, not because I needed the money. I'm kind of the definition of privileged. "That's not it, Coach. It's, uh, it's not bad news, but the responsible thing is for me to tell you. So... I am. Telling you."

The dread on his face is terrifying. "Tell me what?"

I take a deep breath. "The thing is... I'm bisexual and I have a boyfriend. I don't want to come out, but some people know, so... if news gets out, now you already know."

He blinks at me in silence. Then, "Is that it?"

"Yes." I nod.

"You weren't photographed underage at a gay sex club?"

What? "No. I've never been to a gay sex club." Is there even one here in San Luco?

"Your boyfriend, is he legal?"

"He's older than me."

His gaze sharpens. "How much older?"

"Uh... he's twenty-three."

"Is he a bikie, gang member, or otherwise involved in crime or a criminal organization?"

This is starting to get weird. "He works at a menswear store and wants to design costumes for TV and movies. Coach, are you feeling okay?" How do I ask if he's having some kind of mental break without potentially making it worse?

"So what you're saying is that you're dating a law-abiding, age-appropriate, ordinary man, but you don't want to make any public statement about it?"

"I don't know about ordinary," I object. "Blaise is pretty special."

Coach nods, then chuckles. "Of course he is. Marks... are

you sure you don't want to come out? Keeping a relationship secret is a pretty big thing."

It's so far from what I expected him to say that for a minute, I don't know how to answer. I sit down in one of the chairs grouped around the screen. "Our closest friends know," I admit. "And my family. I don't like the idea of sneaking around, like Blaise is something to be ashamed of, but... I'm not planning a career in baseball, Coach. Why bring all this attention that neither of us want, when in a couple of years, we can be open and nobody will care?"

"It sounds like you've thought this through. You're a sensible kid. I know what your ex-teammate did this year has made things more difficult, but if you change your mind and decide you want to come out..." His face gets a pained expression, but he pushes on. "I and the athletic department would support you."

"Even though it would bring down a media shitstorm that isn't focused on our game?" I'm only half teasing—part of me can't believe he actually brought himself to say that.

"Even though. My players matter, Marks."

Aw. "Thanks, Coach. I don't think we'll change our minds on this, though. I just wanted you to know so you wouldn't be surprised if it somehow gets out."

"Thank you. I appreciate that."

I stand to go, and I'm nearly to the door before he calls, "Marks?"

"Yeah, Coach?" I turn back. He's watching me closely.

"You're having a killer season so far, and you're only a sophomore. Are you really sure you don't want to consider the pros?"

"Positive," I say confidently.

He nods. "It's just... I had a call about you last week."

I frown. "A call?"

"It might be nothing. Like I said, you're still only a sophomore. But if you keep playing like this, people are going to show interest."

"People?" I don't get it.

Coach sighs exasperatedly. "Scouts, Marks. There's a chance you'll be scouted."

Whoa. "Me? No way." I'm not that level of player.

"There aren't any definites. But if playing pro ball was ever something you wanted, it might not be out of reach. Think about it."

"I don't want to go pro," I tell him, but for the first time in years, I'm not sure that's completely true.

That conversation is still circling through my head when I park outside Blaise's place. It's early—he won't be home for another half hour, at least—but I'm too restless to go back to my dorm, and if I call my friends, I know we'll end up talking about this. Which I don't want to do yet. Not until I get my head around the idea myself.

I really wish my dads weren't currently on a plane heading back to Georgia, because this is the kind of thing they usually talk me through. I could call Mila, but there's a good chance she'd just call me an idiot a few more times, and I'm not in the mood for that today. Sisters can be harsh, man.

A couple of Blaise's neighbors that I recognize are standing at the entrance, talking, and I decide to see if they'll let me in. Sitting on the floor outside his door won't be more comfortable than my car, but it'll be a change of scenery. Besides, sitting in my car outside a residential building for too long makes me feel like a creeper.

Sure enough, as I near them, one of the women smiles at me. "Here to see Blaise?"

"Yeah. He's due any minute—mind if I wait for him inside?"

They both shrug, and one swipes the door open for me. "Knock yourself out."

I take the steps two at a time, then slide to the floor in front of his door and lean against it. There's something almost therapeutic about letting my head thunk against the wood, so I do it three more times. Thunk, thunk, thu—whooooaaaa!

Blinking, flat on my back, I stare up at the blond stranger looming above me.

"You're not my Chinese food," he observes. "Not unless you forgot the food and plan to offer something else instead."

What the fuck? Oh, *shit*. "You're the roommate," I realize, scrambling to my feet. Crap, what's his name? I'm sure Blaise told me at some point. "Uh, hi. I'm Jordan, a friend of Blaise's."

"He's not here right now," the roommate points out, folding his arms across his chest. He doesn't look pissed off, though—kind of amused, actually.

"No, I know—he's at work. But he'll be home soon, so I thought I'd wait." God, that must sound so weird to someone who doesn't know we're boyfriends, and I don't know if Blaise would tell him or not.

"You were going to wait in the hall? Like this is some made-for-TV rom-com?"

Ouch. "I felt like a creeper waiting in the car," I excuse weakly.

He nods sagely. "Yeah, I get that. Waiting in the hallway outside the door is so much less creepy."

This isn't going well, and I think the smart thing to do right now is say buh-bye. "So, I'm just gonna..." I gesture vaguely toward the stairs.

Roommate smiles. "You don't happen to be the owner of the

green Vans sitting in the middle of my living room, do you? The ones that are two sizes too big for Blaise and way more worn out than he'd ever let them get?"

I don't know why, but heat rises from my neck all the way up to my hairline, and I know I'm blushing. "Uh, yeah, those are mine. I was going to wear them last night, but Blaise made me change..." I trail off. I doubt he even cares.

He laughs. "I'm totally messing with you, Jordan. Blaise told me about you—come in and wait for him." He holds the door wide, and I manage to smile as I walk past him.

"I'm Drey, by the way," he adds, closing it once I'm inside, and memory floods in.

"Oh sure, I know. Dreyton Langtry the third," I say casually. I can't believe I forgot that—I even cracked a joke about how pretentious it was when Blaise told me. The way he smirks tells me he knows I forgot.

"I'm glad we got a chance to meet," he says, waving me toward the couch, and it's kind of awks. I'm used to just flopping down like I belong here, but I guess I'm a guest? So I sit like I'm visiting my grandmother, except I never had a grandmother to visit and I just end up feeling hella uncomfortable and out of place. "I got in this morning and I'm leaving in a couple of hours, so I didn't think we would. But Blaise mentions you almost every time we talk—apparently you're the reason my Pop-Tart stash now lives in my room instead of the kitchen?"

I gasp and sit bolt upright. "What? Oh my god, all he had to do was say they were yours! I wasn't gonna eat someone else's food." I can't believe Blaise did me dirty like that.

"He said that," Drey agrees, sitting in the armchair opposite me, "but he also thought having them where you could see them would be like waving crack under the nose of a recovering addict."

"I have a will of steel," I protest indignantly.

One blond eyebrow rises. "Oh? Want one right now?"

Fuck. I really, really do, but this is a test. There's never been a more obvious test in the history of them. If I say yes, I fail. If I say no, I'll be proven victorious... but I won't have a Pop-Tart.

Damn Drey and his wiliness.

"No, thank you," I say, and even to me it sounds sulky.

He laughs again, then asks, "You like Chinese food? I can order more."

"Isn't it already on its way?"

Drey shrugs. "No idea. I just assumed thumping on the door meant food, but I only ordered it ten minutes ago, so that could just be my brain being in a different time zone." He hauls out his phone and taps the screen. "App says it's still being made. Let me call—what do you want? I already got enough for Blaise."

He updates the order, then leans back in the chair and studies me thoughtfully. "Just so we're both on the same page, I know about you and Blaise," he says. "We've been friends for a long time. I can keep your secret."

"Thanks. It's not that I want it to be a secret," I feel compelled to add. "I just don't want it to be a circus."

He nods. "I get it, man. I work for a private charter company, and that means sometimes flying with athletes. I've heard all the dramas that come with the press. The thing is..." He leans forward, his piercing blue gaze pinning me. "Blaise is an amazing guy. Best friend anyone could have, will always step up for you if you need him. You wanting to keep this under the radar short-term is fine, but if it turns into a permanent thing..."

I meet his gaze dead-on. "He met my dads last night. It doesn't get more serious than that for me."

He nods. "Good."

TWENTY
BLAISE

Jordan texted me earlier to say he was coming over when I finished work, and I saw his car on the street when I pulled in, but he's not in it. Maybe he went for a walk? As soon as I get out of this suit, I'll call and see where he got to.

A car pulls into the waiting bay as I approach the door, and I recognize it as belonging to Ricky, the son of the owner of Drey's favorite Chinese takeout place. Ricky does most of the deliveries, since his dad believes Uber Eats and DoorDash are evil, and he's delivered here a *lot* of times.

Sure enough, he smiles at me as he gets out of the car. "Hey, Blaise. Order for Drey—do you mind taking it up? I've got another one to drop off still."

"Sure." I grab the bags, tip him, and swipe myself into the building. It's only when I'm halfway up the stairs that I realize Drey ordered a lot of food, even if he was planning on me sharing it.

Then I get into the apartment and realize why. My roommate and my boyfriend are sitting on the floor beside the coffee table, arguing animatedly while they inexplicably move random items around. Is that a toilet paper roll? Why's that in the living room?

"This is a weird kind of party," I observe, kicking the door shut behind me and carrying the food to the kitchen. They both turn.

"You're home!" Jordan exclaims, his face lighting up.

"I am. I see you've met Drey." And bonded over... a pencil holder and the weird statue Drey's mom insisted on putting on the TV cabinet?

"We were just discussing why baseball is so much better than basketball," my adorable boyfriend says smugly, and Drey snorts.

"The other way around, jock. Lucky they make you wear a helmet, or your brain might be even more scrambled than it is."

"I've never been hit in the head... in the past five years," he tacks on, and I laugh.

"I'm going to change. Start dishing up this food, or I'll be eating the furniture when I get back."

Jordan trails after me into my bedroom, leaving Drey to handle dinner, and throws himself onto my bed, sighing.

"What's wrong?" I ask, taking off my jacket and hanging it. "Did something happen with your parents?" Oh god, please don't let them have told him they hate me. I thought last night went so well!

He waves that off. "Nah, brunch was fine. They should be landing in a couple hours, and they'll text me when they're home."

Phew. I nudge off my shoes and say, "What is it, then? You seem down."

"Not down," he corrects, staring at the ceiling. "Just... thinky. I told Coach."

I stop halfway through unbuttoning my shirt. "Oh." Ohhhhh. "Was he mad?" Jordan was completely convinced his coach wouldn't be homophobic, but I can't deny it's been a tiny worry for me that he's wrong.

"No, he was totally cool. As long as you're not associated with a gang or other crime organization, too young or old for me, and nobody got pics of me at a gay sex club, he really doesn't care. Even said that if we changed our minds and decided we did want to go public, he'd support us." He pauses. "Though he looked like the thought gave him an ulcer."

I chuckle. "At least he said it. That sounds like it went well, then."

"Yeah. Yeah, it did."

Wearing only my pants, I sit on the bed beside him. "So why are you so thinky, then?" I lightly tug one of his earlobes. Now that they've healed, he's discovered they're more sensitive, and touching them always gets a good reaction from him.

Sure enough, he shivers a little and smiles. "He said he got a call about me last week. A scouting kind of call."

"Wow." That's so not what I expected him to say. "Flattering—but also, you definitely earned it. You've been on fire lately."

"I guess."

I'm not sure why this has got him so introspective, but I figure distraction is the way to go. "It makes sense that they'd put feelers out now, while you're a sophomore, right? But they probably wouldn't even want to talk to you for another year, when you're closer to graduating and you've really proven yourself." I'm talking out of my ass—I have no idea how this all works. But that seems to perk him up a bit, so I keep going. "And just think of the bragging rights in the meantime."

Laughing, he sits up and leans over to kiss me. "You creative people know how to think right. Come on, let's eat. Drey said he has to leave soon, and I was thinking, since we're gonna have the place to ourselves and there's a whole week until my next game... maybe we could try anal tonight?"

My mouth goes dry, and it's only his hopeful expression that stirs me to croak, "Sounds good."

Drey's long gone, and Jordan and I have been making out on the couch for ages when he pulls back and sits up. "So... sex."

Sitting up beside him, I wrap an arm around his shoulders, and he leans his head against me. "It all counts as sex," I remind him. "Not everyone likes anal."

"I want to try it, though. I, uh..." He squirms a little. "You know I like it when you finger me. Sometimes when I'm in the shower, I... experiment."

My lips twitch, but I'm careful not to sound like I'm laughing when I say, "I'm guessing you like that too."

He nods. "I think I want to try bottoming first. Is that okay with you?" We've talked about this before, when we talked about sexual health and condoms. He knows I'm vers but prefer to top, and I hope that hasn't influenced his decision here.

"Of course it's okay with me," I assure him. "As long as you're sure that's what *you* want."

Lifting his head, he meets my gaze. "I really do. I mean, I want to try it the other way too, but this first time, I'm kind of excited to bottom." His face gets red, but from the way his breath hitches in his chest, I know he means he's literally excited, and that gets me revved up too.

"Let's go into the bedroom, then. You'll be more comfortable on the bed." Plus the lube is in there, and we're definitely going to need it.

He bounces up and grabs my hand, making me laugh as he

tows me along. "Just you wait," he promises over his shoulder. "My ass is going to *ruin* you for any other man."

My eyes drop to said ass, and I smirk. "That mission has already been accomplished."

It's his turn to laugh as he gives his booty a shake, and I tackle him onto the bed, where we get distracted with more kisses. Kissing Jordan is addictive. I could spend a lifetime doing just this.

The press of his hard cock against my thigh redirects my thoughts. Okay, so I'd probably want to spend *some* of that lifetime up close and personal with his dick. "How do you want to do this?" I murmur between kisses.

"Shouldn't you be telling me? I'm the novice here."

I snort. "Please, let's not pretend you're not going to be the bossiest bottom ever born. How do you feel more comfortable? Hands and knees? On your back? Riding me?"

He hesitates, and vulnerability flashes across his face. "I think... on my back? I want to see you, and I don't want to drive until I know what I'm doing."

"Sounds great," I assure him. "Want me to prep you?" I lean over to get the lube from the nightstand, and when I turn back, he's wearing a wicked smile.

"I want you to watch."

"Exhibitionist," I tease, as if the idea didn't make my dick jerk in my pants. "Let's get naked, then."

To say that Jordan puts on a show for me would be vastly understating it. I strip off quickly, but he... He turns the act of removing jeans and a tee into a three-act performance, even without music. By the end, I have a firm grip on my cock just to keep from coming. "If you don't want this to be over too soon, you better get a move on," I croak, and he saunters toward the bed.

"I guess Mila making me watch *Magic Mike* wasn't such a bad thing after all," he muses, lying down beside me and grabbing the lube.

"Channing Tatum?" I ask. I know all about his thing for celebrities.

"Joe Manganiello." He squirts lube onto his fingers, bends his knees up, and inserts the first digit like a pro.

"Whoa. You really have been playing in the shower." I bite my lip as I watch.

"Yeahhh," he breathes. "Lube's better than conditioner, though."

I glance up in time to see his eyes drift half-closed, a tiny smile on his mouth, and I lean in to kiss him.

When I break away, we're both panting a little, and he insists, "Don't... distract me. I'm busy."

I don't bother to respond, just stroke a hand down his chest the way I did the day we met, leaving my palm on his lower abs as he adds a second finger.

"You're so fucking hot, Jordan," I murmur, eyes glued to those fingers sliding in and out, loosening him up for my dick. "I can't wait to get inside you."

He whimpers. "Fuck, yeah. Me too."

By the time he's taking three fingers easily, his face is flushed, lips parted, and I'm at the edge of my control just having watched him. How I'm going to make this good for him, I have no damn clue, but I will. "Ready?" I whisper, and he nods.

I've never gotten a condom on so damn fast in my life.

This is far from the first time I've ever done this—so, so far. And yet, the moment when he slides his fingers free and I position the head of my cock against his hole, I meet his gaze, and... I can't deny the feelings that swamp me.

This is special. It means... more.

"Stop me if it hurts," I remind him, my voice as unsteady as my emotions, and when he nods, I push forward.

There's the usual resistance, and then he relaxes, and I slowly slide in, deeper and deeper until I'm fully seated. I look anxiously at his face, but that hint of a smile is back. "Okay?" I check.

"Yeah. It's... weird, but good. I thought it would hurt, or be uncomfortable, but I guess I might be born to bottom."

I snort. "Or you're an athlete with really good muscle control, and you've been fingering yourself for a while."

He gives an experimental little wiggle that makes us both gasp. "Whatever it is, I think this is the part where you start thrusting and make me see heaven."

"I knew you'd be a bossy bottom." But I obey, pulling back almost all the way before pushing home again... and again. He moans, a deep, drawn-out sound that sends shivers through me, and I pick up the pace a little.

It's his first time; be gentle, I remind myself, but he's so into it, urging me on, meeting my thrusts, making the most arousing, delicious noises, that I can't hold back, driving in harder, faster, until we're both sweaty and panting and incoherent.

I'm going to come. I can't stop it. Fumbling desperately, I hook one hand under Jordan's knee and adjust our position, and on the next thrust, he screams.

Yes!

"Holy—"

I thrust again, drilling his prostate, and his words cut off, his eyes rolling back.

On the third thrust, he comes, the hot clamp of his ass tightening around me, and I let go, let myself experience the best orgasm of my life before I carefully pull out and collapse beside him.

"Jesus," he whispers, long minutes later, and I smile at the ceiling.

"No, just me."

He snorts and fumbles for my hand. "I'm definitely not someone who doesn't like anal."

TWENTY-ONE
JORDAN

IS THERE ANYTHING AS GOOD AS A LAZY SUNDAY IN SPRING? I love March. Blaise isn't working today, and we smashed it at our game yesterday, so I spent the night and we had awesome, drowsy sex in the gray light of dawn before snoozing again.

He's up now, and I can hear him puttering in the kitchen—hopefully something breakfast-y, since my usual Sunday breakfast of Pop-Tarts is banned in this apartment. So rude. I'm still in bed, scrolling Insta and pretending to be a man of leisure and not someone who needs to finish a stats assignment sometime in the next few days.

Oooh, this is cool! Blaise has been tagged a bunch of times in posts and reels from the book convention he made those costumes for. I guess it must be this weekend. Wow, they really do look fucking epic, and judging by the comments, I'm not the only one who thinks so.

I click into one of the hashtags for the event to see if anyone else had costumes that good, and the answer is... not many. It actually looks kind of fun, for a convention about books. The scale of it is bigger than I expected, and it's not just a room with tables and people—from what I'm seeing, there are panels and meet-and-greets and mini-events too. This is the kind of thing I want to get into when I'm working—large-scale events with intricate themes.

I stop scrolling suddenly when a post that's mostly text catches my eye.

DUE TO THE WEATHER IN DENVER, A LARGE NUMBER OF TICKET HOLDERS ARE UNABLE TO ATTEND. THESE TICKETS CAN BE RESOLD—COMMENT BELOW IF YOU HAVE A TICKET TO SELL.

There's the usual disclaimer that organizers take no responsibility and it's up to buyers to take every precaution, but I click into the comments.

I've had an idea.

The event's at the Anaheim Convention Center, and according to the Sunday Schedule post I scrolled past not long ago, there's stuff happening right up until something called "The Unholy Supper" tonight. I want to get into event planning. Blaise is breaking into costume design. What better way for us to spend a Sunday afternoon than at a big event with lots of costumes?

I find someone claiming to have two tickets and DM them to see if they're still for sale. I get a reply immediately.

> **CORYNISMYHONEY:**
> OMG yes! I'll sell them 2 for 1 if you'll get me a signature from Halle Manx pleeeeeeease! Or at least try. Her line will probs be a mile long.

Okay. That's... unexpected.

> **JMBALL4LIFE:**
> I'll try? If I can't, I'll pay the difference in ticket price.

> **CORYNISMYHONEY:**
> I love you!!! TYSM!

We make the transaction, and I get her details, including the name she wants signed on "any paper is fine, even the back of a gum wrapper." Then I get up and go in search of Blaise.

"I can't believe you talked me into this," he grumbles four hours later, but his gaze is already tracking a bunch of people in costumes.

"Oh, please. You'll love it. Okay, let's get the lay of the land, find out where this Halle Manx is, and then we can decide whether to see her now or walk around a bit first."

Blaise drags his eyes back to me. "Did you say Halle Manx?"

"Yeah. That's the author Desi wants me to get a signature from for her."

"She's also the author who wrote the books I designed those costumes for," Blaise says.

"No way! That's so cool. Now we definitely have to meet her."

Luckily, we were given maps at the door, and we find Halle Manx's booth easily enough. Unluckily, the line is, as Desi guessed, a mile long. Maybe two.

"I guess people really love these books." I take in the clusters of mostly women, but also a lot more men than I would have expected, since the books supposedly have a lot of romance in them. There are a lot in cosplay, but most of them seem so excited, clutching books or hauling along roller suitcases or carts. They're talking animatedly to each other, and every once in a while, someone will call out to a passerby and there'll be shrieks and hugs and exclamations of "I haven't seen you since last year!" The whole vibe of community is really strong, and I wonder how the event organizers tap into that to play the whole weekend up.

"That corset is gorgeous," Blaise says, and I follow his gaze toward a woman standing in front of a nearby booth selling bookmarks.

"Let's go ask her where she got it," I suggest. "I want to see the event, and if we join the line now, we'll probably be here all afternoon. We can try again later." I did tell Desi I'd only *try*.

We talk to purple-corset woman and the couple selling the leather and resin bookmarks, then we crash a couple of the panels. I find myself taking notes on my phone. Not so much about what's being said—though I'll admit to sitting with my mouth open and listening in shocked awe to a five-minute discussion about "the throne scene"—but about the setup, the way the panels are structured and rooms set up, the way people are interacting with the whole thing. Even the flow of traffic gets a mention—this is the afternoon of the second day, and I've heard a few people say it's quieter than yesterday, but it still seems pretty busy to me. Yet there's no "chaos." This is the art I need to learn, and I have a pile of questions to ask Toby, my events mentor and kind-of uncle, later.

Blaise finds a section of booths that sell costumes, and although most of them are just vendors of mass-produced generic stuff, there are two he beelines toward—one run by a woman who makes velvet cloaks and intricate tiaras and headpieces, and another by a lesbian couple who make cosplay components, like chainmail, corsets, and stuff I don't know the names of. After a few minutes chatting, we learn that they also take commissions to make full cosplay outfits, and they show us photos of some of the ones they did for this event. They were interested to hear Blaise had made some too, and when I showed them the pics from Insta, they got super excited.

"We *saw* those!" Kyra, the shorter one, exclaims. "You made them? They're fabulous! Oh my god, you need to contact the event organizers and get on the list of cosplay designers for next year. Once people know you did those costumes, you'll be flooded with commissions."

"How does he do that?" I demand, because Blaise looks a little shell-shocked. I don't think it occurred to him to connect in a serious way with fandom communities—he just waits for people to find him through word of mouth. Maybe because he's so focused on breaking into film costuming and considers this a step along the way instead of a career.

Kyra tells me who to get in touch with and reminds me twice that planning for next year's event is already well underway, so not to dawdle. Then she goes to help a customer, and I leave Blaise talking to Helen about the difficulties of making chainmail, which I have no interest in.

I find a booth selling books, and even though there are a lot of big gaps where things are sold out, I spot a hardcover with Halle Manx's name on it. That would be way cooler for her to sign than a piece of paper, and I grab it and wait my turn to pay.

"Heh," the seller says as she scans the book. "I didn't think it would last long. We sold out of all Halle's books yesterday. This one somehow got mixed in with the extra copies of regular stock, and I only found it five minutes ago."

"Lucky for me, then." Seriously, maybe I should read one of these books, just to see what all the hype is.

The woman looks at me like I'm crazy. "To get an event-exclusive-edition hardcover with sprayed edges at four o'clock on Sunday? Yeah, hon, you should buy a lottery ticket."

Oh-kaaaay. I look at the book with new eyes as she hands it back to me. It did seem kinda expensive for a book.

Blaise joins me, and we decide to go check out Halle's line again. It's not really any shorter, but we join it anyway. It takes about three seconds before someone sees the book in my hands, squeals, and announces how jealous they are. That turns into me sheepishly admitting it's for someone else and how I haven't read it, which somehow is an invitation for the people around us to begin telling us about the series. Not gonna lie, even though romantic fantasy isn't my thing, it doesn't sound all that bad. Plus, these people... they take the fandom seriously, but they're so nice and so welcoming.

Next thing I know, an hour has passed and it's my turn. I leave Blaise talking costume ideas with the people behind us and step up to the table. Halle Manx is a pretty, middle-aged woman with a really nice smile, though her eyes look a little tired. No wonder, if she's been talking to people all day.

"Hi," she says, taking the book one of her assistants already stuck a Post-it in. "It's great to meet you—" She glances at the Post-it. "—Desi."

"Oh, thanks, but I'm not Desi. She got stuck in the weather in Denver and sold me her tickets, and I said I'd get your signature for her."

She looks up, surprise and then a bigger smile crossing her face. "That's really nice of you...?"

"Jordan."

"Well, Jordan, do you want to video call Desi so I can say hey to her? I don't mind."

That might be weird, but why not? "Let me see if she's around," I hedge, tapping out a quick DM. It's no wonder the line takes so long, if Halle takes the time to talk to everyone, but it's also really nice of her. "I can see why people like you so much," I tell her, stalling while I wait to see if Desi gets the message. "I think I'm going to read one of your books."

Her mouth drops open, but before she can say anything, my phone lights up with a video call, and I hand it over.

"Hi, Desi," Halle says, and screams erupt from the handset. I wince, but Halle just laughs. "Your friend Jordan did you a solid. I'm sorry we didn't get to meet this time, but I've just finished signing your book." She holds up the hardcover, bringing on a wave of new screams. She looks at me questioningly. "Was it a surprise?"

I shrug. "Not really, just a last-minute find."

Halle talks to Desi for another few seconds, then ends the call and hands me back the phone, which already has DMs from Desi popping up. I shove it in my pocket to deal with later.

"Thanks for being so cool," I say. "People really love you. We came today because I saw all the pics and thought it was worth checking out. My boyfriend, Blaise, designed some cosplay costumes for some of your readers." I smile at her again and turn away to let the next people have their turn, but her hand clamps around my wrist. I look down at it and then back at her suddenly weird face.

"Did you say your boyfriend is Blaise?"

TWENTY-TWO
BLAISE

"Your boyfriend is Blaise?" I hear, and look over to where Jordan is *still* talking to Halle Manx. For someone who's never read her books, he sure is hogging her time.

"Uh-oh," Jenny, who I've been talking to about the best way to construct wearable wings, says with a chuckle. "Sounds like you're being summoned."

"Sounds like it's time for me to move him along so you can have your turn," I reply. "It was great meeting you. Text if you run into trouble with the modelling wire, and I'll walk you through it."

"Thank you!"

I step away from her and join my boyfriend, who's looking a bit wary. "Uh, yeah. Here he is, actually." He puts an arm around my shoulders.

Halle's eyes widen as she stares at me. "You're Blaise? Wait." She holds out a hand to her assistant, who hands over a phone, and a second later, she's leaning across the table to shove the screen in my face. "This Blaise?"

I blink a few times and pull my head back so I can actually focus. "That's not me—oh, wait, do you mean did I make those costumes?" I can't believe how many people semi-recognize me here, just from those four costumes. It's wild. And fucking amazing. But mostly wild.

"Yes! Was that you?"

Suddenly I'm wary about answering. What if she decides to sue me or something? I know she doesn't have a legal leg to stand on—it's cosplay, and it's not like I'm advertising and selling them using the names of her characters. It was a custom commission based on a basic description. But still...

"It was," I venture warily. I can't lie—enough people know I made them that I'd never get away with it.

She drops the phone and races around the table, and just as I'm raising my hands to fend off an attack, I find myself with an armful of author. She squeezes me tight, and I look over her head at an equally bewildered Jordan.

"Oh my god, I love you!" she cries, pulling back. "Thank you so much! When I saw those costumes... I swear, I came this close to crying." She sniffles, as though she's about to cry now. "It's like you got into my head and *saw* my characters."

Okay, wow, that's... I put a hand on my chest. "Really? That's such a compliment. I just envisioned them based on the descriptions—you have really great descriptions, by the way. You made it so easy."

"That's the nicest thing you could have said," she gushes. "Do you mind if we get a video together for me to share on my socials? You can cross-post it too. I already shared pics of the cosplayers, and those posts got great interaction."

Coming as this does right on the heels of my thoughts about maybe signing up as an event affiliate to do costumes for next year—something to add to my portfolio, even if I am doing the internship by then—I agree. An author with a line this long has to have a few thousand followers, right? Maybe even as many as fifty thousand. I might be able to get a couple of commissions from this.

"Hope will take the video," Halle says with a bright smile at her assistant, then adds to me, "This is my sister, Hope. She keeps me sane."

"I try," the woman says wryly, scooping up the phone from the table. "Come and stand in front of the banner. Branding, girl, remember?"

Halle rolls her eyes. "I don't need to remember with you to remind me."

We arrange ourselves beside the standing banner that has Halle's name and the blown-up cover of one of her books on it, and then when Hope nods, Halle says, "Yesterday I posted some cosplay pics that blew us all away, and, you will not believe it, but today I got to meet the man who designed and made them!" She slings an arm around my waist. "This is Blaise, and he brought my vision to life in the best way. If you haven't seen the pics yet, I'll link them below—and I'll link Blaise's profile too." She winks. "Oh, and a shout out to Desi, who couldn't make it and had to sell her tickets to Blaise's boyfriend. We missed you, but I'm so glad I got to meet Blaise!"

Hope lowers the phone, and I wait three seconds longer before letting go of the awkward smile I plastered on my face. I hope it doesn't look as weird as it felt.

Halle hugs me again. "I'm so glad I got to meet you," she repeats. "Do you have any other pictures of those costumes?"

I nod. "Sure. Some on dress forms, some on Jordan, who helped me make sure everything had freedom of movement, and a whole bunch I took while I was making them."

"Could you send them to me? Hope—" She half turns toward her sister, but Hope is already stepping forward with a business card. "Send them to the email on there, and Hope will make sure I get them. Thank you so much."

"Thank you," I say genuinely. "You've made me feel great today. I'm trying to get into wardrobe and costuming for film and television, and it's hard. Some days it feels..." I stop. I can't believe I'm unloading on this stranger.

"It feels like no matter how hard you try, you'll never get there?" she asks, and her face is full of understanding. "I remember that. I submitted over a thousand queries across six books before an agent offered me a contract, and that book never even sold. Some of the older ones eventually did, though, which is ironic. So I know how you feel, and I'm so glad I could give you some of the happy you gave me. We creatives need to stick together."

"Not to interrupt or anything, but they're going to kick us out soon and there are still people waiting, Halle," Hope says quietly.

Jordan and I say our farewells and leave, apologizing as we pass all the people waiting. Some give us dirty looks, but others just smile and call out things like, "Isn't she great?"

It's one of the most surreal experiences I've ever had.

The whole drive home, Jordan and I talk about the event. Considering neither of us is much of a reader and when we do pick up a book, it's not romance, fantasy, or a combination of the two, it surprises me that we can fill the time so easily. But it flies by—Jordan has ideas and questions about the planning and management of something on that scale, stuff that his current classes haven't really begun to touch on yet. He's been to his fair share of sports-related events, team open days and games and round robins and a whole bunch of other things I've never heard of, plus the usual career fairs, music festivals, and the like that everyone our age has been to, but this was a new experience for us both.

It had never occurred to me that so many people would be interested in costuming to meet an author. I've seen the scope of things like Comic Con, of course, but those characters are already visual—we see them, know what they look like, the details of their costumes. And of course, they're owned by studios that have no trouble licensing them and mass-producing costumes for anyone to purchase. Sure, there are dedicated cosplayers who'll make their own from scratch, but those aren't the people who hire the job out.

Book characters, on the other hand... I've done a few cosplay outfits for people found on the page, but I never realized how impactful it could be. Seeing so many people dressed up today, talking to Kyra and Helen and especially Halle, really opened my eyes. In a very real sense, *this* is exactly what I want to do with my life—take someone's written description of a character and bring them to life visually.

I've always known the impact clothing and style can have in conveying personality on the screen. I was mentally adjusting sitcom characters' costumes to better suit the actors' mannerisms when I was a little kid. It was a reflex—*she should have a bracelet to fidget with; his collar needs to be wider.* But in my mind, books belonged in the realm of the imagination. Unless they were adapted into screenplays, any visual component lived in the mind of the reader. It never struck me that they could also be brought to life this way.

"What are you thinking?" Jordan asks when we finally make it to my place and he's thrown himself onto the couch. "Also, what should we have for dinner?"

"I have leftover chili and cornbread. There's enough for us both," I say absently, frowning at my phone. It's been on silent in my pocket since we left Anaheim, but somehow, it completely blew up in that time. My Insta notifications are *insane*.

"What's up?" Jordan gets off the couch and comes to look over my shoulder. "Whoa. Looks like Halle posted that video and tagged you."

"I have two hundred DMs," I say faintly. "What the hell? How many people could have seen that post already?"

He takes my phone from me and starts scrolling through. "Well, she's got over two million followers, so probably a lot."

Ex-fucking-cuse me? "*How* many followers?"

"Some of these are scams, or those annoying sales messages," he says, ignoring the question. "So those can be deleted. But a lot are questions about your prices for commissions." He looks up at me. "What do you want to do?"

I rub my hand over my mouth. I want to take them, of course, but I'm only one person and there's no way I can do them all. Plus, this is a side business for me. My main goal is still the same. I like the idea of bringing an author's vision to life, but designing the same costume over and over again doesn't do it for me.

But the money would get me closer to my goal. It might even get me there a lot faster.

I take my phone back from Jordan and update my profile to say "Currently closed for commissions. Check back soon for updates." That will buy me time to work things out. Maybe I can set a guideline that I'll only do a certain "look" once—like, one of the costumes I did for Halle's character was a dress from a specific scene. Not repeating costumes once they've been done will let me have some variety in interpreting characters. I also need to work out pricing, and a schedule—how many can I take on at a time?

Once I have that clear, I'll be in a better position to reply to some of these messages. It might even weed out a lot of the requests. But this will definitely be good for my portfolio.

"You're going to do it, aren't you?" Jordan says, grinning as he watches my face. "This is fucking epic. I get to be the dressmaker's dummy or whatever, okay? That way when you're famous, there will be tons of photos of me in your early designs."

"It's a dress form," I correct, not for the first time, "and you're ridiculous." I kiss him. "But yeah, definitely. You can be my model." I kiss him again, letting my phone fall to the floor. "Thank you for today. This never would have happened without you." I hesitate. I want to tell him I love him, but is it too soon?

Like always, Jordan knows me better than I think. "You're welcome. You know I'd do anything for you, right?" he says. "I'm pretty sure you're the love of my life."

What else is there to do but kiss him again? "I love you."

TWENTY-THREE
JORDAN

I truly hadn't planned on telling the rest of the team about me being queer. Even though Polly thinks they'd be cool with it, and he wants us all to feel like a family or brotherhood or whatever, it just isn't something I think they need to know right now. Not with everything gelling so well.

For the first time in about twenty years, our team has a shot at making regionals. It's nearly the end of March, and we've only lost *one* game. That's not just good, it's *phenomenal*, and Coach is so happy, he's almost smiled a bunch of times. So nope, no way do I want to mess with the good mojo. If even one of my teammates turns out to be the tiniest bit uncomfortable with me being queer, that could get in their head and throw off the vibe for the whole team. I'm not taking that risk. I can let them know when the season's done—or next year, even. It's not like I'm going anywhere anytime soon.

Fuck knows I'm not letting Blaise go, either... in a non-chained-in-my-basement way. We haven't been together that long, so I might be jumping the gun, but I kind of think he's it. Like... *it*, it. I'm not usually the heart-eyes, start dating and think forever type, so I don't think I'm fooling myself.

Forever's a long time, though, so if I'm right, there's no need for us to race through the stages of commitment or whatever. We've both got things to focus on right now: for me, finishing college and enjoying baseball while I still can. For him, getting that internship and kickstarting his career. It's most likely that next year, while I'm still here at Franklin, he'll be in LA working his ass off bringing people coffee and taking notes. We're going to need to be prepared to do long-distance for at least twelve months—realistically, when he gets a job up there, longer—and I'm already prepared to go through those tough times.

I mean... assuming he wants to. We haven't exactly talked about it yet. But we did talk about taking a short weekend trip over the summer, so I don't think he's planning to ditch me. Plus, we both said the L word. I know him well enough to know he didn't do that lightly.

On top of Blaise's budding business as cosplay designer for fantasy readers, Dimi called me two days after my dads' visit. He said if the Joy Inc. internship doesn't work out for Blaise, he wants to talk to him about an assistant costume designer job for Joy Village Theater Company. Which is basically a great job offer already, though I'm not sure how Blaise would feel about moving to Joyville. It's essentially Nowhere, Georgia—the whole town exists just to support Joy Universe. And the job's in theater, not film, which is where he really wants to work. But the fact that Dimi reacted like that tells me I won't have any issues convincing my other uncles to activate their contacts if need be.

Which it won't. He's getting that internship. I can feel it.

So... yeah. Things are good, future looks bright, no need to mess with the good vibes.

I sit on the bench in front of my locker to tie my shoes, whistling. I'm headed to Blaise's next—his friends are coming over to mock some show that starts streaming its second season tonight. I don't know what it is, but apparently they've all got deeply held opinions on everything from costume design to lighting, acting, and script, so I'm prepared to sit back with my popcorn and enjoy the snark. Butch and Harold alone would make the producers weep.

"New earrings?" Laringo asks, a little too casually. I'm not sure why—he hasn't cared about the piercings before. Maybe he wants to get some himself and needs my encouragement.

"Yep! Blaise got 'em for me after last week's win. I think they bring out my eyes." I bat my eyelashes exaggeratedly, but instead of laughing, he exchanges a look with Reiner.

"Listen, uh, Marks," he begins, sounding awkward as fuck. "Don't you think him buying you earrings is a bit... weird?"

A hush falls over the room, and even though everyone continues what they were doing, I can sense their attention on us. "Weird?" I repeat. "Not really. He's investing in our wins."

"Yeah, but..." He trails off, glancing over at Reiner.

"It's just, buying someone jewelry—a lot of jewelry—that's a personal thing," Reiner jumps in. "And Blaise is gay, you know? I mean, he's great and it's been fun seeing him become a baseball fan, but he's... gay."

If one of them had punched me in the gut, I don't think I would have felt this shitty. I can't believe they're saying this. To my face. They know my dads—Laringo has actually been out to dinner with them. How can they somehow feel like Blaise being gay makes him less or whatever it is they're implying?

"I don't like what I'm hearing," Polly says in his captain voice, taking two steps forward. "Do I need to remind everyone that this is a no-hate team?"

The horror that crosses Laringo's and Reiner's faces is reassuring. "Fuck no!" Laringo bursts out. "That's not what we meant! It's just... Blaise is gay, and Marks is letting him buy him presents, and we thought..."

"Leading him on is not okay, man," Reiner finishes. "Don't give him the wrong idea—it's not fair to him."

The strangling band around my chest snaps, and I can breathe again. They're looking out for Blaise's feelings? Calling me out for "using" him? I love my team so much.

Boyle makes a strangled sound that I'm pretty sure is him trying to hide a laugh. Polly stares at them, then slowly turns to me, his gaze questioning. What do I want to do?

I wasn't going to come out to the whole team this season. I had reasons, good ones. But with all my guys watching me now, at least some of them ready to throw down for someone they don't know well just because it's the right thing to do, how can I stay quiet?

Standing, I smile at everyone. "Blaise is my boyfriend. I swear, I'm not leading him on."

Jaws drop. Eyes blink rapidly. Someone coughs.

"What?" Timmins asks. "Like... seriously, what? I thought you were straight! You were dating that Nina chick last semester."

I shrug. "I thought I was straight too. Then I thought maybe I was celeb-sexual, but turns out, I'm bi. Or pan. I'm still not sure."

"The fuck is celeb-sexual?" someone mutters.

"Marks is a dumb shit who thinks celebrities aren't real people, so for him, wanting to bone Chris Hemsworth didn't mean he wasn't straight," Boyle says matter-of-factly.

"Ryan Gosling," I correct. "Did you *see* him in that movie, *Crazy, Stupid, Love*?"

"No, because I was *eight years old*." Polly looks at me like I'm crazy.

"I did," Timmins volunteers, and when a dozen incredulous stares turn to him, he says, "What? I have four older sisters. Marks, man, I'm sorry, but I did not want to bone Ryan

Gosling. Not the first time I saw it or the fifty million times after."

"Wait, wait, hold up." Laringo's frowning. "Why Ryan Gosling and not Chris Hemsworth?"

"Is that really what we're focusing on here?" Polly asks incredulously. "*Really?*"

"I'm just saying, why would you go for Ken over Thor?"

"Attraction is a strange and wondrous thing," Boyle says sagely, and we all crack up laughing. "What? I'm serious!"

"So..." Reiner looks me in the eye when we all settle down again. "You're not leading Blaise on just so he'll buy you earrings?"

I shake my head. "We're together. One-hundred-percent dating."

"Why didn't you say anything?" There's an edge of hurt in his voice. "Did you think we'd—"

"Nope." I cut him off. "But Blaise and I don't want the publicity of me being an out collegiate athlete, so we only told a few people to start. You guys were on my list to tell next, but our juju is really good right now, and I didn't want to risk it."

"What the juju are you all blathering about?" Coach demands from the doorway. "Since when is this locker room used for talk therapy?"

I grin at him. "I told the team I'm dating Blaise."

A howl goes up. "Coach *knew*?" Laringo slaps a hand to his chest. "I'm dead, dude. You told Coach before you told us?"

"If you're reacting with all this drama, do you blame him?" Coach snaps. "I hope I don't need to remind anyone that this is an inclusive team, and the FU athletic department stands by its diversity policy in all its sports."

"As long as Marks keeps playing the way he is, I don't care if he dates those earrings he loves so much," Timmins says dryly, and even Coach's lips twitch at that one.

"Maybe you should all get your ears pierced," he says dryly. "Marks did, and he's having one of the best seasons I've ever seen."

Boyle's eyes light up, and Coach is quick to add, "That's not a requirement, request, or official directive. Any decision you make is not connected to this team, its coaches, or the Franklin U athletic department." He shakes his head, then turns on his heel and stalks out, muttering something about dumbass kids.

"Aww, he really loves us," Reiner says, shoving his stuff in his bag. "Okay, so Marks has a boyfriend, but we're keeping it on the down-low."

"Are we all clear on that?" Polly asks, his captain hat firmly in place. "Let's not drag the limelight away from how awesome we're playing." He hesitates, then adds, "And like Coach said, this is an inclusive team. Marks is still the same player he's been all season, and last year too. Who he's dating doesn't change that."

"Except that he's dating my sister's girlfriend's friend, who is also Polly's girlfriend's friend, and they're not only the best cheer squad we've ever had in a crowd, but they organized some kind of drive with the arts students to get ticket sales up," Boyle tacks on.

"They did?" How come I didn't know that?

Boyle shrugs, but Polly goes pink. "Uh... Calla wanted me to talk to you all about that. There's this drawing class that has a form and movement component that needs models, and they told a bunch of the students that if they showed support for the team, we might be persuaded to... model."

Reiner's bag hits the floor. "Naked?"

Polly shakes his head frantically. "No! Nope. It's not *that* class. They hire models for that. This is just, like, people. Moving. And maybe shirtless if you were comfortable. I modeled for Calla. It doesn't take long—she mostly did sketches while I was just working out. They need to see how arms and legs and muscles move."

I pull out my phone to text Blaise. I can't believe he didn't tell me about this. I mean, sure, he graduated and doesn't need a model, but it's his friends masterminding it all. And using it to raise support and awareness for my team.

"I could get on board with this," Laringo muses. "I like hot artsy chicks, and I look great without my shirt on."

"I'll, uh, tell Calla there'll be at least one volunteer, then," Polly mumbles. It seems like he's a little embarrassed by this. Dude needs to learn to own it. His hot, smart, ambitious girlfriend is thinking outside the box in a way that benefits her classmates and his team. There's no losers here.

"Let's have a party," I suggest impulsively, then re-think it. "Not a *party*, party. But like a mixer. The team and the arts kids. After a game, maybe?"

"And the art geeks can be all, 'Wow, Laringo is sooooo perfect to model, we have to have him.' I like this idea," Laringo announces.

"Oh, are we talking about things that will never happen?" Reiner teases. "But seriously, sure. Let's do it."

Polly sighs, then laughs. "I'll tell Calla. She'll be all over it."

And just like that, me being queer is just another piece of locker room news.

TWENTY-FOUR
BLAISE

I'VE HAD DAYS IN MY LIFE THAT WERE SO SHITTY, EVEN remembering them hurts. Like when my mom died, or a storm blew half a freaking tree and about a million gallons of rain through the window of my dorm and trashed my stuff. Having a dickhead for a dad wasn't bad enough; I lost my remaining childhood memories to fucking rain.

Then there are the gold star days. Days that were so completely amazing, I can hardly believe I was so lucky as to live them. Today's been one of those days. I had a huge commission at work, a guy whose ex-girlfriend cut up all his clothes, claiming their relationship failed because he loved them more than her. The judge awarded him ten thousand dollars in damages, and I'm the lucky bastard who got to help him replace his "basic" wardrobe. As if that wasn't good enough, while I was on lunch, I got an email from Halle Manx, asking me to give her a call. Of course I did.

She said she'd looked at the photos I sent her after the convention, and she and her team had this idea. Would I be interested in designing and patternmaking costumes for some of her characters that she could sell through her website? She wants to offer the option of just the pattern, the pattern plus a kit of everything a cosplayer would need to make it themselves, or a fully made-up version. I warned her I could only handle the design and patternmaking, plus one made-up sample and all the notes about materials, and she assured me her team could find people to do the rest. The flat fee for each design and pattern that she suggested was way more generous than I expected, and I think I might have zoned out for a second before telling her yes, I would definitely watch my email for the contract.

So yeah, total gold star day. Jordan came out to his team over a week ago, and even though I know he was worried it would mess with their winning streak, it did not. They've won both games since, including their away game against Arizona State, and the articles about the team no longer begin with, "The Kings, the team alleged sex offender Greg Hannaway played for," and now only mention him in a throwaway line toward the end, if at all. Plus, the team's really gotten into the idea of modeling for the arts school—there was an informal mixer the other week, and now there's talk of making it an official partnership between the arts school and the baseball team, a collaborative effort going forward. I *have* noticed a wider range of people in the stands lately—and not just because winning games means more people come to watch.

I think I'll stop and pick up something for dinner—chicken, maybe, or curry from that Thai place Jordan loves. He's meeting me at my place and texted me this morning to announce that he has no studying to do tonight. So it'll just be us and the whole night to do whateve—

Clunk.

What the fuck?

My whole car starts to rattle, practically vibrating, and there's smoke coming from under the hood, so I quickly steer to the side, grateful I'm not on a busy road. As soon as I turn the engine off, it clunks again.

It's fine. This is fine. It's just a minor hiccup. Not something that's going to ruin my gold star day.

I pop the hood, then get out and go have a look. That's my first mistake—the hood is fucking hot, and when I get it up, with much swearing, all I see is smoke and engine. I don't know why I bothered looking.

Pulling out my phone, I google for the closest garage. It's two blocks away, which bodes well if I'm going to need a tow. Not that I will. This is something that can be fixed in two minutes.

The guy who answers the phone doesn't seem so sure. "Wait, so it was rattling *and* there's smoke?"

"It also made a weird clunking sound, twice. I haven't tried to start it again, though—should I?"

"Not yet," he says slowly. "Is it smoke or steam?"

I look at the dissipating plume. "I think both? It looks like steam, but I can smell smoke—like burning rubber kind of smoke, but not rubber, exactly."

He's silent for a second. "Where did you say you are?"

"Portland Street—according to Maps, I'm about four minutes' walk from you."

"Okay, stay there. I'm just closing up, but Imma swing by and take a look. If I need to, I can tow you back and get started on it tomorrow morning." He hangs up before I can ask anything else.

Oh well. A tow and minor repairs are going to be a hit to my savings, but it's still fine. This new job is going to put me over the top of my living fund goal before the end of June. I'm going to soothe the sting of my car breaking down by applying for the internship tonight.

While I wait for the mechanic, I send Jordan a text saying I'll be late and can he grab dinner for us. With Drey's agreement, I gave him a key to the apartment a couple of weeks ago. He immediately texts back a thumbs-up and a kissy face emoji, and I can't help smiling. Gold. Star. Day.

Fifteen minutes later, the smile is gone.

"I don't understand," I say numbly, even though I very much do understand. I just don't want to. "How can it not be repairable?"

The mechanic—whose name is Dave—grimaces. "I guess it could be repaired, but it's not worth it, man. It's an old car, and it'll cost more to get it up and running than it would to buy something five years newer. I'd be a dick to tell you anything else."

That's thousands of dollars. He's talking about *thousands* of dollars. Because if I buy a new used car, it has to be something reliable. I don't know what my living situation's going to be like when I move to LA, and I can't count on the idea of public transit being able to get me to and from work. Even now, getting a bus to the mall for work would turn my ten-minute commute into a forty-five-minute one, and it would be *worse* for my night and weekend shifts. A car that I can depend on is a must-have.

So... I guess I'm not applying for the internship tonight after all. Or this year.

Swallowing down my bitter disappointment, I ask Dave, "Can you tell me exactly what's wrong with it?" Maybe I can get a second opinion.

He shrugs. "Sure. The engine block's got about seven cracks in it that I can see, and those are your biggest issues. In layman's terms, it means you've got to replace the engine." Shaking his head, he says, "I honestly don't know how that happened. *Seven?* That's not normal. The car overheated because your coolant's low, and it looks like your oil hasn't been changed in a couple of years, maybe. When was your last service?"

"Six months ago," I whisper, because stuff like that—

coolant, oil change—that's all supposed to be done during a service. I might not know much about cars, but I know that. From the shock on Dave's face, quickly chased away by anger, my regular mechanic has been ripping me the fuck off.

"I'll give you a quote for a full repair that lists all the problems and the details for you to file a complaint with BAR," he says grimly.

"BAR?"

"Bureau of Automotive Repair. Whoever you used should get a hard smack for this. You could probably sue too."

Like that doesn't cost money I'm not going to have. Not to mention *time*. Either way, I'm staying in San Luco for another year.

"What happens now?" I ask. "It's not like I can just leave it here, but what you're saying is that it's not worth towing."

He winces. "Look, I'll take it back to the garage for tonight, and tomorrow I'll call the parts yard. The engine's shot, nobody's going to want anything from that, but the body's in great shape, and I can tell it's been taken care of. They might offer something for it, at worst enough to cover the cost of the tow."

I sigh. That's something, at least. "Thank you. Let me just get my stuff out." Not that I keep much in there—a couple of reusable grocery bags, a bottle of water, my spare sunglasses, and one of Jordan's hoodies that I borrowed a while back. I'm usually pretty good about bringing things inside and cleaning out any trash.

Standing safely on the sidewalk, I watch as Dave hooks up my ex-car, and then he comes over and gives me a business card. "Need a lift anywhere around here?" he offers, but I shake my head.

"Thanks, but I'll call my boyfriend. He'll be wondering

what's keeping me anyway. Do I need to call or stop by tomorrow?"

"Yeah, I'm going to need you to sign some papers, and I'll have that information for you to file your complaint. Want me to ask around, see if anyone is selling a half-decent car?"

"That would be great, thanks." I give him my details, then wait forlornly until he's pulled away before calling Jordan.

"Hey," he says, "did you get another customer fall in love and keep you late to throw money at you? Because I'd be okay with being a kept man."

Any other time, I'd laugh and make a joke about already buying him pretty things, but instead I cringe. "I wish. Uh... my car broke down. Could you come and pick me up?"

"Oh, fuck. Yeah, of course. Where are you? Do you need me to call AAA or something?"

I can hear him moving, a door closing and then the sound of footsteps on the stairs. He's so sweet, but right now, I just feel envy that in his life, AAA is a go-to option, whereas in mine, it was an expense I chose to forgo. And it's not like they could help me now anyway.

"It's all taken care of," I say. It's not his fault he's got parents with money. "I just want to get home." I tell him where I am, and he's already starting his car when I end the call.

I'm really not that far from home—if Jordan hadn't been there, waiting for me, I would have walked it—and his car pulls up just a few minutes later. First I dump the bag of stuff in the back seat, then I climb in the front.

"Don't worry," Jordan declares, "dinner's keeping warm in the oven, and I also got ice cream. Plus, Reiner's cousin's husband is a mechanic here in town, so we'll get him to look over whatever your guy says, make sure you get the best deal. We got this, babe." He leans over to kiss my cheek, and tears prick my eyes.

I swipe them away angrily.

"Blaise?" Jordan's tone changes, becoming quieter, more worried. "What happened? The tow truck came already?"

"Yeah. I need a new car."

He puts the car in Park and turns off the engine. "Say what? I thought it just broke down! How can they know that already?"

I shrug. "Sometimes shit's just that bad. Take me home, please." I just want to be home.

So much for my gold star day.

TWENTY-FIVE

JORDAN

I sneak worried looks at Blaise the whole way back to his place. This is a lot worse than I thought—for starters, what the fuck happened to his car that it can't be repaired?

Once we get inside, he sighs. "Will dinner keep a while longer? I want to take a shower."

"Go. It'll be fine." Normally I'd ask if he wants company, but now doesn't seem like the time. He dumps the bag of stuff from his car on the kitchen counter, then trudges off to the bathroom like he's going to his doom. Not good.

Yanking out my phone, I send a text to Reiner.

JORDAN:
> Can you ask your cousin what kind of car problem would be completely unrepairable?

While I'm waiting for a reply, I spot the card Blaise put next to the bag—it's got the name of a garage on it, as well as the phone number for some dude called Dave Purdy.

> **JORDAN:**
> And ask if he knows anything about Dave Purdy from San Luco Automotive.

Maybe this Dave guy is trying to take Blaise for a ride. Though I'm not sure how he'd benefit from saying the car is unrepairable.

I putter around the kitchen, getting out dishes for our fried chicken and potatoes, opening a beer for Blaise—because this is definitely a beer kind of night—and my phone chimes with a text just as I hear the water go off.

> **REINER:**
> Dude, what happened to your car?! Also, my cousin is Dave Purdy from SL Auto, so he knows everything about him.

Huh. Small world. Also, fuck. I might not know the guy, but Reiner thinks he's decent, so it doesn't seem likely he'd be ripping anyone off. There goes that hope.

> **JORDAN:**
> Not mine, Blaise's. Your cousin said it's dead. Gotta go.

I put the handset down as Blaise comes out wearing boxers and an old T-shirt. He looks tired, but not physically. More like all the hope has been sucked out of him. Is this situation really all that bad? I mean, I know it's not good, but it's not the end of the world, either. He's still got his job, his talent, his home, and his prospects. And me. I'm not going to let anything shitty happen to him if I can help it.

"Come and eat," I suggest. Hunger probably isn't helping the situation.

He joins me at the counter, looks at his plate with a distinct lack of enthusiasm, then sighs and picks up a wing. We eat quietly for a few minutes before he wipes his fingers on a napkin and says, "I guess I'm not really hungry."

"Do you mind sitting with me while I eat?" Maybe if he does, he'll pick at his food some more. He hasn't had much, and I know how long it's been since his last break.

"Sure. I guess you want to know what happened."

"Only if you want to talk about it." That sounds more supportive than "Fuck yes, tell me everything right this second."

"My car broke down. I googled the nearest place that offered towing, and the guy came out, looked at it, and said it would cost more to repair than to buy a new car. Something about cracks in the engine because of overheating. Turns out, my regular mechanic's been taking my money and not servicing the car."

Hot outrage rises in me. "What? That asshole!"

Blaise shrugs. "Pretty much. But now I need to buy a new car."

"You can use mine," I offer immediately, and his brow furrows.

"What?"

"It's not like I need it all that much. The only reason I talked Uncle Luke into letting me drive it back after Christmas break is because Polly came with me, and we spent New Year's at a friend's place in Texas. A road trip was more fun than a bunch of expensive flights in holiday crowds."

"You still drive it," he points out.

"Mostly to get here, or to the mall. I live on campus and walk to all my classes anyway. It just means that I grab an Uber or whatever to come here."

"I can't make you pay to visit me because I have your car, Jordan."

"Then come and pick me up," I insist stubbornly. "Or you

can hang out in the dorm with me sometimes. Nostalgia, and all that."

He smiles at me, but it's lacking its usual authenticity. "That's really sweet, but it's still only a short-term solution. If I'm going to go to LA for the internship, I need a car, and I can't take yours with me. Buying a car means using a chunk of my savings, and that means it's going to take a little longer before I can go. It's fine. Nothing's changed except the timeline, and honestly, I was ahead of the original one anyway. So... nothing's changed at all, when you think about it."

He's so clearly trying to be positive about this, but I'm still stuck on the fact that this is going to delay his internship. That hadn't occurred to me, which probably makes me a dumbass. On the one hand, a delay means he'll be here next year, with me, which isn't something I'm mad about. Buuuuut I want him to be happy. Blaise wants this internship. He wants to kickstart the rest of his life. So yeah, I'm mad about anything that's gonna get in his way.

"Let's think outside the box for a second," I suggest, then hesitate, desperately trying to come up with something. "Apply for the internship, use my car, and I'll bet we can find a way to get you a car for cheap before you have to leave."

"I need a car that won't break down, Jordan. And even cheap equals money."

"Yeah, but something will come up." I'm not giving up on this. "Franklin is full of rich kids who are about to graduate. I bet a whole bunch of them bought a car to use while they were here and are going to sell them in June before they leave." That happens, right? Sure, Uncle Luke would have literally murdered me if I suggested it—then resurrected me to lecture about fiscal responsibility and understanding the value of money—but I'm sure some of these trust fund babies have parents who don't care.

"Be serious," he chides, but at least he's smiling more genuinely now. "Cars aren't like sofas, Jordan. Nobody buys one for college and then leaves it behind when they graduate."

"They might." Mila might have been right when she screeched about how stubborn I am.

"No. They don't. Because unlike sofas, cars are *mobile*. People just drive them to their next destination."

Dammit. I hate that he's right. Though I still think it could be something that happens sometimes. "Okay, so maybe there isn't going to be a bunch of great cars being sold for cheap in June. That doesn't mean you should give up. Apply for the internship like you planned, borrow my car for as long as you need, and in the meantime, not only will we find the perfect car for you at the right price, we'll find the money to pay for it."

Every fiber of me is itching to offer him a loan. Not that I have thousands of dollars just lying around, but I know if I called Uncle Luke, he'd agree. He really likes Blaise. He likes that he's got a plan, that he's focused and determined, and especially that he likes me. But I know Blaise wouldn't take it, not even if we had a contract with repayment plans laid out. He'd just get mad if I offered. So I'm not going to offer.

Yet.

But I *am* going to encourage him to stay on track with his plans, and if it gets to crunch time and he's still short on cash, I'll talk him into it.

"Can we not talk about this anymore?" he asks. "I know you're trying to help, but right now it just makes me feel worse, because there really isn't a way to magic up the money. It's not the apocalypse, and the internship will still be there next year. I'll even be in a better position to take it, because I'll for sure have the money I need and more. I might be able to get a place in LA with less crappy roommates." He gives a fake little laugh. "So... it's all going to be fine. I'm disappointed and frustrated, sure, and looking for a new car wasn't on my to-do list for this year, but until this happened, I was having a great day, and I just want to... I don't know. I want to go back to the good part of the day."

"I like good things," I say affably, even though what I really want to do is hug him and pet him and croon that I'll fix everything. "Tell me about the great day you had."

He visibly shifts gears. "Well... you know how you think I make too big of a deal about clothes?"

I snort. "Yeah. You do." It was dinner with my dads, for crying out loud. Jeans would have been *fine*.

"I had a customer this morning whose ex-girlfriend thought the same thing. He disagreed, obviously, and so did the judge."

I put my fork down. "Judge?" This sounds interesting.

Blaise nods, grinning. "The one who awarded him ten grand in damages after she slashed his clothes to bits with a filleting knife."

"Oh my god, she did *not*!" That's the stuff of TV. "Do we know these people? Please tell me they go to Franklin."

He gives me a "get real" look. "No, they're both fortysomething real estate agents. I don't know them, and I'd be surprised if you did."

"That's kind of epic, though. Not that I'd ever do that," I hasten to add when his face changes. "I might think you care too much about me wearing jeans to a restaurant, but the way you are with clothes is one of the things that makes you so great."

The faint pink flush and soft look he gives me spur me to ask, "So... how much of the ten grand did he spend, and what did he get?" I might not care about suits and the difference between tie styles, but Blaise does, and watching him relax and begin to eat again as he lists off the clothes the guy bought is worth having to listen to it. Then my eyes bug out when he tells me what his commission will be from the sale. "Fuck, that *is* a great day!"

"That's not even all of it. You remember Halle Manx?"

"How could I forget? Me taking you to meet her was one of my best ideas," I say smugly. He opened for commissions last week and has already had to close again, because he's booked up for the year. I suggested he could quit the menswear store and take more cosplay commissions, because the per-hour rate is higher, and I think he might be considering it.

"Haha, yeah, you're the brains of this operation. Anyway, I sent her the making-of photos, and they inspired her."

"Was it my modeling that did it? She wants to write a book about me."

"Yeah, that's totally it," he says dryly. "But actually, kind of. Not the book part. She wants me to design costumes for some of the characters in the series so she can sell them."

It takes my brain a minute to process that. "That's fucking awesome!"

"Yeah. She said her agent would send me the contract to look over, but the terms we talked about were good."

"I looked her up, and she's got more than one series. Maybe once you do this one, she'll want you to do the others. Or she'll talk to her author friends. You'll have the money for a car in no time, babe." I smile brightly, determined to manifest this into reality. Blaise is going to get his dreams.

TWENTY-SIX
BLAISE

I HAVE A SWEET, CONSIDERATE, GENEROUS BOYFRIEND WHO loves me, and I hate it. Okay, no. I don't hate it—I love it. I love *him*. But I hate that he insisted on lending me his car, and I hate that I gave in and took it. Because really, it *is* the sensible short-term solution.

But aside from the battering to my pride—which is considerable—it also highlights the different lives we've lived. Jordan has no money worries. He has a decent model car that his dads bought new for him when he got his license. It's not fancy or flashy, but it's a goddamn new car that they bought for a sixteen-year-old. My car was actually my mom's old car, and when I say "old," I mean it. She bought it secondhand (or maybe thirdhand) when Dad left and she had to sell the perfectly good, nearly new BMW he'd bought her in order to pay her lawyer and some of the bills. She said at the time that a more modest car suited her better anyway, but even though she wasn't a flashy person, I didn't believe it. She was socking as much cash aside as she could to give me a head start, because she knew Dad wouldn't pay for college for his queer son.

Which is point number two... my mom loved me, but she's

gone, and Dad's not in the picture. Jordan, on the other hand, has a swarm of loving family who embrace the queer part of him and are constantly in and out of his life. Seriously, he's living across the country from them all, but they may as well be next door. Messages, emails, social media, the occasional phone call... all things that keep him dialed into the lives of his many sort-of relatives.

He loves his sport. I... well, I don't hate it. I'm actually kind of starting to love it too. As long as he never makes me play. But I want to design costumes for a living. Fabric and fashion and style are my milieu. How can that possibly blend with cleats and dirt?

"Blaise, there's practically steam coming out of your ears," Harold says. "What's troubling your little head badly enough to put those bags under your eyes?"

I raise a brow. Bags? "Bitch."

"True," he agrees. "But so was my statement. Now come on, you dragged me here to the mall to eat a sandwich with you, so tell me what's on your mind."

I sigh. "I'm just... annoyed by life."

"Now who's being a little bitch?" he asks. "Annoyed by life? Honey, so are we all. Be specific, so I can help you fix it."

"It's Jordan." I go for broke.

Harold sits back, shocked. "*Jordan?* That's not what I expected you to say. What happened? Is he sick? Oh my god, he cheated."

"What? No!" No matter what relationship doubts I have, Jordan's fidelity isn't one of them. "Why would you say that?"

He shrugs. "What the hell am I supposed to think? Jordan's the last person I would have picked to be your boyfriend, and yet somehow he's perfect for you. So... what's the problem?"

"He..." I pause. This is going to come out all wrong. "He lent me his car."

"Yeah, I know. Does he want it back or something? Is he being all overbearing about how much you drive it and what gas station you go to?"

"No, none of that. I offered to keep track of mileage and work out some kind of reimbursement, but he laughed it off."

"Okaaaaay." Harold rolls his wrist, asking for more detail.

"It's not just the car. That he lent me to use for as long as I need it. He also asked around his team if anyone knew someone selling a car, and when they didn't, he made flyers and put them up on all the student noticeboards on campus."

"This isn't clearing anything up. Are you... getting nuisance calls because of the flyers?"

I shake my head. "No, he put his number on them so he could weed those out. But, like... that author who wants me to design costumes for her sent me the contract, and Jordan suggested I show it to his friend Cara, who's apparently a lawyer? Junior associate or something at a firm with six names in it. And then he called her, and she said to send it over."

"Free legal advice about a contract? That's great," Harold encourages. "What did she say about it?"

I pull a face.

"Blaise... no. You haven't sent it? Why not?"

"Because of Jordan!"

Harold, who's been one of my best friends since freshman year and helped to get me through the mess after Mom died, shakes his head. "You're going to need to explain this one to me, because I don't see the problem. Jordan was the one who suggested it. He set this up. Why would he be the reason you don't want to— Oh my god, Blaise, did *you* cheat? Because if you did, so help me, I'm going to throw red wine all over that shirt."

"Of course I didn't... Wait. What red wine?"

He pats his insulated water bottle smugly. "Never you mind. So... you didn't—"

"Nobody cheated," I interrupt, just to keep the story moving. "But don't you see how Jordan's doing all the giving in this relationship, while all I do is take? It's unbalanced. Just like we are."

Harold puts down the remains of his sandwich. "I'm not the best person to give relationship advice," he begins slowly, and I snort.

"I'll say."

"*But*," he glares at me, "I think the point of a relationship is that you support each other during the bad times. And that it works in cycles—so you might need a little more from Jordan now, but who's to say he won't need you later on? You can't tell me you didn't give him a lot of support when he was working out his sexuality. And you've basically... okay, not gone back into the closet, but you're behind one of those weird hippy bead curtains because him coming out to the whole campus would be a debacle. So, you see—you give too."

I can't argue with those points, but at the same time, I'm not convinced. "It's just... what I give, it's... emotional. He's giving stuff that saves me money, a *lot* of money. And he has a lot of money. I don't want that to be a thing between us, but I can't help feeling like it's getting to be."

"He's saving you money, but is it *costing* him money?" Harold points out.

Reluctantly, I shake my head. "Not since I told him I'd lock him outside if he tried to Uber to my place."

"So what's the big deal then?"

"It doesn't feel right!" My voice rises in frustration. "I don't want him or anyone thinking I'm with him for what he can give me." I know he wants to offer me money for a new car. Hell, it wouldn't surprise me if he found me something that was an "amazing bargain" that he was actually subsidizing. He hasn't—yet—because he knows me and I don't want that.

Except part of me really wishes he would. It would make things so much easier. And I'm tired of everything being hard. What would it be like, for once, if I didn't have to work for *something*? For bills to be covered, for my family to accept me, for my goals to be achievable?

Even thinking it makes me feel like shit, because I'm so much luckier than most people. Things *are* easy for me, relatively speaking. I like my life, and I don't think I'd want a silver spoon.

There are just times that I can't help wishing for an easier way.

I look up and see Harold watching me. "Send the email, Blaise. Nobody thinks you're with Jordan for any other reason than that you two belong together, and you're doing him and all of us a disservice by thinking otherwise."

"Yeah, I know. But—"

"No. Send the email to his friend. Get her to look at the contract. And start the next step to not needing Jordan's car, so you can get past whiny diva mode and let those of us who know how to do it properly take back the role."

I stare at him for a second, then dissolve into laughter. "I hate you sometimes."

"I'm waiting for you to send that email."

Sighing, I pull out my phone, find the email from Halle's agent, and forward it to the email address Jordan gave me three days ago, along with a short note introducing myself and thanking her for the help. Then I show Harold the screen with the email clearly marked Sent. "Happy now?"

"Ecstatic. Now finish your lunch, and then you can use your employee discount to sell me the lemon paisley shirt I saw when I came to get you."

Some things never change.

Jordan doesn't come over that night—he's got an assignment due tomorrow that he needs to finish—so I'm alone, lying on the couch eating dinner and mentally adjusting everyone's outfits on the TV, when my phone rings.

It's a Chicago number, which is unusual enough to make me consider answering. Wrong number or telemarketer? Or it could be a scammer, giving me the opportunity to take all my current frustration out on someone who actually deserves it.

I answer. "Hello?"

"Hi," a cheerful female voice says. "Is this Blaise?"

Not a wrong number, then. "It is. Who's calling?"

"Hey, I'm Cara, Jordan's lawyer friend. And according to him, kind-of cousin, though we're actually not related in any way. He's a little weird sometimes."

I huff a laugh. "In the best way, though. Hi, Cara. Thanks for doing this—I hope Jordan didn't bulldoze you into it."

"Nah, he never bulldozes. He's just so charming you have to give in. But this was one of the easier things he's asked me for. Seriously, Blaise, this contract is beautiful."

I blink. "It is?"

"Yup. I showed it to one of the senior associates, just to prove to myself that I wasn't losing my mind. It's extremely fair. You retain full copyright of your designs, which the author will license from you—that's a big deal, since they're based on her IP. They've even got a clause saying you'll be clearly acknowledged as the designer on all packaging, marketing, and promotional materials, including the website listing. She must really like you."

"That's..." Wow. "So there are no problems with me signing it? Nothing that might come back to bite me later?"

"Nope." She pops the *p*. "Unless you wanted to negotiate the fee?"

I shake my head before realizing she can't see me. "No, that's more than fair. I probably would have quoted her less, to be honest."

"Don't tell her that. What about the timelines—are you okay with those?"

Halle has allowed six months for four costumes, which is doable around my current workload, but if something comes up, that might throw me off track. "I think so, but what happens if I fall behind? Is there a penalty?"

"Not like you're thinking. You'll get a deposit of 25 percent per costume when the contracts are signed, so you can start work. Another 25 percent will be paid as each design is completed and approved by the author. The final 50 percent payment comes after you deliver fully completed designs with all the agreed-upon materials, including one sample costume and the written instructions. So the longer you take, the longer you wait to get paid. There's also an expiry clause—if you haven't delivered everything twelve months after the signing date, the contract becomes defunct. You get to keep any money she's paid you, and she gets to keep—and use—anything you've given her, but unless you agree to an extension before that—"

"It's over. Okay, got it. That sounds workable to me."

"Then my advice to you is to go ahead and sign."

"Thank you, Cara. I'm so grateful for your help—and again, I hope it wasn't too much of a bother."

She hesitates. "That's... Listen, Blaise, we don't know each other, so feel free to tell me to fuck off, but Jordan's really into you, and Mila says her dads liked you too... so in the interest of you being future family, it's never a bother when family asks for a little favor."

My throat goes dry. "Uh... that's kind. I-I..." Fuck, I'm losing it. "I don't have a lot of experience with that kind of family. And I really don't want any of you to think I'm taking advantage."

She's quiet for another moment, then asks, "Family kick you out for being queer?"

"Not exactly, but... yeah." Because if Mom and Dad had stayed married, I'm honestly not sure how my coming out would have gone. I like to think she would have stuck up for me, but chances are, she would have gone along with Dad's wishes and snuck me money on the side.

"I can't relate to that, but I can tell you that nobody thinks you're taking advantage. The family phone tree and group chat have been active, and everything that's been said about you is good. So just keep making Jordan this happy, and don't worry about the details."

If only life was that easy. "Thanks, Cara," I say instead, and end the call.

I might still be unsure of my footing with Jordan right now, but at least I have a contract that's going to get me one step closer to making up the ground I lost.

TWENTY-SEVEN
JORDAN

Something's going on with Blaise, and it's killing me that I can't help. Or more to the point, it's killing me that he doesn't want me to help... and every time I try, it just makes him more distant.

I know what the problem is, of course. This setback in his plans has really hurt him, and now that we're getting toward the end of April and applications for the internship are about to close, he's feeling it twice as hard. Last week when we were hanging out with his friends, Calla asked me if I was going to stick around San Luco after regionals, and I (awkwardly) said that once my ball commitments were done, I'd be heading back to Georgia for the summer internship I have lined up. Blaise didn't say anything, but he was quiet for the rest of the night, and I don't blame him. He's worked his ass off and has to delay his goals, and yet here I am, with an internship I got partly due to nepotism and that Toby was fine with having me start late because of regionals.

So... yeah.

From my perspective, the worst part of all this is that I could make it go away for him. I *know* my dads would lend him the money. Or Uncle Luke would call around people he knows and see if anyone has a pool house he can stay in. Fuck, they've just moved back to LA—they'd probably let him stay in my room in their house (because of course they have a room for me. I'm their favorite kid when Mila's not around).

But he won't take help from me. The one time I got up the nerve to bring it up, he shut me down so fast, I barely got the words out. As far as he's concerned, borrowing my car is already too much, and that's the end of it. Cara messaged to tell me she liked him and that he'd said something about not wanting to take advantage, but that's ridiculous—how can he be taking advantage of me when it's not costing me anything? Plus, he's my boyfriend and I love him.

Which is why I dropped the subject. I don't want this to come between us any more than it already has.

"C'mon, Marks," Boyle says, slapping me on the shoulder. "Smile. No sad faces allowed after a game like that. Wanna listen while I call my mom and remind her of her promise?" He's grinning from ear to ear. He got that third home run today, and he's been crowing through four innings, Coach's victory pep talk, and showers. It would be annoying if he didn't earn it... and promise we could all come over to hang out at his place next year. He asked if I wanted to be his roommate, and I'm kind of thinking about it. I love the dorms, but spending so much time at Blaise's place this semester has shown me how nice it can be to have a bit more privacy... and a bathroom that's not being used by thirty other guys.

Part of me is hoping Blaise will ask me to move in with him. I'm sure Drey won't care—the five times we've met, we got along really well.

"I don't think your mom wants an audience to hear you gloat," I say, "but thanks for the offer."

"Why so glum, chum?" he asks, dropping onto the bench

beside me. He's fully dressed in his suit, ready to go, whereas I'm still just in pants and socks. "You've got good looks, good grades, a boyfriend who tolerates you, my friendship, and *we're going to regionals!*" He shouts the last part, and everyone breaks out into hollers and cheers.

I can't help grinning the way I always do when I think of it. I picked Franklin for the academic program and the location—the fact that I'd been offered the chance to play D1 baseball here was just a bonus. The team hasn't been more than mediocre for a long time, and I didn't expect my college baseball career to include a trip to regionals.

But we did it.

"I'm fine," I assure Boyle. "Just... thinking about stuff that doesn't belong in your moment of victory. No more dorms for you, buddy."

He pumps both fists in the air. "No more dorms for me! Xera blew my phone up with about a million texts already. She's pissed she'll be graduating this year and can't take advantage of my new place."

"So am I," Polly says as he passes by to throw his towel in the hamper. "You couldn't have made this deal with your mom last year?"

"Dude, I don't think I could have hit three homers last year, and I don't like to lose," Boyle admits with surprising modesty. Then ruins it by adding, "We smart guys weigh the odds and strike when the time is right. You'll learn that one day."

Polly narrows his eyes. "Marks, do me a favor and—"

"On it." I shove my sweaty jersey in Boyle's face. It's hot today, and I worked up a good stink.

He rips it away and is swearing vengeance when Coach's voice cuts through the room. "Polling! Marks! My office!"

I freeze, and the room hushes. Usually when Coach calls someone to his office after a game—especially at this point in the season—it's because a scout wants to talk to them. And there *was* a scout at today's game; I heard the others talking about it earlier. It's no surprise Polly got called... but me?

I've never spoken to a scout before. I never thought I'd need to... or want to. And the guys all know that my plans don't include the big leagues.

"Am I in trouble?" I ask stupidly, and then horror strikes. Maybe someone saw me and Blaise together and Coach wants to warn me. Maybe there's a journalist in his office, not a scout. He could have called Polly as well in his role as captain to support me... or something.

Coach gives me a withering look and leaves, which does *not* answer my question or make me feel better.

"Get dressed," Polly says. "C'mon, hurry up. I'll wait for you."

"No, I think he wants me for something else. You go on." There's a very faint tremor in my voice that I'm sure nobody notices.

Except Boyle leans his shoulder against mine and says, "I bet you're wrong. I bet there's a scout there waiting to talk to you. So get the fuck up and put on a shirt."

I'm not completely convinced, but even if it is bad news, I can't go out there half-dressed. Not unless I want to feature in headlines like "College Baseball Coach Murders Own Player" and "Queer Baseball Player Killed While Half Naked."

Taking three deep breaths like my uncle Derek taught me, I race to put on my shirt and jacket before nearly strangling myself with the tie. Boyle busts a gut laughing, but Polly shoves my hands out of the way and takes over. Then he pushes me toward the door.

"Good luck," Laringo calls after us, and I have no idea if he thinks it's a scout or my big bisexual outing.

By the time we get to Coach's office, my palms are sweating.

I wipe them on my pants, and Polly pauses with his hand on the doorknob. "Bro, chill," he whispers. "It's fine." Then he opens the door and we go in.

The guy waiting for us is wearing slacks, a shirt, and tie, but no jacket, and he's got a warm smile on his face. That's a good sign, right?

"Polling, hey," he says, holding out his hand to shake. "Good to see you again. You're having a great season."

I relax. A scout. Not a journalist.

Fuck. A scout!

"Thanks," Polly says. "It feels great to have a team that's so in sync."

Aw, that's Polly. The perfect captain and team player.

As if hearing me, he half turns and says, "Marks, this is Don Kettering. He works for the White Sox."

It gets cold in Illinois.

That probably shouldn't be my first thought right now. I paste on a wobbly smile and shake his offered hand. "Nice to meet you." There, that sounded... sane.

God, why am I being like this? I don't even want to play pro. Do I?

"Good to meet you too," he says warmly. "You've surprised us all this year, in the best way possible."

"Thanks. It's, uh, been a great season for us." I hold on to the smile and relax again when he turns back to Polly.

"You guys are looking hot going into regionals. How are you feeling?"

"Thrilled to be here and confident that we'll give it our best," he says with an assured air that makes me so jealous. I need to pull it together.

"And how are you feeling about joining our fine organization come July?" Kettering asks slyly, and Polly laughs.

"I do like Chicago."

"And you, Marks? Ever been to Chi-town?"

"Uh, no. Winters there are a little on the cold side for me." Yes, I just said that. "But I have a friend who lives there and loves it," I add hastily.

His smile widens. "That's right, you're a Georgia boy."

"Actually, Cali first, then southern Georgia. So, you know..." I shrug. "Sun."

"Well, baseball's a summer sport, which leaves those nasty winters free for tropical vacations... paid for by a generous signing bonus, maybe."

Oh my god, he's serious. He's a scout, talking to me. About playing for the White Sox.

"I gotta be honest," I say, "playing for the majors wasn't in my plans. Not that I'm not flattered. A lot. A whole lot, actually."

He cocks his head. "How do you feel about changing those plans? Because in my job, we talk to our colleagues, and I can tell you that if you keep playing like this, next season I won't be the only one asking for a meeting."

Next year. When I'm a junior. I'll be eligible for the draft next year.

"I'd want to do like Polly and wait till I'm a senior." The words leave my mouth without any thought whatsoever.

Kettering nods. "A long-term thinker, huh? And I bet you want the extra time to get more interest too."

That hadn't occurred to me. Is that how it works? Why have I not paid attention to this shit?

Why am I even participating in this conversation?

"Long-term plan," I echo weakly.

"Well, no need to make any decisions yet. Keep on like you're doing, think over your plans, and keep in mind that I've got my eye on you. Maybe you should pay a visit to your friend in Chicago, see how you like it."

"I've got a boyfriend," I blurt, then instantly wish I hadn't. Heat rages in my face, but it's too late now. "That's not public. Uh. The team knows, but..." I don't know how to finish that sentence.

There's low-level surprise on Kettering's face, but no judgment. "We're an inclusive organization, which you probably know from the media. Your boyfriend would be welcome at Guaranteed Rate Field too." He almost manages to hide his wince, but I'm not sure if it's the mention of my boyfriend or the name of the stadium that causes it.

I nod a couple of times. "Cool. Well. Like I said... life plan. But it was really great to meet you, and I'll... I'll think about what you've said."

He and Polly talk a little more, mostly confirming that the team is strongly interested in him for the draft, and then Kettering shakes both our hands again and leaves.

"Dude." Polly punches my shoulder. "What the fuck? I thought you and Blaise were keeping things quiet."

"I don't know why I said half the things I just said," I confess.

"You did seem a little spacey. But hey... how cool would it be if we both ended up on the same team?"

The grin overtakes my face, because yeah, that would be cool.

But then it flees. How do I tell my boyfriend whose career plans have been put on hold that mine are looking up?

And, more importantly... am I seriously thinking about this?

TWENTY-EIGHT
BLAISE

ALL I CAN THINK ABOUT IS THE EMAIL.

It's haunting me. Since it arrived two days ago, it's overshadowed everything I've thought and said and done. All through the ball game this afternoon, including the wild celebrations we had in the stands when Marty hit his third home run of the season, it's been a tiny, horrible seed in my mind.

Even now, as we wait with a pitcher at Shenanigans for the guys on the team to arrive, I can't stop my thoughts from going back to it. I only read it once, and it was only a few sentences, but they're burned into my brain.

Hi Blaise,

Touching base about the Joy Inc. Costume & Wardrobe internship that we discussed last year. Applications for the July intake close at the end of this month, and I haven't seen one from you yet, so I thought I'd remind you.

Look forward to your application,
Dinesh Bakshi

Coordinator
Joy Incorporated Internship Program

"Blaise?" Xera says, and it sounds like it's not the first time. "Do you want wings?"

"Uh…" My stomach is churning, and I've barely touched food since I read the email the first time, so my instinctive reaction is to say no. But I can't keep skipping meals.

I need to deal with this. Reply to the email and close the issue.

"Yeah, wings sound good. Want some cash?"

She waves me off. "They're on Marty. He just doesn't know it yet."

That makes everyone laugh, because it's not the first time she's done that, and Marty always rolls his eyes, threatens to tell their mom on her, and then pays for it from the account the two of them share that their mom puts money into. Jordan said once that Marty calls it "the friendship fund," because their mom thinks they need to buy friends. I'm not sure if I'd like her.

Under the cover of everyone's merriment, I slip my phone out of my pocket, open the right app, and hit reply on the email.

Hi Dinesh,
Thanks for thinking of me, but I won't be applying this year.
Maybe next year.
Best wishes,
Blaise

Hitting Send is the hardest thing I've done since Mom's funeral, and my hand is literally shaking as I return my phone to my pocket. So much, in fact, that I fumble and it falls to the floor with a clatter.

Then clatters some more as it rings.

I scramble to pick it up. I don't recognize the number, but I really need a few minutes to pull myself together before someone asks me what's wrong, so I say brightly, "Just going to take this," and head for the door.

"Hello?"

"Blaise? It's Dinesh here."

I freeze two steps outside and get a bunch of dirty looks from people going inside who have to dodge around me. Fuck. Moving to the side, I swallow and say, "Oh, hi."

"I swear I don't normally work on a Saturday," he says wryly. "Well, not often, anyway. But I was checking on something that was due yesterday, and I saw your email come in. You're not applying this year?"

"I'd hoped to," I admit, "but some things came up, and my financial position won't allow it. But I definitely will next year." It's a promise more to myself than to him.

He sighs. "I can't deny I'm disappointed. The Costume & Wardrobe Director will be, too, when I tell her. We've both been waiting for your application."

Jesus, does he want to stab that knife a little deeper into my heart?

"I'm disappointed as well," I manage. "Things will be different next year, though, and I hope you'll still be happy to see my application then."

"We will," he assures me. "Imani saw you tagged on social media for some cosplay outfits, and she's told me three times since then that I need to prioritize your interview for the program."

Imani Jennings is the head of costume and wardrobe for Joy Inc., and the thought that she liked my designs makes me want to dance a jig... and break down in tears. Because that interview isn't happening.

"In the meantime, keep doing as much side work as you

can," Dinesh continues. "The more experience you have, the better the chance we can hire you for an actual paying assistant job if the right project comes along. I just wish we could pay you for the internship, get you on board right away." The clear frustration in his voice makes me feel a little better. Not much, but anything's an improvement on rock bottom.

"Thank you," I say politely. "I'll keep my Instagram updated with my work. If a project that does seem like a good fit for me comes up, I'd appreciate the chance to send over my latest résumé and portfolio." Jobs like that don't get advertised, so I'm basically asking him for a heads-up. It's pushier than I usually am.

"I'll let Imani know you're interested," he assures me, which means exactly zero. "Thanks for taking my call."

"No problem. Bye."

I stare at the black screen of my phone, then rub my palm over my eyes and sigh. That was painful, but it's done. It's over. Finished. I'm not applying for the internship this year.

To draw a line under the whole thing and put it completely out of my mind, I open my email app and file his message away, out of the inbox. Out of sight.

Then I take a deep breath, letting the tang of briny air soothe me, and go back inside.

"Who was that?" Calla asks as I sit down.

"Nobody."

"You were talking to nobody for a while," Xera observes. "Is this like 'nobody I want to tell you about,' or 'nobody it was a telemarketer but I've started smoking and don't want my friends to know'?"

Phil immediately leans over, sniffs me, then shakes his head.

"Thanks for that," I tell him, and his shy smile gets a cheeky quirk. "It's not important," I continue, knowing I have to tell them something or they'll nag about it until the end of time.

And I don't want us to be talking about this when Jordan gets here. He still thinks I should apply and hope things work out, money-wise. "I got an email from the guy running the internship." I don't need to give details—even Xera knows my plans. "He wanted to know why I hadn't applied yet. I told him I wasn't going to, and he called to follow up." I shrug. "That's it."

From the expressions on my friends' faces, you'd think someone had died.

"You're really not going to apply?" Butch asks.

"Not this year." I shake my head. "I haven't even found a car within the price range I'm willing to pay, but if I had, I still have no chance of making up the gap to what I'd need. Not in time. And the last thing I need halfway through the internship is to run out of money and be living in my not-so-new car somewhere in LA."

"But..." Calla looks like she's going to cry. "You're *so close*."

God, why are they doing this to me? I get that they're sad on my behalf, but can't they see they're just rubbing salt into the wound?

"I was, but life happens. It's fine. And it means that next year, I'll have a nice fat safety cushion in my bank account."

Harold clears his throat and glances around the table. "Maybe you should apply anyway. We were talking about it, and between all of us, we can—"

"No."

"Blaise," Butch starts, using her most cajoling voice, but I hold up a hand.

"Stop. I'm grateful, I really am, and I love you all so much for the offer, but I'm not borrowing money from you. Especially when I know you don't really have it to lend."

"I do," Xera says coolly, her gaze almost a challenge. She's wearing her usual game-day makeup colors of purple and gold, with her favorite red lipstick that somehow doesn't clash, and nobody would guess from looking at her rah-rah Franklin outfit that she's a double major in finance and economics, planning to take over her mom's investment banking firm one day. "I've got plenty of money, I've seen your work, and I'm willing to invest in you. We'll draw up a contract with repayments and interest rates and everything. Not a favor; a genuine investment."

I can't deny it—the temptation is real. I've known Xera long enough now to know she doesn't fuck around with money. If she says this isn't a pity thing, a charitable donation of sorts, then I believe that.

But what if the internship doesn't go as well as I'd hoped? Or there's another strike just as I'm finishing it, and work dries up for a while? There's no 100 percent guarantee I'll get a paying job when I'm done, and then where will I be? Owing money to a friend. Worse, it'll put Butch in the middle. Things are going so well with them, and I don't want to be the cause of any hiccups.

Reluctantly, I shake my head. "Thank you, but no. I won't borrow from a friend. If I decide to get a loan, I'll go to a bank."

She looks me dead in the eye. "You have no collateral and plan to leave your job in July. A bank won't lend to you—definitely not with the terms I'm prepared to offer."

I smile, suddenly so grateful for my friends. "And that's why I won't borrow from you." Looking around the table, I add, "Really, it's fine. This is just a temporary setback, not the end. Applying this year was always the reach goal, remember? I'll still get there, and in the meantime, I get to hang out with you again next year."

None of them look all that convinced by my fake bravado, but they rally, and the wings arrive thirty seconds later, providing a much-needed distraction.

We've decimated half the platter when the team starts dribbling in, most of them stopping by our table to say hi and accept our congratulations, or at least waving on their way to the bar. Then Marty arrives with Jordan and Polly, and we all stand up and cheer, applauding and hollering. Butch even whistles. The non-baseball-supporting patrons look at us as though we're crazy, but Marty laps it up, waving like a celebrity and taking an elaborate bow when he gets to our table.

"Your conquering hero has arrived," he announces. "Where's the beer?"

Phil passes him the pitcher, and we make room for them to join us. Jordan slides into the seat beside me and squeezes my knee under the table. It's times like this I wish we could just be completely public; I really want a kiss and a cuddle right now.

"Have you called Mom yet?" Xera asks. "Because it's killing me. Call her."

"I called on the way over here, and she was just as unimpressed as always by my miraculous feats. But she agreed that a deal is a deal and told me I could start looking from now."

"So you might be moving before the semester's even over?" Calla asks. "Are you going to leave it empty all summer?"

"Fuck, no," both siblings say in unison.

"If he finds somewhere before end of semester, we'll be staying here in Cali for the summer," Xera explains. "I'm using the excuse of needing to sort out accommodation near UCLA before my postgrad starts as a reason not to go home and have Mom explain all the ways I'm failing at life." She casts a sidelong glance at Butch. "You'll stay with us for part of the summer at least, won't you?"

"Are you inviting your girlfriend to live in my apartment?" Marty turns to us, a teasing gleam in his eye. "You all heard her treat my home like she owns it, right?"

"Oh please, like you wouldn—"

"Before this turns into a family fight," Butch interrupts

Xera, giving her a kiss on the cheek, "let's all toast to the man of the hour. Congratulations on the homer, Marty!"

"To Marty!" we yell, lifting our glasses, and he grins and blushes.

"Aww, shucks. Sure, I *am* a hero"—he ignores the laughter that erupts—"but I couldn't do it without my teammates to support me. And hey, I'm not the only one whose amazingness got recognized today. Jordan got scouted!"

I hang on to my smile with sheer grit. *What?*

"Oh my god, that's great!" Calla squeals. "Who by?"

Jordan shrugs modestly, but he's grinning. "The White Sox. It's nothing... I don't even know if that's what I want."

My head's spinning. Seriously? This is such amazing news, but I don't have the emotional bandwidth to process it right now. I'm thrilled for Jordan, but the dark part of me, the whiny, horrible side that drowns me in feelings of failure and inadequacy and makes me want to crawl into bed for a week and cry... that part of me wants to know why *today*? Why is my boyfriend getting an amazing opportunity on the same day my career got officially put on hold?

And what does he mean, he doesn't know if that's what he wants?

TWENTY-NINE
JORDAN

"I thought you didn't want to play for..." Harold waves his hands. "You know, the grown-up teams."

"*Grown-up?*" Calla echoes incredulously. "Seriously?"

He rolls his eyes. "What? You're lucky I've gotten this involved in a sport. You can't expect me to know all the terminology, too. But," he turns his expectant gaze back to me, "have your plans changed now?"

I'm the focus of all eyes, and I shrug. "I don't know," I admit. "I always figured no, but... I mean, I love ball. So..." I shrug again, extremely conscious that beside me, Blaise hasn't said anything. "I'd want to graduate first. It seems like a waste not to finish my degree when that was my plan all along. Maybe by then nobody will want me. I'm not even eligible to be drafted for another year, anyway." Even to me, it sounds like I'm making excuses, delaying having to make an actual decision.

Which I am.

"You've got time," Butch agrees, "but does that mean coming out publicly? You said you didn't want to because you weren't going to play pro and it wasn't going to be an issue."

I open my mouth to reply, then stop. Fuck. "Also unknown. But I guess ultimately that's not just my decision." Isn't that how relationships work? I look uncertainly at my boyfriend.

"What? No! I'm not going to be a factor in outing you," he hisses. The skin around his eyes is tense and tight. "That's your call. You get to decide who knows that about you."

"That's not fair to you," I point out.

"You decide who you want to be out to," he insists stubbornly. "And then I decide where I want to go from there. We can talk about this later. You've had great news; let's not spoil it. Congratulations." His lips stretch in what I think is supposed to be a smile. "Um... Excuse me for a second." He pushes back his chair and stalks away while I blink after him in shock, the air in my chest stuck.

"Uhhh," Boyle says. "What the fuck? Did he just...?"

"It's fine," Xera says. "He's... having a bad day. I'm sure he didn't mean it the way it sounded."

"Really?" Polly sounds mad, but his expression is thunderstruck. "Because it sounded like he'll break up with Marks. What the fuck kind of bad day did he have? Wasn't he at the game?"

There's an uncomfortable silence as everyone who's *not* on the team looks awkwardly away.

"You should go after him," someone says, and I glance around to see who.

It's Phil, leaning across Blaise's chair between us, his face red but his eyes determined.

"Dude," Boyle breathes. "He talked to you!"

Phil ignores him. "Go after him," he repeats. "He's upset."

Okay, I don't know what the fuck happened between Blaise dropping me off on campus this morning and now, but nobody's talking about it. Whatever it is has knocked my guy off-balance, and *it's prompted Phil to speak*. I get up and follow Blaise through the crowd toward the door.

He's outside, about ten paces down from the entrance, leaning against the wall with his head tipped back and his eyes closed. His face is pure misery, but worse, as I get closer, I hear him mutter, "Get it together. This is good for him. Don't be that guy. Don't ruin it."

Is he talking about me? Because if he is... fuck that shit. Just because I get good news doesn't mean I can't be there for my boyfriend on a bad day.

"Hey," I say softly, and his head jerks around.

"Shit. I'm sorry. I just needed some air. It's..." He trails off and swallows.

"I heard you're having a bad day. Anything you want to talk about?"

His sigh could fill a balloon. "It's fine. I don't want to ruin the mood."

"As far as I'm concerned, you could never ruin anything. Please tell me. I want to help." As soon as the words are out of my mouth, I know it was the wrong thing to say. His expression shuts down completely.

"Sometimes you can't fix things, Jordan."

"I know," I say quickly. "I mean... I want to be supportive. You don't have to tell me. Just let me... be with you."

His face softens, and the warm look in his eyes tells me I haven't fucked this up.

"I want that too. I'm sorry, I'm being a dick. And you had such an exciting day." The smile isn't quite genuine, but he's trying. "That's so cool, being scouted."

I brush it off. "You're not being a dick. You had a bad day, and... my news would have been a surprise. I'm not blind to the fact that it could cause problems if I decide I want a career in the pros. You probably didn't need that piled on top of... everything." I don't mean for my voice to rise inquiringly on that last word, but it does.

Scrubbing his hands over his face, he says, "The internship coordinator contacted me, and I told him I wasn't applying this year."

"No." The denial is instinctive and instant, and again, the wrong thing to say. But I can't take it back. "There was still time—and you have so much time to make the extra money before July." I haven't had a chance to talk to my dads about it yet.

"That's wishful thinking."

"It's not. Okay, maybe I'm looking at it through a positive lens, but you *do* have options. I was thinking—"

"I'm not borrowing money, Jordan. Not when I don't have a definite way to pay it back."

"I get that." Fuck, there goes idea number one. "But it's not the only possibility. My dads have just moved to LA, and I know they'd let you stay at their place—"

"Move in with my boyfriend's dads?" His incredulous tone cuts me off. "Are you serious? I've met them once, and we've been dating less than six months!"

Ouch. "I'm just saying, you have options still. And it's not the worst idea," I can't resist adding. "They like you, and they like me being with someone who has career goals and makes me happy. Plus, you and Uncle Luke could carpool to work."

"So then what would happen if we broke up?" he demands. "If I wasn't making you happy anymore? I'd be homeless and scrambling to find somewhere to live in the middle of an intense internship."

"They wouldn't throw you out," I argue. "Not that we're breaking up anyway. Do you want to break up?" Suddenly I feel incredibly vulnerable.

But he's not listening. His eyes have narrowed. "What do you mean, I could carpool to work with your uncle?"

Shit. *Shit.* "I was just—" I change my mind about lying and meet his gaze squarely. "Uncle Luke works for Joy Inc. So did Grant until he got this new job."

Blaise's jaw drops. "But they lived in Georgia," he says blankly. I see the exact second he realizes. "They worked at Joy Universe?"

"Grant did. Uncle Luke's always worked for the head office, but he had to go to Georgia for a while to do some work at the theme parks and then we decided to stay because—" I see his face and stop. "That's not important. It's a cute story, though."

"I'll be sure to read the book when it comes out," he snipes. "How could you not tell me this? You *knew* I wanted to apply for the Joy internship—oh my god, you let me talk about it at dinner with your dads! And this whole time… Who else knows? Your friends? Do they know where your dads work? Have they been thinking what an *idiot* I am this whole time, talking about going for an internship for my *boyfriend's dad* like it's a big deal for me to get it?"

"It's not like that," I protest. "Nobody thinks you're an idiot."

"Oh, so they just think I'm using you, then."

"No! God, Blaise, you didn't even know, how could you be using me? Uncle Luke has nothing to do with the internship program, and anyway, you already had the coordinator practically begging you to apply a year before we even met. This is all just a dumb coincidence."

He pushes his hands into his hair and turns away from me, then spins back. "I just… I can't believe you wouldn't tell me this when it's so clearly relevant. What the fuck, Jordan? When was I going to find out? When I ran into your dad in the break room?"

I shake my head. "Of course not. At first I didn't mention it because we barely knew each other. People... Look, when I was in grade school, I told all my friends that my uncle worked for Joy Inc. because that's so cool, right? Even though he's a business consultant and I didn't even know what that meant. And one of their moms was a sound engineer for an audiobook company, but she really wanted to get into movies. So she—"

He holds up a hand. "Stop. I get It. She used you."

"Uncle Luke doesn't have anything to do with that side of it. His job is business processes and troubleshooting. But he knows people all over the company, and he didn't want to make things hard for me at school, so he hooked her up with an interview." I cringe as I remember. "She didn't get the job, and she wouldn't let her kid be friends with me anymore. Since then, I just don't tell random people where my dads work."

"Maybe that explains why you didn't say anything at first, but I didn't think I was a random person anymore," he says sarcastically.

"Don't do that. You know you're not." I take a deep breath. He's being a colossal asshat right now, but I get why. Nothing has gone right for him lately, and today's just been an avalanche of new information for him to deal with. "But when things changed between us, I didn't know how to bring it up. I figured I'd wait until you got the internship and it couldn't be a thing anymore."

"How can it not be a thing? What must your dads *think*?" His face is pale in the deepening twilight, eyes big.

"They think you're great," I insist, putting as much force into the word as I can. "They think you're dedicated and goal oriented, just like they are. They think you're good for me. And yeah, they know I hadn't told you, but they've seen your work and they like it, Blaise. That wasn't bullshit. They showed it to my uncles, and they..." Fuck. I keep talking myself into corners. "Okay, so, full disclosure."

He moans, but I push on.

"One of the uncles is Jason Phillips."

It takes him a second to make the connection. "The Broadway director? The one who moved to... Joy Universe. And married the head of the theater production company there." He shakes his head hopelessly. "Jesus, Jordan."

"Dimi—the head of the production company—took one look at the photos Uncle Luke showed him and said he'd interview you for a job. That's not a favor," I add hastily. "Dimi doesn't do favors like that, trust me. When it comes to business, he's a piranha."

"Sure," he agrees tiredly, and I sense that I'm losing him.

"Jason would reach out to his contacts if we asked him to. I know he's got friends who transitioned from theater to screen. But my point is, I didn't have to ask any of them to do that, because you already had the internship in the bag! And it's not too late. You can still apply. Call the guy and tell him things have changed."

"Why are you so set on me getting this internship *now*?" he demands. "Why does it matter so much to you that it's this year and not next year?"

I blink, surprised he can ask me that. "You want it," I say, confused. "I want you to be happy. I want you to achieve your goals."

"Is it that? Or is it just that having a boyfriend in town is inconvenient when you're being scouted by the pros?"

My teeth snap together. "What?" I whisper. I can't believe he just said that.

"Because since we met, you've been so adamant about how you don't want baseball to be your whole life, you want to be able to enjoy it as a hobby. Less than a month ago, you were getting big ideas about ways to coordinate book conventions. Us being together was only going to be a secret until you graduated. But now... now you're thinking about going pro, but you still don't want to come out. Is that why you want me to take the internship? Would it be easier if I was in LA, and long-distance became an excuse for us to drift apart?"

THIRTY
BLAISE

In the four days since I walked away from Jordan's shocked and devastated face, I've done nothing but work, mope, and reply to Calla's daily "You alive?" message. I started out ignoring my friends' calls and texts, but that lasted all of three hours before they turned up on my doorstep, pounding on my door so hard that the neighbors came to see what was going on. After that first drunken pity party, I convinced them to leave me to sulk over the fight by myself, but Calla's check-ins were the only compromise they'd accept.

God. I can't believe I'm *such* an idiot.

I need to call Jordan and apologize. Beg for forgiveness, more like, with plenty of groveling. But every time I think of how often I went on and on and *on* about the internship, about how I'd love to work for Joy Inc., about what a hard industry it is to break into... I just want to die.

I said it all to his dads, too, who work for the damn company. And the whole time, he had all those contacts at his fingertips. I can't help wondering if deep down, he thinks that's why I'm with him. That I somehow knew, found out from a friend of a friend on campus, and that I've been hinting all this time.

That's the last thing I want, for him to doubt that I recognize how amazing he is. How sweet and cute and sometimes clueless in a way that makes me want to wrap him in cotton and keep him safe forever. How focused he gets when he's got a goal.

And yet... I also feel like a fool. He kept this huge secret—because he didn't trust me? Because he figured we were only a good time, not a long time, and it wasn't worth telling me? I don't want to believe that, but I don't know what to think anymore. He was so eager for me to apply for the internship this year... was it because he wanted to end us but didn't know how?

The memory of his face when I accused him of that rises in my mind's eye, and I shake my head. No. Whatever it is he's thinking, I don't think he wants to break up. He'll be mad, especially after what I said, and fuck knows he's got the right to be. I can't even believe I said it—I was overwhelmed and disheartened and feeling so damn low, and the words just came out. But even if he's confused about how he'd manage a career in the pros as a queer athlete, I don't believe ending us is what he wants.

Which just means that the longer I let this fight continue, the more he's going to think that I *do*. I don't... but...

Wouldn't it be easier?

My mind hasn't changed about wanting him to come out—I don't want to be known as the bisexual baseball player's boyfriend. I don't want to have to dodge the media to see him. I don't want some jackass digging up the details of my history, or worse, getting a soundbite from my dad... if he would even admit to knowing me. Let's face it, him denying he has a gay son would be clickbait-worthy on its own. So yeah, keeping our relationship quiet is fine with me. More than fine.

But not forever.

If Jordan's being scouted—which, god, he's earned it, and I'm so proud of him—if he decides he wants a career in professional baseball after all... well, that changes everything.

For one, it could turn a year or two of long-distance into a decade of cross-country distance. Illinois isn't exactly known as a hub for film and television. Even if he goes elsewhere or is traded around to different teams, there's no guarantee any of them will be on the West Coast. Most of my work will be here in California, maybe Vancouver or New York. And... what changes then? Do I want to be the boyfriend of a pro bisexual baseball player? It would be all the same issues, just on a bigger scale.

Or what if he doesn't want to be a bisexual baseball player? Do I want to be his secret boyfriend? I don't think I'm cut out for that.

Which is why I haven't called him yet. How can I grovel for forgiveness if we're just going to be back in the exact same place? If I don't even know what I want?

I sigh and rub my eyes. This is not a fun way to spend a Wednesday night... or the Sunday, Monday, and Tuesday that came before it. Saturday night was just a drunken haze.

The strident ring of my phone startles me. Who the hell could be calling? I don't recognize the number, but it's a California area code.

What the hell. Talking to a stranger for a minute will at least distract me from thinking about Jordan. "Hello?"

"Blaise?" The voice is familiar, but I can't quite place it.

"Yeah, this is he."

"It's Luke Durrant. Jordan's dad. Please don't hang up."

"I wouldn't," I protest instinctively, but *shit*. Why is— "Has something happened to Jordan?"

"Oh—no." He hesitates. "He's... upset, but he's fine."

I breathe a little easier, then tense up again. If Jordan's okay, why's he calling me? Is he going to warn me off his son? Or maybe he knows I know where he works and he's calling to threaten my future career? I mean, I don't think he'd do something like that, but I barely know him except through Jordan, and most kids are biased toward their parents—

"I apologize for calling out of the blue like this," Luke says, breaking the awkward pause. "I wouldn't normally interfere in Jordan's life, as much as the rest of the family disagrees. But I thought you might need a listening ear."

He... what?

"Excuse me?" I ask blankly.

"I hope you don't mind, but Jordan's told us a little about your family. He might have mentioned to you that my parents disowned me when I came out to them—I was still in high school, and they kicked me out. I know friends can be amazing—god knows mine have been, all my life—but there were a lot of times I missed having a parental figure to talk to."

Tears burn my eyes, and I swallow hard to dislodge the painful knot in my throat. It doesn't work, and as the silence begins to draw out, he says, "I'm sorry, you probably think I'm being presumptuous. I'll let you go—"

"No!" The word bursts out on a sob, and I suck in a wheezing breath. "I mean—" I have to stop, give myself a second to fight back the tears.

"It's okay, Blaise," he murmurs. "You're okay."

God. The sobs that rack me *hurt*, but it's such a release. I cried when Mom died—of course I did—but I never let myself cry about what Dad did. Or the fact that Mom never really accepted me being gay—it was something she just preferred not to think about. Since the day I came out, I haven't felt like I had a parent I could confide in... who would listen, no matter what, and still think every part of me was perfect.

And I've missed it.

When the tears finally peter off, I let out a shaky sigh. "Sorry. That's... sorry." I'd be embarrassed, but honestly, I don't have the energy.

"Don't be sorry. Do you want to talk about it?" he offers.

I clear my throat. "Uh... wouldn't that be weird? Jordan's your son."

His chuckle is warm and comforting and everything I ever wanted from my own dad. "Maybe that gives me a unique perspective. As much as I love my kid and think he's incredible, I know he's not always right, Blaise. He messes up just like any other person. In this case, I'm going to guess keeping secrets for too long was part of the problem."

I groan. "I'm so embarrassed. I swear, I didn't know—I wasn't using him, and when I went on and on at dinner that night—"

"Relax. I know. This is partly my fault—we've spent a lot of years warning Jordan not to be too trusting. He's such a sweet kid, and he always wants to help people, but that makes it easy for them to hurt him."

"I never wanted to do that," I whisper. "This whole thing has just been a mess."

"Why don't you tell me your side?" he suggests. "It'll stay between us, but it might help to just talk it out."

I take a second to gather my thoughts, then start slowly, back when my car broke down. By the time I'm done, I'm shocked by how much stress I've been feeling about all this. How much I really wanted to be able to lean on Jordan and accept his help, but also... not. Because I want to do this *myself*.

"Is it so bad that I want to do this without handouts?" I ask, feeling stupid and vulnerable. "I know this industry runs on who you know, and I'm not opposed to making contacts and leveraging them, but I don't want to feel like... like I didn't earn it. Like I never would have made it if my boyfriend didn't lend me money or... or call his dad for a favor."

Luke's quiet for a moment. "I'm going to ask you to stop that line of thinking," he finally says, more firmly than I've heard from him before. "Because I've seen your work, my friends who work in the industry have seen your work, and at a senior management meeting on Monday, the Wardrobe Director for the whole damn studio made an impassioned—if fruitless—plea that the company give the internship program the budget to pay the interns. It's not a coincidence that she did that two days after you said you couldn't afford to apply."

I hesitate, because... it *could* be a coincidence.

"It's not a coincidence," he repeats firmly, as though he knows what I'm thinking. "You're talented and you've worked hard. You've already earned this, Blaise. If you had money, this wouldn't be an issue, and the lack of money to support yourself for a year is not your fault. Most people can't afford to do that. When I was your age, there was no way I could have done it, and the only reason I could now is because I've been in an executive job for nearly twenty years and made a pile of good investments along the way. Stop beating yourself up for things you can't control."

Taking a quiet breath, I let go of my fear that Jordan's dad might still think I only wanted him for what he could do for me. "I still don't want to borrow money from my boyfriend or my friends," I admit. "I just... the idea stresses me out. I need them in my life, and I don't ever want anything to come between us."

"I get that. Did Jordan tell you how I'm related to him?"

I frown. "He said you were married to his uncle and then adopted him after his parents died."

"That's right. His mom was my first husband's sister. I met Matt when I was at college, and don't get me wrong, I loved him, but I think I loved Mandy more." He laughs quietly. "She used to joke that if Matt and I ever broke up, she was keeping me. I had no family, and she was the big sister I always needed. Losing her hurt me more than any other loss I ever experienced, because she loved me unconditionally—so much, she named me as the guardian of her children."

I swallow. That's... a lot.

"I understand needing your friends and being afraid to lose them, but part of friendship is supporting each other when you can. That's definitely part of a relationship. I'm not saying you need to borrow money from anyone, especially since this isn't an emergency situation, but I think you need to let yourself be open to the idea that your friends won't leave you if you need them. Mandy knew I would gladly spend the rest of my life parenting her kids, and I know I could have asked her for a kidney, and she'd have reached for a knife." He pauses. "Okay, that's a little more macabre than I intended it to be. But do you hear what I'm saying?"

I laugh—it's a little rusty, but it's real. "Yeah."

"Now, I'm not going to offer you money, and I completely understand why you might feel awkward staying with us, but if you want, I can ask around and see if anyone is willing to let a hardworking, talented intern live in their spare room."

I think about it—really think about it. "That's kind of you," I say finally, "and I don't want you to think I haven't been listening. But I don't think I'm ready for that."

"You have to be comfortable. Despite what my impatient son thinks, if you prefer to wait until next year, that's not the end of the world."

An hour ago, I would have said it felt like it, but... it's really not. And hey, the extra time will let me play around more with the cosplay business.

"So that brings us to the other part of the problem," Luke continues.

"Jordan being scouted," I confirm. "I'm so happy for him, but..."

"But," he agrees. "The only thing I've ever wanted for my

kids, both of them, is that they're happy. If Jordan decides this is the path he wants to take, I'll support him completely in that. But I'll be honest with you, Blaise—it's not the future I want for him."

"Honestly, it's not the future I want for *us*. If there even is an us." Since I haven't yet called to grovel. "But I don't want him to make decisions about his future based on what I want."

"I'm pretty confident you and Jordan have a future," Luke says wryly. "I guess what it's going to look like all comes down to Jordan."

I might feel more confident in my decisions now—and more aware of the steps I need to take in letting my friends help me when I need it—but I'm still scared shitless about calling Jordan.

Because right now, that's the only thing that matters.

THIRTY-ONE
JORDAN

THE WORST PART ABOUT THIS WEEK IS THAT I DON'T KNOW what the fuck to do. Should I be trying to call Blaise? Or would that be harassment? He made it pretty clear when he walked away that he wasn't happy with me, so I assumed the ball was in his court to make the next move... but maybe I should give him some kind of sign I want to make up?

If he even wants to make up.

Fuck, what if he wants to end things? What if what he said about making his decision after I've made mine meant that he was looking for a reason to break up?

My teammates are sick to death of hearing me ask these questions. Their answers, every time, have been to call him or text him. That he was already upset before our fight, that he said things he didn't mean. That he'd found out I'd been keeping secrets from him. As Boyle put it, "You were both douchenozzles, but he's the one going through a hard time right now, while your life is beer and beaches. You gotta be the one to step up."

Blaise's friends have all refused to give me any information, though they weren't assholes about it. I got the feeling they want us to sort things out, so maybe Blaise hasn't told them it's definitely over. That's gotta be a good sign, right?

Calla and Xera, who were kind of shared friends, both told me I needed to work out what I wanted before asking Blaise to change his life for me. And fuck, that's hard. I don't know what I want.

None of these questions have easy answers, and I still don't know what to do on Thursday morning. I blew off class because my brain is too full of things that are more important than education, but staring at the ceiling of my dorm room isn't helping me work out the answers to my problems.

My phone rings, and my heart leaps the way it has every time in the past few days, but it's not Blaise, just Mila. I ignore it like I have been for three days and return to my contemplation of the ceiling. Somewhere in the cracked plaster, there has to be a clue about what my next steps are.

Mila calls again, and again I ignore it, but when she calls for a third time, I huff and swipe to answer.

"Wha—"

"Do not *ever* ignore my calls like that again, Jordan Stephen Marks, do you understand me? Or I swear to god, I'll make you regret it until your dying damn day."

Yikes. She's in a mood.

"Sorry," I mumble. "But... I'm sufferiiiiiing." The word draws out on a sigh. There are only a few people I'd whine like this to, and my big sis is one of them. Even if she's not always all that sympathetic.

"Yeah, whatever, I know. Where are you?"

"Uh... in class?"

"Try again."

Fuck, she knows me too well. She's always been able to pick it when I lie.

"I'm moping in my dorm," I admit.

"Perfect. Come down and meet me."

Sitting up so fast, my head spins, I say, "What?"

Her longsuffering sigh is a thing of art. "Jordy. Come downstairs. And meet me. Now."

"You're *here*?" I swing my legs off the bed and look around for shoes, then realize I'm only in boxers still. Switching the phone to speaker mode, I toss it on the bed and grab my jeans.

"Yes, I'm here. I flew in to see you, so the goddamn least you can do is *come downstairs and meet me.*" She ends the call before I can reply.

I've never gotten dressed so fast in my life, and my fly is still undone as I race down the stairs and out the door. At first, I can't see her, but then a couple of girls move out of the way, and there she is, talking to a guy I don't know.

"Mila!" I call, and she turns, her face lighting up in a smile. I reach her in record time, and I swear, I didn't know I needed a hug from my sister this much.

She gives me one last squeeze, then lets me go and declares, "You stink."

"Hey!" My injured tone is real. "I have *problems*, Mila. I need help with how to talk to Blaise, not insults."

"Roommate problems?" the guy she was talking to—who I'd forgotten about—interjects. "Because I'm an expert on that."

I blink at him. "Uhhhh... no."

He shrugs. "Too bad. I'm Jay."

"Jordan." I glance between them. "Do you two know each other?" I thought he was just a random guy who stopped to flirt with her, but maybe—

"Nope," Mila says cheerfully. "Jay was telling me about the protest that's happening this weekend." She waves a flyer I didn't even notice she was holding. Maybe I'm losing touch with reality.

"Oh. Well, it's not roommate trouble, but it *is* guy trouble."

Yes, I've reached the level of disaster where I tell a complete stranger about my woes. Right after my sister told him that I stink.

To be fair, I might not have showered properly after practice yesterday. It was more of a quick rinse.

He shrugs. "My troublesome roommate's a guy. Is yours a jocky gamer stoner whose elitist fuck family is hell-bent on destroying the world we live in?"

I don't even know how to answer that. "Um. No."

"Too bad. We could have exchanged tips. Good luck anyway." He walks off, stopping not far away to offer someone else a flyer.

"What was that?" I ask my sister.

"Just because you've been lucky with your roommates doesn't mean we all are," she chides, still watching Jay. "But I think his problems might run a little deeper than incompatibility."

"That's great, but can we focus on me?" I hesitate. "And maybe a little bit on why you're here?"

Mila tosses her hair, exactly the same as mine except long, and gives me an incredulous look. "Are you kidding me? You call me all upset and saying you've fucked things up and don't know what to do, then ignore all my texts and calls for three days? What the fuck did you think I'd do, take up making friendship bracelets? You're damn lucky I didn't call the cops and ask them to do a wellness check or something."

"Calling my RA would probably be easier. And faster," I point out.

"Jordy!"

I shut my mouth. She sounds so mad, I don't think this is the time to remind her I prefer to be called Jordan now.

"Where can we talk?"

My mind blanks. My dorm room is twenty feet away, but

aside from not showering properly yesterday, I also haven't been taking care of my stuff. I don't want to give her another reason to yell. Plus, my roommate will be finishing his morning classes soon, and sometimes he comes back after.

"What about under that tree?" I suggest. "It's a nice day."

"That bad, huh? Fine. Let's enjoy the fresh air. Since you're alive and relatively coherent, my flight back is at four. I could only get today off from work."

I wince. Maybe it's time for me to stop with the self-pity, since it's made my sister disrupt her life. "I'm sorry," I say sincerely. "Thanks for coming, but you really didn't have to."

Her face softens as we settle onto the grass under a shady tree. "I know. But this is what big sisters are for. So... tell me everything from the beginning. I could barely understand you the other day."

She interrupts me only once, when I mention the scout. "Yeah, about that... again, congratulations. Jamie's been super conflicted about whether he can be excited about that or if he needs to be worried about you. But we both thought that wasn't what you wanted?"

"I don't know!" I practically wail, getting the attention of a group of girls walking past. I muster a halfhearted smile and wave, but they still look at me weird.

"I can see we have a lot of work to do here," Mila mutters. "Continue, and we'll come back to this."

I get through the rest, cringing when I tell her what Blaise said, then I give her big puppy dog eyes. "Help me. What do I do?"

If her expression is anything to go by, I've given her indigestion. "For starters, you need to shower. Then you need to *call Blaise*. Dumbass."

"But—"

"No. None of this gets sorted out if the two of you don't talk about it. Yes, that's going to be a painful conversation. Yes, your feelings might get a little bruised... or his. But you sulking in your dorm room and him doing whatever the fuck he's doing isn't going to give you closure."

"I don't want closure." That means breaking up and letting go. "I just want things the way they were."

"Where you were keeping secrets from him, he resented your attempts to 'fix' his life, and your relationship was a secret?"

Ouch. Words *really* hurt.

"Okay... not like that, exactly."

She sighs. "Jordy—"

"Jordan."

"Jordan, I love you. Honestly and sincerely, if I could choose a different brother, I wouldn't. You and me, we were a team, always. But right now, you suck."

"Definitely feeling the love," I mutter.

"No. Listen to me. What Blaise said during your fight was shitty and inexcusable. Honestly, if you tell me right now that he talks to you like that all the time, then not only will I apologize to you and advise you to dump him, I'll also go find him and tell him exactly what I think of him."

"He doesn't," I assure her. "He never has before."

"Okay, so—and I want to preface this by saying that when you talk to him, if he doesn't apologize for what he said, my advice to dump him still stands—but the guy was having a bad day, week, month. Right? And then he finds out that his boyfriend's been keeping secrets from him that kinda have an impact on his future, and that nearly everyone else already knew those secrets. So he's wondering if people think he's a gold digger or whatever, and then bam, here's the extra whammy of 'you know those future plans we talked about? I might change them in a way that will *also* impact your life.' He had a lot to think about and no time to process."

"Fine. I get it. I need to talk to Blaise, find out where he stands, at least. But what if he wants me to decide now about the pros? I'm not ready to make that decision, Mila. I..." I suck in a deep breath. "I thought I'd decided years ago, but now that it's a real possibility, I think maybe I was..." My gaze slides away from hers. "Maybe I was scared that if I wanted it, if I went for it, I wouldn't make it, and then I'd have to deal with being a failure." I shudder. "I don't like who that makes me."

"What do you mean?"

I look at my hands in my lap. "Uncle Matt ran away when things got hard, and here I am, afraid to even *try* the hard things."

Mila's silent for a second, and my stomach churns. Does she hate me now? She hasn't spoken to Uncle Matt since she was fifteen. I glance up to find tears in her eyes.

"Oh, Jordy," she whispers. "You're nothing like Uncle Matt."

"But—"

"When he left, it took him *years* to decide to even contact us again. Uncle Luke kept tabs on him, and he went right back to the life he'd been living before Mom and Dad died. He walked out on his husband and two dependent children—what he did affected three other people. You decided between two possible careers, the outcome of which—at the time, anyway—affected only you. And it's not like you gave up baseball. You've still been training and working just as hard as you would have been if you'd been aiming for the pros, you just chose different future goals. That's not a bad thing. You planning a career in a different field, knowing how hard professional sports are to break into, is smart. It's also not a bad thing if you change your mind now."

"I'd still want to finish my degree," I tell her, but my mind is distracted, processing what she said.

"Good. I think that's a smart call, too, and I know the dads will agree with me." She gives my knee a squeeze. "If you decide to give the pros a shot, your future career in events management will still be there when you're done. The thing is, though, you don't have to decide now. You're not even eligible for the draft for another year, and you just said you wouldn't want to go for it until the year after."

My mood, which was lifting, thuds back to the depths of hell. "That doesn't solve the problem with Blaise. What do I tell him?"

She leans back against the tree, lips pursed thoughtfully. "Remind me... the plan was always for you two to fly under the radar while you were playing ball, because it would only be until you graduate and neither of you wanted the attention, right?"

I nod. "Right."

"And if you *do* decide to go pro, would you want to be an out player? Or not?"

I think about it. "I'd want to be out," I say slowly. "Whatever gender my partner is, I wouldn't want to keep them secret under that kind of scrutiny and for what could be a long time." How could I? What if we wanted to live together or get married?

Mila shrugs. "Problem solved."

"No, it's not." I glare at her in exasperation. "First, I don't know if I want to go pro, and you just finished telling me I don't have to decide yet. And second, what if Blaise decides he doesn't want to live the life of an athlete's partner?"

The pitying look she gives me makes me feel like we're still little kids. "You're trying to answer all the questions right now, when some of them can wait. Talk to Blaise. Tell him you're not sure what you want to do, but you have a year before you need to give it serious consideration. This time next year, if you decide baseball is what you want, you can come out your senior year. Do it before baseball season starts, so by the time you're actually on the field, it's old news. People will have almost a whole year to get used to it before the draft." She grins. "You're not the first bisexual ball player, you know."

Fuck. She's right.

"And," she continues, "in another year, Blaise will be starting that internship, right? So if he's not around that much, the media might not pay that much attention to him. But this also gives him time to think about what he wants. You guys haven't been together that long, and the pros have only been in the mix for literal days, Jordy. You both need to consider your options and how much you're willing to sacrifice, and you have a whole year to do that before decisions need to be made."

My sister is a goddamn genius.

"But none of that can happen if you don't talk to him. So definitely call or go over." She wrinkles her nose. "But shower first."

THIRTY-TWO
BLAISE

I wait until I get home from work on Thursday and I know he's done with practice to call Jordan. I wanted to call him last night, right after I spoke with Luke, but it was late and I was already emotionally wrung out. Probably not the right headspace for what needed to be said. Today I worked, and I wasn't going to call him from the back room on my lunch break—plus, he has classes all day on a Thursday.

So now's the best time. We need to talk it all out.

The phone doesn't even ring before his breathless voice in my ear says, "Blaise? I was just about to call you."

He sounds anxious but also glad I called, and that gives me the courage to say, "Can we meet up? I think we should talk."

"Yeah, me too. Are you home yet? I can be there in twenty."

I hesitate. Do I want to do this here? What if it doesn't go well? I wait too long to answer.

"Or we can meet somewhere else, but if you just want to break up with me, please tell me now. I still want to meet, but I need time to plan how I'll get you to change your mind."

The burst of relieved laughter that explodes from me is stupidly loud, and I clear my throat. "I don't want to break up."

His huge sigh of relief is balm to all my injured feelings. "Okay. That's great. What about the beach, then? Have you eaten? We can get something from the food trucks."

I don't think I could choke anything down right now, but if this goes well, maybe after. And if it doesn't, Shenanigans is right across the street from there. I'll call Calla and she can come and drown me in booze.

Twenty minutes later, I get out of the Uber and squint out over the ocean. At this time of year, the sun is setting, and tonight it's putting on a spectacular show. There are little groups and couples dotting the sand, enjoying the warm night. But my gut is a mess of knots.

"Blaise!"

I turn to see Jordan waving at me from where the pavement meets the sand, a hesitant smile on his face, and, squaring my shoulders, I go to meet him.

"I'm sorry," we say in unison, then freeze, staring at each other.

Neither of us knows what to say next.

Finally, though, I remind myself what an asshole I was to him and break the silence. "I said a lot of horrible things, and I'm really sorry. I don't think you set out to deceive me or that our relationship is an inconvenience to you. I know you were only thinking of helping me." I take a deep breath. "But there are some things I really want to do for myself, and this internship is one of them. I'm grateful—so grateful—for everything you've done for me, but I don't need you in my life for the things you can do for me." I stop and replay that. "Except for the usual things guys do for their boyfriends."

He cracks a smile. "Oh, good. I like sucking you off." He reaches out and tentatively grabs my hand. I look around, worried that someone might see but not wanting to pull away. Nobody's paying us any attention, though, and as the sun dips below the horizon, the shadows deepen, giving us more privacy. "I also like messaging you all the time and hanging out with you and touching you. Cuddles and talking about random stuff while we eat together, and helping you with costumes. Knowing that you're at my games—I swear, I can hear you cheering the loudest."

I blink, not wanting to get emotional again, and he sucks in a deep breath.

"But, Blaise, I also like being able to help you. Not... I'm not saying I need you to be dependent on me or anything. I love you for the independent, driven high achiever that you are. But when you're having a shitty day, I like being able to bring you dinner and rub your shoulders. When a design's not working, I like that you bounce ideas off me even though I have no clue what half the words mean. And when you don't have a car, I like knowing that I can lend you mine and make your life just a little bit easier. The same way you like buying me new earrings when we win and Pop-Tarts when we lose."

I snort, because I can't deny it. The only time I ever let him have Pop-Tarts at my place is if the Kings have lost. He gets a box of Pop-Tarts, a backrub, and a commiserating blowjob, and then I listen to him talk through what the problems were and how he thinks he could have done better.

"Maybe I took it too far," he continues. "I know money is a tough subject for you, and maybe I shouldn't have pushed so hard about the internship. But I swear, I only did it because I knew how much you wanted it. It wasn't because I wanted you gone."

My turn now.

"I know. I overreacted. I should have made it clear that my mind was made up. I knew you were hoping to offer me money when the deadline got closer, and I didn't want to deal with that whole conversation, so I just... didn't. But that made things worse in the end." I shake my head. "I can't tell you how much I regret what I said to you on Saturday. I'd been sitting on the email for two days, and I'd finally replied to it. I felt shitty and like I was never going to get anywhere. It was just not a good day for me." Making eye contact so he can see I mean it, I say, "I really was—am—so happy that you got scouted, Jordan. You deserve *every* opportunity, even if you decide you don't want it. But I'd just talked to the guy, and it was tough for me to process right then. I'm sorry I ruined such a big day for you."

"You didn't," he's quick to interject. "I swear, you didn't. Not like you mean. I... Look, since it's pretty clear that neither of us wants to break up, can we go sit down? This is going to take a while, I think."

I nod. "Want a coffee?" I offer. From what he said on the phone, he probably hasn't eaten, and I know he's always starving after practice, so I add, "Or tacos?"

"Tacos," he agrees gratefully, and we line up at the truck. I'm kind of glad for the breather. While there's a lot more to say, and I don't think we're completely out of the woods yet, I feel a lot better and want a second to get my thoughts together.

By the time we find a place to sit on the sand, the sun has completely gone and most of the other people have wandered off. It's a lot cooler now, and I'm glad for my sweater as the breeze wafts around us.

"I never intended to keep where Uncle Luke works a secret for this long," Jordan starts, jumping right into the heart of things. "I know I should have told you sooner." He pulls a face. "But I knew it would be a thing for you, and so I just... didn't. Looks like we're both guilty of avoiding the tough stuff."

"Part of that is probably because we're still new," I admit. "It's hard to talk about difficult issues when it's someone you've known for years, never mind months. We'll get better at it." I'm determined we will. "You should know, I talked to your dad."

Jordan nearly chokes on his taco. "What?"

"He called me."

If I hadn't believed Luke when he said Jordan didn't know he was calling, the horror on Jordan's face now would convince me. "Oh my god, I am *so* sorry. I can't believe he would do that!"

"No, it's... it was good. He didn't call to yell at me or anything. He thought I might need a dad to talk to."

Phone in his hand like he's about to call his dad and yell, Jordan freezes. "Oh."

"Yeah. He was right."

He puts his phone away. "He's a good listener, isn't he?"

I nod. "I never had that before. My dad... He's not... Anyway. It was nice. And it helped me get some things clear in my head. What you were saying before, about liking to do stuff for me, I like that too. I need to be better about telling you what my boundaries are, but I think the better we get to know each other, the more we'll learn that stuff. I'm just not used to people being in a position to do so much for me. My friends would help more if they could. I know that, but..."

"It makes you uncomfortable when there's money involved," he guesses. "Okay, so I know the internship is off the table, and I won't offer you a loan, but until you find a car, I really want you to keep using mine. It's just sitting there most of the time. Please."

"Until you leave for the summer," I bargain, just in case he has any ideas of leaving it behind and renting something when he gets back to Georgia for his internship.

"That's a fair compromise," he agrees. Then he sighs. "We need to talk about baseball."

My stomach lurches, and I wish I hadn't had those tacos after all. This is the big one. The issue that could make or break us.

Jordan's next words surprise me. "My sister came to see me yesterday."

"Mila? But doesn't she live in Philadelphia?"

"Yep."

I shake my head, but I can't hold back a smile. "Wow, your family doesn't believe in hands-off, do they?"

"Not even close. But she actually said some smart things that made me feel like an idiot." He tells me about Mila's visit and everything she said.

And then I feel like an idiot too.

"So... basically, we might be getting a bit ahead of ourselves," I summarize.

"We need to agree on this," he reiterates earnestly. "I want to be with you, and if you want me to make this decision now, I'll try—"

"No." I trip over my own tongue getting it out. "No. If you don't know what you really want, I don't want to be the reason you're making this decision. I appreciate that you're considering me, but I mean it when I say I love you too much to force you to do something you're not ready for.

"Your sister is right—we have time to work this out. In another year, we'll know each other a lot better. We'll be at a different stage in our relationship, and you'll have had time to really think through what you want from life." I take a deep breath, feeling like the weight of the world has lifted from me. "Right now, you need to be focused on finals and regionals. The rest can wait." I smile at him. "We have time."

His return grin is the most beautiful thing I've seen in forever. "We have time," he echoes. Then his face falls. "I hate that we'll be apart over the summer, though."

"That was always going to happen," I remind him. "And if I'd gone for the internship, we would have been three hours apart for all of next year, too."

"Yeah, but I could have told myself how amazing it was for your career."

I sneak a look around, then lean over and kiss his cheek. "That's what I'm going to tell myself while you're in Georgia. Plus, I totally plan to drive up to see your dads a few times. I've been invited. So think of how amazing it is for our relationship that I'm getting to know your family."

His face lights up, and I can't resist adding, "Something was said about baby photos."

Instead of groaning like I expected, he laughs. "Dude, I was the cutest baby ever, bar none. And I love the idea of my dads welcoming you the way my mom did for Uncle Luke. So make sure you ask to see the photo of me fingerpainting the wall with my poop."

No guy would ever say that if he didn't truly love me and trust that I felt the same.

EPILOGUE

JORDAN

December

Drey is coming out of the building with his wheelie overnight bag as I approach. "Leaving already?" I call, and he grins.

"Last-minute celebrity holiday vacay. I got a look at the flight manifest, and believe me, I'm gonna have stories when I get back."

I laugh, but I'm looking forward to it. He can't ever name names, but the stories are always good. "We're leaving on Friday, so if I don't see you before then, I hope your holidays are awesome."

"You too." He offers me a fist bump, and then he's off.

Inside, I run up the stairs and let myself into the apartment. "Blaise?"

"Here," he yells, and a second later, he comes out of the bedroom. "You're earlier than I expected."

"The mall was scary and I need a hug." It's completely true but also a blatant hint that I need his help to finish my Christmas shopping.

"Aww, did the crazy holiday shoppers frighten you?" he teases, enveloping me in his arms. I lean into his body. It's been eleven months since we first met, and I've been held by him more times than I can count, but I'll never get tired of it. I'm surrounded by warmth and affection and *Blaise*.

"Some of those people have serious issues," I mutter into his neck. "I went into Sephora and a ten-year-old nearly knocked me over."

He pulls back. "Why were you in Sephora?"

"I need a gift for Mila still." I shrug. "I was looking for a gift pack or something."

"Didn't she send you a list of things she wanted, along with links to the places you could buy them online? I seem to remember a conversation about wanting to avoid the home wax kit debacle."

"I was fifteen!" I protest. "Nobody's ever going to let me forget that." Mila had been bitching about the cost of her regular waxing appointment, so I bought her a self-wax kit for Christmas that year. I thought I was doing a good thing—saving her money. It's still a running joke in the family.

"Okay, but why are you looking for gift packs if she sent you a list?" Blaise quirks an eyebrow.

"It's the principle," I mutter, and he laughs.

"Jordan, honey, I love you, but trust me on this. Get that list, pick something, order it online, and then add some fancy chocolates or something so you can say you made an extra effort."

That's... a great idea. "You're fucking brilliant." I smack a big kiss on his mouth. "Did I leave my blue hoodie here? I can't find it, and I want to pack it." We're leaving Friday afternoon to spend the holidays with my dads, and we're both really looking forward to it.

Blaise and Uncle Luke have bonded a lot over the past six months, and he just fits in seamlessly with the family in general.

Mila and Jamie are coming too, though they won't arrive until Sunday, and it's going to be the first time Blaise has been in a room with all of us.

We talked about living together this year—Drey was actually the one who suggested it, which surprised us both—but ultimately, we decided it was too soon, especially with all the other stuff we've both got going on. So I moved in with Boyle, but I spend about half my nights here anyway. Our relationship has gotten a lot stronger, and though we still have the occasional fight, we're both better about communicating and defining our boundaries.

The team put up a good fight in regionals last season, but we didn't manage to progress to the World Series. Nobody was surprised, since that's the furthest we've gotten in a long time. We got a whole lot of media attention for making it that far, plus a bit extra when Hannaway pled guilty to all charges and we got dragged peripherally into that. At least there isn't going to be a trial, though, and it won't be drawn out. It's basically all over now, bar the strict new policies the athletics department has introduced.

When we get back from break, we'll be diving straight into preseason, and I'm pumped—though I miss Polly. He got drafted by the White Sox, and the team's already trying to work out if we can get to one of their games out here. Coach told me that he got two more calls about me during regionals, though no other scout visits. We think they're waiting to see how I start this season, if I can bring the same level of play, before they show real interest.

I'm waiting to see how this season goes too. I feel good about my game, and I'm confident I can deliver again what I did last year, but this time, with the knowledge that people are watching, I'll have a better perspective on whether I want to take things further. That decision still hasn't been made, but I feel like I'm in a better headspace to make it when the time comes.

Either way, I'll be finishing my degree first—I'm firm on that, especially after my summer interning with Toby at Joy Universe. I do really love event management; the question is whether I want to put it on hold for a while and live the baseball dream first.

"Your blue hoodie's in my room," Blaise says, looking around as his phone rings. He locates it on the kitchen counter and picks it up. "It's Halle Manx," he says, surprised, and I leave him to take the call and go in search of my missing hoodie. She's probably calling about commissioning more design work for her characters. He fulfilled that first contract by September, and she contracted another one of her series with him then, which he finished up just a few weeks ago.

His cosplay work has been going amazingly well, and he finally decided to leave his job at the menswear store in October, when he had enough put aside in savings not only to cover his living expenses during the internship, but to—in his words—find a place to live where his roommates wouldn't steal his organs while he was sleeping. He's still making as much, if not more, as he was before, but the work is a lot more fun for him than selling suits to clueless college students.

Though he says I'm always going to be his favorite customer.

"No way! That's amazing news, congratulations!" I hear him say, and I wander back into the living room to see him grinning.

"What?" I ask, but he shakes his head, listening to whatever she's saying.

Then his face changes, going blank with shock.

"Blaise?" I cross the room in three strides. "What's wrong?"

He pulls the phone away from his ear and taps the screen, then says, "Halle, could you repeat that, please?"

"The Ferowethe Chronicles is being developed for streaming, and I want to specify in the contract that you be part of the costume design. Is that something you'd be interested in?"

My jaw drops, and I grab his arm. I don't think my eyes could get any wider. Blaise is shaking, but he sounds surprisingly calm when he says, "I would, but I don't think studios usually go for that kind of condition. They like to pick their own people. So maybe ask, but don't let it screw the deal up for you."

I squeeze his arm. What the fuck is he doing? This isn't the time for him to be selfless. What if she decides she doesn't want to risk asking?

"That's so sweet, Blaise," she replies, and I can hear the smile in her voice. "But I already asked them. They were iffy, like you thought, but then I sent them pictures of the work you've done for me, and after they talked to their costume people, they agreed. All I need is the okay from you to give them your details, and someone will be in touch to talk contracts."

I slap both hands over my mouth to keep from yelling, and not even super-professional Blaise can keep his cool.

"Oh my god, Halle, really? Oh my *god*."

She laughs. "So that's a yes?"

"Hell yes! Thank you so much. Oh my god, thank you!"

"I need somebody else there who gets my vision, and you're it. And hey, we creatives stick together, remember?"

"Still, thank you. This is... unbelievable." He thanks her a few more times, promises to call her in the new year, and ends the call with his hands still shaking.

I tackle him in a hug, and we dance around in a jumble of excited half-sentences for a few minutes before we collapse on the couch.

"You heard that, right?" he asks me. "I didn't hallucinate it?"

"I heard every amazing word. That's one of her biggest series, isn't it?" I vaguely remember him saying that back in October. He wondered why she'd asked him to do the costumes for another series instead, when this one was more popular. I guess we have the answer now.

"Yep. The book world is going to go insane when it's announced." He shakes his head. "Fuck, I didn't even ask which streaming service or production company."

"Call her back," I suggest. "Or email and ask for more details."

"No, it doesn't matter. Even if it turns out to be an unpaid internship, I'm taking it. It's an actual project job."

My grin widens. "We need to celebrate. Let's message everyone and—"

"No. Don't tell anyone until they get in touch with me. I don't want to jinx it."

I want to protest, but as an athlete, I understand superstition, so instead I groan and let my head fall back. "I hope they call soon, then. Keeping this a secret might kill me. I want to tell everyone how amazing you are."

"It probably won't be until after the holidays." He's trying to sound practical and reasonable, but I know him too well.

"I hope not. But just in case it is, you and me will celebrate tonight. Just us; nobody else has to know. We'll go out for dinner somewhere fancy and get an overpriced steak or something."

Blaise laughs and leans over to kiss me. "There's no way you'll get a table anywhere fancy at the last minute a week before Christmas. We'll have plenty of time to cele—"

His phone rings.

We both sit bolt upright and look at it like it might bite. "Who is it?" I whisper.

"LA number." His voice trembles. "It could be anyone." He

sounds like he's trying to convince himself more than anything. "Probably a telemarketer."

Probably. I mean... it's only been fifteen minutes since Halle called. But, on the other hand... "Answer it."

"Hello?" His eyes widen. "Yes, this is he... Oh, hello... No, I just wasn't expecting to hear from you so soon."

Fuck, it *is* them. That's got to be a good sign, right? They want to get things moving? I wish I knew more about this stuff.

"Thank you, that's so flattering... Yes, I do... Sure, I can send you my résumé and full portfolio. Okay... Yes... That sounds great... Perfect. Did Halle give you my email address? Okay, then I'll wait for your email, and we'll go from there. Thanks so much for calling... You, too. Bye." He ends the call, drops the phone in his lap, and collapses back against the couch.

"I'm dying here, Blaise. Talk to me." His face is telling me nothing.

"That was the head of wardrobe for Green Chest Productions. He offered me an assistant costume designer job for the project. He's going to email me the job specs and the draft contract, and then after the holidays set up a meeting for me to meet the rest of the team and the showrunners. Halle's signing the deal today, and they want to get started first thing in the new year." His head rolls toward me, and his stunned gaze meets mine. "He said he was really impressed by my work and looks forward to hearing my ideas." As if to punctuate his words, his phone dings with an incoming email, and we look at the notification on the screen. "That's him."

"See? Can we celebrate now?" I seriously don't think I can hold in my excitement.

A grin slowly spreads over Blaise's face, and he says, "Fuck it. Text everyone. Let's celebrate."

I cheer and unlock my phone to send a message in the group

chat, while beside me, Blaise starts to chuckle in that "I can't believe it; this can't be real" way. That's okay—it'll sink in soon.

I ignore the fact that he'll probably need to move to LA sooner than we'd planned; ignore the fact that if he's already building a name for himself when—if—I decide to go pro, we'll get even more media attention. None of that matters right now. They're tomorrow's problems.

Tonight, we celebrate.

Thanks for reading *Batting Style*! For the bonus scene that shows Jordan and Blaise ten years from now, subscribe to my newsletter: bit.ly/LouisaMBonus

If you want to read Jordan's dads' story (and meet PopTart-loving preteen Jordan), check out *In Your Hands*.

We talk spoilers and updates in my Facebook reader group, RoMMance with Becca & Louisa.

And if you want more, check out my Patreon (patreon.com/user?u=84207502) for early access to chapters, artwork, and other bonus material, including exclusive serials!

MEET ALL THE COUPLES OF FRANKLIN U 2!

Perry and Theo
The Hookup Mix-up

Harrison and Benny
A Stealthy Situation

Blaise and Jordan
Batting Style

Jay and Ryan
Level Up

Silas and Everly
Full Service

Dex and Austin
Tongue-Tied

Chase and Amos
Method Acting

Emmett and Jonah
Twincerely Yours

ALSO BY LOUISA MASTERS

The Collective

Higher Demon

Demon Hunter

Demons-In-Law

Asher

Micah

Zachary

Franklin U

Mr. Romance

The Holigay Hookup *related novella

Batting Style

Ghostly Guardians

Spirited Situation

Vortex Conundrum

Conduit Crisis

Gateway Catastrophe

Here Be Dragons

Dragon Ever After

The Professor's Dragon

The Dragon Experiment

Conspiracy of Dragons

Hidden Species

Demons Do It Better

One Bite With A Vampire

Hijinks With A Hellhound

Sorcerers Always Satisfy

Hidden Species Box Set

Met His Match

[Charming Him](#)

[Offside Rules](#)

[A Christmas Chance (novella)](#)

[Between the Covers (M/F)](#)

Joy Universe

I've Got This

[Follow My Lead](#)

[In Your Hands](#)

[Take Us There](#)

Novellas

Fake It 'Til You Make It (permafree)

One Golden Night

O Hell, All Ye Shoppers

Out of the Office

After the Blaze

Blokes Down Under Novella Collection

ABOUT THE AUTHOR

Louisa Masters started reading romance much earlier than her mother thought she should. While other teenagers were sneaking out of the house, Louisa was sneaking romance novels in and working out how to read them without being discovered. As an adult, she feeds her addiction in every spare second. She spent years trying to build a "sensible" career, working in bookstores, recruitment, resource management, administration, and as a travel agent, before finally conceding defeat and devoting herself to the world of romance novels.

Louisa has a long list of places first discovered in books that she wants to visit, and every so often she overcomes her loathing of jet lag and takes a trip that charges her imagination. She lives in Melbourne, Australia, where she whines about the weather for most of the year while secretly admitting she'll probably never move.

http://www.louisamasters.com

Milton Keynes UK
Ingram Content Group UK Ltd.
UKHW041622120824
1235UKWH00054B/782